■ □ ■ □ ■

SHAMARA AND OTHER STORIES

■ □ ■ □ ■

SVETLANA VASILENKO

SHAMARA AND OTHER STORIES

Translated from the Russian

Edited and with an introduction and notes
by Helena Goscilo

NORTHWESTERN UNIVERSITY PRESS

EVANSTON, ILLINOIS

Northwestern University Press
Evanston, Illinois 60208-4210

Svetlana Vasilenko's fiction originally published in Russian in the following
sources: "Shamara," in *Zvonkoe imia* (1991); "Piggy" ("Khriusha"), in *Zvonkoe
imia* (1991; first English translation in *Present Imperfect: Stories by Russian Women*,
ed. Ayesha Kagal and Natasha Perova [Boulder, Colo.: Westview, 1996]); "The
Gopher" ("Suslik"), in *Zvonkoe imia* (1991); "Going after Goat Antelopes" ("Za
saigakami"), in *Zhenskaia logika* (1982, 1989; first English translation in *Lives in
Transit: A Collection of Recent Russian Women's Writing*, ed. Helena Goscilo [Ann
Arbor, Mich.: Ardis, 1995]); "Little Fool" ("Durochka"), in *Novyi mir* 11 (1998).

Printed in the United States of America

ISBN 0-8101-1721-5 (CLOTH)
ISBN 0-8101-1722-3 (PAPER)

Library of Congress Cataloging-in-Publication Data

Vasilenko, S. V. (Svetlana Vladimirovna)
[Short stories. English. Selections]
Shamara and other stories / Svetlana Vasilenko ; translated from the
Russian by Andrew Bromfield . . . [et al.] ; edited and with an introduction
by Helena Goscilo.
p. cm. — (Writings from an unbound Europe)
Contents: Editor's acknowledgments — Editor's introduction —
Shamara — Piggy — The gopher — Going after goat antelopes — Poplar,
Poplar's daughter — Little fool.
ISBN 0-8101-1721-5 (cloth) — ISBN 0-8101-1722-3 (pbk.)
1. Bromfield, Andrew. 11. Goscilo, Helena, 1945– 111. Title.
1V. Series.
PG3489.3.A747 A23 1999
891.73'5—dc21   99-056625

To Petre Petrov, the Iurodivyi Web Wonder,
and
Sasha Prokhorov, the Supreme Kino King,
for impassioned conversations about pleasures of
the text, the voice, and the screen

—Helena Goscilo

■ □ ■ □ ■

CONTENTS

■ □ ■ □ ■

EDITOR'S
ACKNOWLEDGMENTS

WHILE EDITING THESE TRANSLATIONS OF VASILENKO'S COMPLEX prose and tracking sundry references, I have leaned on the expertise and largesse of two Russian saviors: Marina Ledkovsky and Sasha Prokhorov, who have my affectionate gratitude. For having nuanced and enriched, obliquely but measurably, my long-standing appreciation of Vasilenko's ways, means, and matrices, I thank the authors of three superlative papers on her fiction: Petre Petrov, "The Embraced Silence: *Iurodivaia* at the End of the Twentieth Century and Her Ancestors"; Elena Prokhorova, "Svetlana Vasilenko's Radioactive Zone: 'Lost Identity' or 'Identity of Loss?'"; and Lika Suris, "Re-writing Motherhood in Vasilenko's 'Khriusha.'" Finally, I present a verbal bouquet to Susan Harris, Susan Betz, Andrew Wachtel, and Andrew Bromfield for their uncommon efficiency and professionalism.

■ □ ■ □ ■

EDITOR'S INTRODUCTION

ZONE, OZONE, BLOOD, AND ASCENDING HOPE

DESPITE THE ROMANTIC *VISSI D'ARTE* PARADIGM OF THE creator's inseparability from her creation, biography rarely, if ever, fully illuminates a writer's fictional worldview or the enigmas of what Russians traditionally call the creative process. As the notorious case of Afanasy Fet illustrates, experience stamps texts in paradoxical and unpredictable ways. Fiction's complex mediating techniques chart detours and dead ends frustrating for both the naïf and the unreconstructed empiricist intent on locating a direct, uncluttered highway between life and page. Yet the story of a creative life, even outside media-hyped celebrity lore, holds potent allure for readers whose desire to unravel the artistic personality often shades into an unacknowledged "guilty" passion for voyeuristic participation in a metanarrative of fame.

Aficionados of biography-based criticism will find heuristic rewards in the accessible facts of Svetlana Vasilenko's biography, which potentially draw several bridges to aspects of her prose. For skeptics and hard-core formalists, of course, reading *Werke* through *Leben* smacks of metaphysics, for the "x factor" at best destabilizes such artless transfers, calling into question the explanatory models of authorial origins and the practices on which they are predicated.

. . .

Facts for Fictions

Born in the Thaw year of 1956 in Kapustin Iar (Russia's equivalent of Cape Canaveral), Vasilenko spent what she ironically calls her "cosmic childhood" in a security zone surrounded by a wire fence and paranoid restrictions. Within this contaminated, postnuclear parody of the fabled "garden" into which autobiographies trope the idyll of early innocence, she enjoyed emotional closeness with her mother, a Ukrainian construction technician from a family of veterinarians. Vasilenko's contrasting remoteness from her perennially absent father, rocketry specialist Vladimir Morev, who ultimately abandoned his family, accounts for her principled decision to adopt not his but her mother's surname.

In retrospect, Vasilenko herself locates the roots of her impassioned feminism in her childhood, blighted by radiation and defense-industry protocols that, apparently, convinced her of the gendered nature of destructive aggression (masculine) and the salvatory impulse (feminine). Indeed, the male-militarist environment of Kapustin Iar variously surfaces as a psychic war zone and Valley of Death in the polluted settings of her fiction, including "Going after Goat Antelopes" ("Za saigakami," 1982), where "humanity [has] become extinct," and her recent novel *Little Fool* (*Durochka*), whose eponymous heroine redeems a world on the brink of nuclear extinction.

At Kapustin Iar, which, Vasilenko contends, endeavored to instill a love of death in its residents, she saw both Gagarin and Tereshkova launched into space, helped her mother minister to the countless animals who overran their all-female household, and, at the age of eight, began to write verses. The thousand-plus letters from enthusiastic readers of a precocious Vasilenko poem that *Komsomolka* printed in 1966 ignited dreams of a career in belles lettres and the resolution to actualize them.

After abortive forays into literature during the early seventies, Vasilenko found employment at a synthetic-fibers plant in Volzhskii (a penal milieu reflected in the habitable background of "Shamara") and, upon moving to Moscow, as a fruit hauler and mail carrier. In 1977 she married the considerably older engineer whose child she was already carrying. Still heeding the Siren call of literature, the following year she enrolled in the Gorky Literary Institute, where she claims to have spent "the happiest period" of her life, studying under Grigorii Baklanov until her graduation in 1983. By then critics had hailed her first adult publication, "Going after Goat Antelopes," as the best story of the year and its author as a formidable, fresh talent. Yet Vasilenko waited six years before seeing her next story, "A Resounding Name" ("Zvonkoe imia"), in print.

During perestroika, the refusal of Moscow's preponderantly male journal editors to accept women into their ranks forced Vasilenko to earn a livelihood through menial labor—a fate shared by such former institute classmates and acquaintances as Nina Sadur, Galina Volodina, Elena Tarasova, and Nina Gorlanova. Goaded by this professional blackballing along gender lines, Vasilenko and fellow prosaist Larisa Vaneeva determined to publish a volume of women's prose. It featured the work of their informal writers' group, the New Amazons, consisting of Vasilenko, Vaneeva, Valeriia Narbikova, Irina Polianskaia, Svetlana Vasil'eva, Nina Gorlanova, Elena Tarasova, Nina Sadur, and Nina Iskrenko. Largely through the tenacious efforts of Natal'ia Ryl'nikova, an editor at the foremost perestroika publishing house of Moskovskii rabochii, the anthology—titled *She Who Bears No Grudge* (*Ne pomniashchaia zla*)—appeared in 1990, followed in 1991 by a similar but genre-diversified women's collection, *The New Amazons* (*Novye Amazonki*). The brutality and ingrained callousness that the New Amazons deemed endemic to Soviet society found fictional refraction in what subsequently acquired the label of "their naturalism." It provided a critical point of departure for vituperative Russian reviews of both publications, which Western Slavists, however, acclaimed for their bold originality.

As perestroika staggered to a close, Vasilenko joined the Writers' Union (1989) and the Pen Club (1990), completed her training in film directing (1989), and began collaboration with Andrei Konchalovsky on a film of *Tristan and Isolde* (1990). With desovietization (1991), the stigma of female authorship gradually evaporated. Vasilenko not only turned to long-contemplated projects in film and fiction but became the first secretary of the Union of Russian Writers, headquartered in Moscow; twice resided at Yaddo, the artists' retreat in upstate New York; and published extracts from her work-in-progress (the novel *Red Flamingoes* [*Krasnye flamingo*]) in both the Estonian journal *Raduga* (1997, no. 2) and the New York–based Russian almanac *Word* (*Slovo,* no. 21). The thick journal *New World* (*Novyi mir*) named her *Little Fool* its best publication of 1998.

Myth and Apocalypse

"Radiation Angel," the oxymoronic title of Pavel Basinskii's brief commentary on Vasilenko's prose, deftly captures the syncretism of polarities that structures her vision. Horror and transcendence are inseparable categories in her fictional world, where an apocalyptic threat looms over both natural and human ecology. Atavistic violence, despoliation, and self-destructive urges rule human conduct and devastate the landscape. To convey this traumatized universe in palpable, vivid form, Vasilenko synthesizes meticulous description with symbolic imagery, the cumulative weight of their combination transforming her narratives into myth. The chlorinated water in "The Gopher" materializes the sixth graders' "spite and hatred," which in turn metonymize the arbitrary cruelty of the world; the inadvertent, thoughtless crushing of a bird by the well-intentioned protagonist in "Going after Goat Antelopes" figures the random inevitability of universal pain and decimation. In Vasilenko's narratives the physiological reality of spilled blood (linked concretely to the lacerations, beatings, abortions, rapes, and killings abounding in her fiction) rhetorically expands into an image of cosmic murder/suicide on the one hand and simultaneously of Christ's Passion—what Susan Sontag has called "the paradigm of the cross," with its promise of redemption—on the other.

For Vasilenko, the Old Testament dictum "the blood is the life" facilitates a conceptual and stylistic modeling of humanity as constantly balanced on a double-edged sword: the hell of annihilation and the heaven of salvation/bliss. That duality establishes the terms for the anagnorisis at the conclusion of "Piggy" ("Khriusha"), where the appalled alienation of the female narrator's son at the bloody spectacle of the family pig's slaughter effects an epiphany that finally unites her sacramentally with both disaffected son and formerly scorned mother. The ritual bloodletting that appeases the mythical gods and exorcises the narrating protagonist's bitter resentments illuminates for her not only life's sanctity but also her indivisibility from her own "flesh and blood"—in a powerful fusion of physical with metaphysical. That moment of revelation cum transubstantiation permits her to "hear the loud beating of her [mother's] heart," the inner perspective transfiguring the "large, ungainly blue bird" of her mother's figure into the avian image of transcendence that reticulates throughout Vasilenko's texts. The triad of death/spilled blood/animal demise metamorphoses into the counter-constellation of intensely felt life/symbolic blood "communion"/human resurrection. Characteristically, the pivotal scene maximally exploits the residue of a profoundly phenomenal experience in terms of its noumenal significance.

Like Liudmila Petrushevskaia, Vasilenko starkly registers the psychic and material casualties of contemporary culture, which presuppose the killer instinct, the gene of death (the title of a Vasilenko story) manifested not only in mortality but also in unspeakable acts and events. Unlike Petrushevskaia, however, Vasilenko discovers rapture amid ravage and rupture. Her characters luxuriate in the sensual riches vouchsafed by nature and their own bodies (Shamara's self-oblivious dance, the familiar aromas and textures of the family home in

"Piggy," the "celebration of the body" in "Going after Goat Antelopes"). However fleetingly and illusorily, they attain ecstasy or a sense of completeness in spiritual and physical union. For the few receptive to its imperiled bounties, the world seems "intact" ("The Gopher") and some of those populating it worthy of salvation ("Little Fool"). But that receptivity originates in neither keen powers of observation nor lived experience. It precedes both, stemming from an irrational, primal faith whose inexplicability accounts for Basinskii's characterization of Vasilenko's stance as religious. Her personae typically shuttle between saintly gestures and visceral reactions, bypassing logic and the civilizing potential of courteous speech and interaction.

Speech, in fact, rarely coalesces into genuine dialogue in Vasilenko's fiction, where the most eloquent events and phenomena either reside beyond spoken discourse or contradict and devalue it. Discourse participates in the zigzags of thwarted expectations, as poetic lyricism alternates with crude ejaculations and gritty, minimal statements of unappetizing fact. Symptomatically, at the midpoint of the video novella "Shamara," Ustin rapes Shamara yet in the aftermath unexpectedly (and at her insistence) professes his love. The two bond in their punitive pursuit of the voyeuristic Lera, who has witnessed their violent coupling. Yet a few moments later both declare hatred for each other. Spoken words ("exhaled instead of air," as the narrator of "Going after Goat Antelopes" muses) remain a mystery, and the unstable, cryptic relationship among word, thought, act, and fact often reduces speech to a haphazard desemanticized accompaniment.

"Little Fool" showcases the inscrutable nature of speech through individual and group rejection of conventional discourse. The novel's protagonist, Ganna, is a mute whose surrogate language consists of animal sounds, shrieks (which ally her with *klikushi*), nods or shakes of the head, urinating, and vomiting—accurately identified by Catherine Clément as the quintessential bodily discourse of the sorceress-hysteric. Like her biblical namesake-predecessor Hannah (grace), who expressed joy in songs of thanksgiving, Ganna finds a comprehensible voice only in hymns glorifying God's word (hence her association with the mythic birds of paradise). Otherwise, she performs "in tongues" through the body. Her independence of everyday discourse overlaps with that of the sui generis locals, who have adopted a vow of silence in a Gandhi-like resistance to the evils of their surroundings. Silence and alternate modes of articulation circumvent the adulterated discourse of a lethal environment sustained by mechanically invoked self-justifying slogans. Nonverbal communication here represents a return to a state that antedates civilization and approximates innocence. As Elena Prokhorova astutely observes, humanity in Vasilenko's fiction is viewed "from an anthropological rather than ideological perspective."

Nothing can redress the wrongs that teem in Vasilenko's fictional world, where individual actions rarely palliate or counter life's inexorable debasement. To establish an aura of unpredictable inevitability, of something dire and ineluctable, Vasilenko implants naturalized omens (noose, knife, broken bottle, injured animal, red/blood, snatches of song) in a technique of foreshadowing that resembles an ever-tightening net. With agency vitiated to the point of irrelevance, humans' sole means of prevailing over the stranglehold of circumstances is through miracle ("Little Fool") or, at a more compromised, secular level, escape into an unknown that may prove merely another version of the unendurable ("Shamara"). The ubiquity of death in Vasilenko's fiction testifies to the absence of feasible solutions, even in her major work, which enlists myth and miracle for its triumphant resolution.

Just as ominous symbols augur people's entrapment by irremediable conditions, the device of cinematic montage conveys the incoherence of the world. Abrupt, unexplained interpolations of strikingly visual scenes (often signaled by use of the present tense) reinforce a narrative rhythm that inscribes the relentless forces buffeting beings whose behavior seems equally disjointed and irrational. Rapid shifts and a diegesis punctuated by a sequence of "shots" capturing dramatic moments of tremendous visual impact evidence Vasilenko's cinematic bent and lend an urgent immediacy to her fiction.

From Pilloried to Post

That fiction is thoroughly gynocentric. Vasilenko's protagonists are invariably female, whether they double as first-person narrators ("Piggy," "Going after Goat Antelopes," "Butterfly" ["Babochka"]), appear in texts that strictly adhere to objective "reporting" ("Shamara," the bulk of "Little Fool"), rely on a male center of consciousness ("Poplar, Poplar's Daughter," the "frame" of "Little Fool"), or favor quasi-direct discourse ("A Resounding Name," "The Death Gene"). On the plot level Vasilenko's concerns coincide with issues Western critics have conflated with feminism: maternity, abortion, nurturing, masochism, domestic violence, female friendship, and propagation (both biological and cultural). Men function as objects of desire in Vasilenko's unabashedly sexualized world but ultimately are incidental to the spiritual and psychological dilemmas at the core of her narratives. They dwell on the periphery, their secondary status inscribed in death, abandonment, irrelevance, or total absence, even though their propensity for violence catalyzes memorable incidents, especially in the realm of sexuality.

While unproblematically crediting women with an unconstrained libidinal drive that Soviet puritanism would have denounced as decadent or promiscuous, Vasilenko tends to attribute sexual violence and "anomaly" solely to males. Although the protagonist of "Going after Goat Antelopes," Shamara, and Traktorina Petrovna in "Little Fool" all indulge fleshly appetites outside the conventionally sanctioned context of love and procreation, it is men who practice sexual sadism ("Shamara," "Little Fool"), kill from sexual jealousy ("Shamara," "Little Fool"), rape ("Shamara"), and engage in "perversions." Lera the voyeuristic "hermaphrodite," who trains and dominates his gang of gay boys, makes Shamara a grotesque marriage proposal after almost killing her on Nesterov's Loop—a symbol simultaneously of frivolous play and of combative masculine aspirations quite literally removed from earthly concerns.

Both "Shamara" and "Little Fool" expose male sexuality as rudimentary, uncontrolled, yet controlling. Individual differences among men dissolve as they revert to what Vasilenko presents as a gender-specific reflex: the compulsion to bully, sexually blackmail, rape, threaten, and murder the women they purportedly love and certainly lust after. The guns, rifles, knives, nooses, manacles, and tanks associated with men in both works underscore their essentially brute nature. They "act like animals," in contrast to the numerous anthropomorphized animals (bird, gopher, goat antelope, pig) whom Vasilenko casts as innocent victims of humans' destructive urges. In general, despite its liberating potential for women, carnality remains ambiguous, for it is implicated in the society's general degradation of humans to mere flesh, meat ground in the machine of implacable circumstances.

While enveloping men in an estranging aura of alterity, Vasilenko far from idealizes women and, moreover, tends to undercut the reliability of their perspective in first-person female narratives. Both "Piggy" and "Going after Goat Antelopes" impugn the veracity of female subjectivity, colored by desire and self-exculpatory strategies. In "Piggy" Vasilenko metafictionally bares the device of narrative construction, parenthetically interjecting her "authorial" voice ("While my heroine carries on shouting") to briefly transform her protagonist-narrator from the orienting subject to the contemplated object of her storytelling. And "Going after Goat Antelopes" submits the protagonist-narrator's viewpoint to a corrective re-presentation of events ("But that's not how it really was"), a direct accusation of misrepresentation ("somewhere around here lies will start cropping up"), and, finally, the option of two possible endings to the story. These tactics caution against equating verisimilar, coherent narratives with facticity, let alone truth. Moreover, as Lika Suris persuasively argues, in "Khriusha" "the denial of a transcendental narrator aids in dissolving the temporal boundaries of the narrative and thereby holds suspect the chronological linearity of the Lacanian script of identity formation." That rejection of a prescripted subjectivity obtains not only in "Khriusha" and "Going after Goat Antelopes" but also, and above all, in "Little Fool."

Slavic Scrabble: From Stain to Saint

Vasilenko's extraordinary "Little Fool" culminates her fiction, condensing multiple motifs from her earlier prose in an ambitious narrative that reconfigures Russia's past and implicitly contemplates its future in a bold interweaving of hagiography, folklore, legend, and history. Like Petr Aleshkovsky's *Skunk: A Life* (*Zhizneopisanie Khor'ka. Povest'*, 1993), "Little Fool" draws on Russian religious traditions for a story of redemption and resurrection through miracle. The salvatory principle is variously and atemporally incarnated in the "little fool" Ganna, who, in Petre Petrov's eloquently summative phrase, functions as "the element of reconstitution and unification" within the novel.

Multiple stories of diverse origins and time periods envisage her successive identities: she is the mute thirteen-year-old Nadia turned orphan Ganna; the Tartar princess Tuba turned mermaid, or, alternatively, the galloping rider who drags victims underground where the miraculous treasure of Sten'ka Razin's kingdom of freedom and truth lies buried; the homeless pilgrim turned Christ-like healer; and, finally, the mysteriously pregnant Virgin Mary, "alone of all her sex." Each hypostasis pairs the abused, peripatetic *iurodivaia* ("holy fool," "fool in Christ") with a male figure rooted in history: Prince Dmitry, Sten'ka Razin, the orphan Marat (during Stalinism), and his quasi-double Marat Sidorov, Nad'ka/Ganna's brother in the

Thaw-era narrative that provides an icon frame for the novel. Conceptually and structurally, Ganna unifies the work, its achronologically presented epochs, its embedded genres, and its preoccupations. Her *caritas,* which replicates the Virgin Mary's traditional Russian role of compassionate intercessor between the human and the divine, serves as the sole hope for Russia's turbulent existence.

Vasilenko's bleak vision projects Russia as a volatile, superstitious, irrational nation, rich in imagination, energy, and stubborn religious faith. Repeated scenes of beating, rape, and murder thus alternate with moments of spiritual beatification, ecstatic visions, and compassionate beneficence. Under Stalinism, Russia appears as a large-scale prison/orphanage administered by ideologically programmed sadists (the signally named Traktorina Petrovna and the watchman, Egorych) who kill off the young they are supposed to protect. Against Traktorina Petrovna's officially sanctioned, doctrinaire policies of repression, Vasilenko pits the ancient Christian values espoused and enacted by the crippled peasant woman Kharyta (in Christianized Greek *Kharis* is "grace" and "benefaction"), a transgendered modern John the Baptist: she delivers Ganna to the orphanage and "marries" her and Marat Sidorov as the "parents" of faith (Vera), hope (Nadezhda), and love (Liubov')— the sororal trinity she baptizes to safeguard their souls. Vasilenko packs the novel with heavily freighted religious and folkloric motifs, ranging from biblical personages (several Marias, the Virgin Mary, fishermen, shepherds) and objects (cross, fish, snake) to crucifixions, visions, and miracles. This reticulation of implanted references prepares the reader for the apotheosis of the conclusion, in which Ganna's fulfillment of her appointed task demands a radical suspension of disbelief: chastely pregnant with the New Word, she ascends to heaven, giving birth to a new sun/son that symbolizes a New World of immortality ("there would be no death"), thereby realizing the promise of her name, Nad'ka/Nadezhda (hope). In Vasilenko's grandiosely conceived scenario, Russia's trajectory mirrors that of the kenotic protagonist, who dies into rebirth, perpetually passing through transfiguring/baptismal waters to emerge as a regenerated other self.

"Little Fool" showcases Vasilenko's command of style, unique blend of tragic and transcendent, and intrepid confrontation with "eternal questions." Like Dostoevsky's *Brothers Karamazov*, Graham Greene's *End of the Affair*, and other novels that posit miracles as both divine intervention and human self-abnegation, it envisions the potentially restorative illumination of life on the brink of an abyss. That Vasilenko produced such a text during Russia's turbulent 1990s in itself constitutes a minor miracle.

New York and Pittsburgh, June 1999

SHAMARA AND OTHER STORIES

■ □ ■ □ ■

SHAMARA

Translated by Daria A. Kirjanov and
Benjamin Sutcliffe

A Video Novella

...THE AIR THERE IS LIKE A GOLDEN SCARF. LIKE THIS: YELLOW,
silken, flowing in the sky like water upstream, like a plant.
Tender-hot to the lips, lips like sunbaked cherries in an orchard,
sweet cherries, sand on your teeth.

Golden sand. The Golden Horde was falling, fell, shattered, turned into golden sand. The river has a non-Russian
name—Akhtuba.

Let's begin.

She stood on the sandy hill and danced. The tape player lay
at her feet. It seemed as though she were all alone on this
bank, by this river, under this May sun, as if she were dancing not for people but for the sun, waiting for the sun to
praise her, to kiss her. And kissing her it was.

Suddenly, on the other bank, the armored troop carriers
appeared. Languid but quick, like crocodiles, they entered the
water, their snouts staring vacantly at her as she danced. They
moved right toward her, overcome by lust. They moved fast,
in a herd.

And the women, not visible earlier, now ran out from under
the hill. Grabbing their blankets and children, they ran clumsily in bathing suits or just in underpants and bras. They ran
slowly, hardly pulling their feet out of the sand, losing their
scarves and dresses.

One of the carriers—the "armadillo"—flashed by, as if flirting with her.

She was dancing.

Then it turned around and went straight at her.

She was dancing.

Before reaching her, it maneuvered a little to the right and dapperly rode up next to her, almost touching her with its hot flank. She bent down. A soda bottle lay in the sand; she took it by the neck and hurled it. The bottle broke against the armor.

It stood awhile, thinking—then went at her angrily with its tail end.

It moved blindly, intending to crush her, trample her down, turn her into a wafer.

She ran along the riverbank, tossing rags under its wheels, as if this would stop it. She yelled something, shaking her fist, pleading with it; it was deaf. And when she could no longer run or walk, when she could only crawl, it caught up with her and stopped.

She lay at its feet, breathing heavily, unable to get up, as if she were booty.

And from the innards of the iron dinosaur, a soldier crawled out, up to his waist: a thin little reed with transparent eyes—a skinny albino.

He looked down at her from up high as though looking at carrion. She looked at him with wounded eyes.

He disappeared. Started the engine. Carefully drove around her.

She looked for her dress, found it. It had been torn by the wheels and was covered with oil stains. She threw it away. The tape player was intact.

She took it and walked off, unsteady on her feet.

She peeked into the window of a fishing cottage.

"Ustin! Open up!"

Silence. Fishing nets are drying in the yard.

She knocked on the door and said to it, "I love you."

Quiet. She started to beat her back against the door.

"I'll die without you! I'll die! Die!"

She moved away from the door and told it, as if it were alive, "I'll hang myself, Ustin! You understand?"

The door opened. A man walked onto the porch. He looked her up and down. He was handsome, swarthy, had a scar on the edge of his lips. He handed her a rope with a noose and said, "Anything else?"

Inside the cottage stands a trestle bed.

They lay on the bed, barely covered by the sheets. She's happy, keeps caressing him, clings to the strong body.

He says to her, "It hurts! Mm-mm-mm! Don't touch me there!"

She says to him, "You touch-me-not!" She says, "You're mine."

Her lips touch his skin. "That hurt?"

"I'm telling you—it burns!"

"Got any sour cream?"

"No."

"Kefir?"

"Yes."

She rubs his back with kefir and leans over him, chattering away. "Tomorrow I'll bring you some mink cream. Kefir's no good. And I'll bring some sour cream. Want me to?"

He lay there and lay there and then exploded. "I don't need any cream! Go away!"

"Ustin!"

"Go away!"

"I . . ."

"I told you! I want you out of my sight!"

"You don't love me?"

"Who are you, anyway—a human being or what?"

"And who are you?"

"Who?"

"A jailbird!"

"What?!"

"A thug!"

He raised himself up. "Asshole," he says. "You asshole!"

She walks with the noose on her neck, holding the rope in her hand; her elbow lags behind, as if she were taking herself for a stroll. She's in her bathing suit, walking around the city, cranking up the tape player.

The men at the beer stall call her over. "Come 'ere, we're all gonna chip in to get you a dress!"

Ugly red mugs. But kind. They're laughing. Everybody's laughing, even the buses.

She walks and sobs over the whole city. Naked, with a noose around her neck, her player blasting.

And suddenly she hears:

"Shamara!!!"

The town jester, Lera the buffoon, runs toward her, running across the street like an idiot, at an idiotically breakneck speed, and behind him seven dogs, seven huge mongrels just as bad as Lera himself. Lera took off his shirt and flung it over her shoulders.

She squats in the middle of the sidewalk and weeps.

"He doesn't love me!" she tells the dogs.

The dogs lick her face.

Shamara sits on the balcony of the fifth floor of a five-floor apartment building. She sits on a barrel and trims her toenails, gathering the clippings into a pile.

"I'm gonna throw up right now!" someone says.

Shamara looks around. Lena is standing in the doorway, round like a ball. Her hair curlers whistle in the wind.

"Throw what?"

"Huh?"

"Throw what up?"

Lena shouts imploringly, "Now she's making fun of me! Why, if I find just *one* of your claws—"

"Toenails—"

"Claws . . . you don't have toenails, you have claws. . . . And if they get into the food—"

"Into the soup . . . tomorrow I'll sprinkle some—"

"Then I'll—"

"You'll eat it. It won't kill you."

Stukalkina and Dolbilkina crawled out onto the balcony: one has black hair, the other red; both are called Galya. They've got chemicals in their hair: one has black chemicals, like a jackdaw. The other has red chemicals, like henna shampoo.

"Get off our barrel!"

"Say the magic word and I'll get off."

Stukalkina and Dolbilkina are from the villages Dolbilkino and Stukalkino.

Stukalkina and Dolbilkina take the board, with Shamara on top of it, and lift it. Shamara sits on the board like the Shah of Persia. Lena takes some pickles out of the barrel.

"Galya, oh, my Galya," sings Shamara, alighting between the two Galyas.

They put the board back and leave.

"Stupid village hicks!" she shouts after them.

She took a handful of toenail clippings and sprinkled them off the balcony like salt. "Here, chick, chick, chick. . . ."

She looked down.

Lera was sitting on a shop bench with some youths. Their faces and shirts were like fruit candy, sweet and gentle. Lera was singing in a low bass to the accompaniment of a guitar. "I'm weeping, I'm sobbing, my dearest!"

A girl approached the entryway. She was so virginal. She walked right into the circle; the gentle youths surrounded her. She's fallen into a pink and blue trap.[1]

They grabbed her breasts, her waist, her legs, their eyes shining with tenderness and purity, and it was impossible to escape from the circle. At first the girl smiled, then she stopped; her tortured smile congealed on her lips, as if from frost, and with this tortured, awkward smile on her face, she started to hit their hands. And their tender gazes also froze;

their tender faces hardened. They tossed her around, and Lera sang, rocking out in imitation of Presley:

"Rock 'n' roll, rock 'n' roll!"

They danced. From afar, it was even beautiful.

Dolbilkina and Stukalkina ran out of the entryway—they were late for work—stopped, shook out their curls, and ran on.

Lena emerged next. And then another woman, with a big belly, followed. They were about to run right by her. But the one with the belly, her face like a Madonna's, only with eyeglasses, stopped and said to Lera, "Let her go!"

Lera made a sweeping gesture over the guitar strings: *thwang!* He asked affectionately, "Marin, what's the point of going through with the pregnancy? You willing to have a caesarean?"

Marina moved off, looking back over her shoulder. Lera entered the circle and patted the girl's shoulder in a fatherly way.

"Good for you! The thermal treatment's over!" And loudly, but as if it were meant only for her, he said, "I'm half woman myself—a big, big secret! And with this half I understand you so well! A woman's soul! Hurt feelings! How well I understand! Walk right through! You're free!"

And he ordered, "Attention!"

The boys came to attention, and she walked through the ranks, who smiled at her tenderly.

Only the last boy blocked her way, gently bleating, "O little cherry, whom do you want?"

The girl said, "What a nursery school!" and she walked off on her long legs.

The boys watched her with heavy eyes.

"Shamarina"—the superintendent walks up the five-floor mountain, panting heavily at each landing, and casting stones with each word—"is a whore. She should be in jail. Her husband works here in the chemical division. Don't get involved with her. She's a disgrace to the whole dormitory. Be careful with her. This apartment's a model of maintenance. Okay, that's it. You go the rest of the way yourself; tell her you're new. The girls are working their shift. Remember. Now, me—I'm afraid of her. She can easily cut your throat. . . ."

"What are you saying, Rimma Sergeevna! You mean me?"

Shamara was standing in the doorway. So affectionate, so gentle, she was. The superintendent gasped and went downstairs.

Shamara asked the new girl, "You new here?"

She offered her hand, smiling in a gentle, flattering way, "Zinaida Petrovna," and added, "'Greetings, and you should use the name more often.'"[2]

She took the new girl into the room and showed her the bed she'd be using. There were four beds in the room. Over one of them, Lenka's, hung a portrait—a photo half the size of the wall.

Zina said, "That's her squeeze."

A nail protruded above Shamara's bed, and on the nail hung a noose—the same one.

Only one bed in the other room, the walls covered with certificates instead of wallpaper.

"We've got a star worker here—Raya lives like she's in paradise."

She showed her the whole apartment, like a hostess receiving a long-awaited guest. But her crazy eyes kept flaring strangely and wildly. In the kitchen she lazily pulled out a drawer, suddenly grabbed a fork, and brought it up it to the new girl's throat.

"Two strokes—eight holes!" She stared hard at her.

"So?" said the other.

"I can bend a steering wheel," said Shamara and bent the tin fork with her hand.

And she instantly cheered up.

"Get to know Shamara! Be Shamara's pal! Shamara's been through everything: fire and the water of life. Shamara's been everywhere. And everywhere there's bosses. But Shamara needs freedom. I'm chasing after freedom, and freedom's running away from me, the bitch. I'll catch up to it!"

"There's inner freedo—," the new girl said shyly.

Shamara flew into a rage, grabbed the new girl by the collar, and shook her like a pear. "You finished high school, you ugly mug, and now you want freedom! Where do you think you've come? You've come to the chemical division! Get your glasses on—we only got convicts working here, stupid. Maybe you think you're gonna read books here? Hey, if I see you with a book. . . . If I want to, I'll have you thrown off the commuter train; if I want to, I'll have them wind you up in elastic fiber at the factory. If I want to, they'll be selling pastry at the train station stuffed with you instead of fruit jam. They'll cut you up into little pieces and squeeze you and your glasses through the meat grinder. Get it?"

"That's enough!" said the new girl and pushed Shamara away as easily as could be. She was ever so light, it turns out.

They sat on the beds, breathing heavily. They stared at each other like enemies.

Suddenly Shamara smiled gently, cajolingly. "Hey, don't be stingy, give me your pants for the dance. The ones you're wearing."

As the girl undressed, Shamara examined her keenly. "Your undies import or export?" she asked.

"What?"

"I'm asking what's your name."

"Natasha."

Natasha was sleeping. And in her sleep she heard the door slam shut, then heard Shamara whisper in the dark.

"If anyone rings, don't open the door. I'll hide on the balcony."

She rushed in the darkness toward the balcony. And immediately a terrifying din resounded—instead of the doorbell ringing, the door was simply removed. The beam of a flashlight slashed over Natasha, in her face, her eyes.

"Get up! Who are you? A new girl? Where's Shamara? Talk to me!"

She's silent, enchanted by the guy's face, visible in the golden rays of the flashlight. Proud, swarthy, light eyed, a scar on his cheek—just like in the movies, like in the movies. . . .

"Where's Shamara? Tell me!" And he goes to the balcony door. Natasha doesn't know who he is, only that she has to save Shamara. She gets up, stands there in her nightshirt, and the guy approaches her, and she backs away, but he keeps coming closer. They move around the room, circling; his flashlight trembles, she can see now in the moonlight—the sky's cloudless, the night's blue-black—how handsome he is; and who is he, and how's Shamara doing? The chairs are scattered all around, something's getting smashed to pieces, and she sees that he sees Shamara on the balcony, Shamara's head is visible. Shamara's in the barrel, sitting there and trembling, and Natasha leads the guy away, drawing him away with her movements, and he follows, laughing, understanding everything, but obediently following her into the other room, and laughing with his beautiful mouth, the scar just above his lips. And Natasha doesn't know what's next—what's next is the wall, the wall with the certificates, Raya lives like she's in paradise, and she asks, "Where did you get the scar?"

She merely thought the words, but her lips exhaled them, and he heard.

"From over there," he says. "From over there."

And for some reason he takes out a knife, the blade shining, and he puts it to her throat.

"From where? You interested? Yeah? I'm a chemical worker. Ever heard of those? Heard of 'em, little chickadee? Two years in the chemical division for nothin'. I'm doin' time in jail. Stocking fiber. You have stockings on? Aha, no stockings. Well, then, fiber for stockings, so your little legs don't freeze. You hear me? I'm telling you—so your legs don't freeze. This one girl walked around without stockings, and her little legs almost froze. And why d'ya think her little legs came so very close to freezing? She was being r-a-a-ped. Eight guys. Nice, huh? I'm asking you, wasn't that nice?

Answer me. You're scared. You're scared right now, scared of a little knife. . . ."

And with a mocking smile he kisses her without removing the knife.

"You're scared, still never been kissed. She'd never been kissed either. We did her, all eight of us. In the snow. Those little legs, those little legs, I tell you. Then into the cellar, on the hot pipes, we warmed up her legs— you hear?—so she could make it home on her own two little legs. We're animals, but hey, we warmed them. . . . You hear?"

She heard his voice choke up.

And at that moment Lera's thin, penetrating voice broke into song in the street:

> "When she was just a kid, still a gal,
> But branded with a nickname foul,
> He had his fun, then dumped the 'whore,'
> And married a 'nice girl,' who suited him more."

The guy glanced at Natasha as though he'd regained his senses. He ran his finger along her lips.

"But you—you're beautiful," he said. Then, with a smirk, "Nice."

He left, shouting, "Say hi to Shamara!"

Shamara was sitting in the barrel. The water in the barrel was silvery from the moonlight. Shamara's head looked as though it lay upon a silver platter.

She crawled out noisily, flinging off some dill.

"These girls have got a kolkhoz going here, a village. . . ." She took a few steps, and almost fell. "Damn! . . . Will you rub my legs? They're frozen for some reason. . . ."

Natasha rubbed Shamara's legs with vodka. Shamara kept wincing.

"Those idiots put ice in the barrel. . . ."

"Who was that?" asked Natasha.

"Ustin. That hurts!"

Natasha kept quiet for a while. She felt ashamed to ask, but finally did so, anyway.

"What was he after?"

"I really laid into this babe at the dance. He got really mad. But you don't dance with other people's husbands! He's my husband!"

"Who?"

"Ustin."

"Husband?"

"Yeah."

Suddenly Natasha said, "Handsome."

She lifted her eyes to Shamara.

"Yeah," Shamara said proudly.

They looked at each other.

In the morning, right at daybreak, the workers stormed the bus as if it were the Winter Palace.

Lena shoved Marina forward with her stomach.

"Let a pregnant woman get through!"

"Hey, maybe I'm pregnant, too, just not showing yet!" What a creep of a guy.

Everybody was dragged into the bus.

Dolbilkina stood in the front, looking for Stukalkina. "Galya! Galya!"

Stukalkina was in the back, looking for Dolbilkina. "Galya! Galya!"

Each of them had saved a place for the other.

Shamara was swept away toward one door, Natasha toward another. They were squeezed in tight. The bus took off.

Natasha buried her nose in someone's chest. It was uncomfortable. She lifted her head: Ustin. His lips were incredibly close. On the edge of his lips—the scar. The bus turned, jolting the passengers. Ustin and Natasha leaned with the crowd to the right, then to the left, but their faces stayed right next to each other.

Shamara watched them from a distance. People got in her way, blocking her view. But she went on watching, nonetheless, right through all the shoulders and heads. They kept riding and riding through the morning city, through the poor, gray city, with the concrete walls of its factories, walls that were like a never-ending fence, and they rode past the garages, past the rusty pipes and dump heaps, they rode through the steppe. She watched as they looked at each other, and there was no end to this torture.

They looked at each other and kept riding, riding, looking into each other's eyes—and there was no end to this happiness.

Then everybody got out of the bus, four people staying. Ustin stayed. Shamara hid behind a seat. They took off. Ustin sat there, eyes closed.

The bus idled at the last stop. Through the window Shamara watched Ustin get out, and all the others suddenly seemed to look alike as soon as they got out. Nearby, a column of convicts from the camp walked past on their way to work. It was like the beginning of a new city on the outskirts of town. Ustin took his place in the column. An officer walked up to him and said something. Ustin answered. The officer said something else. Ustin answered. And the officer hit Ustin so hard in the face that Ustin almost fell over, breaking his fall with his hand. He got up, wiped himself off. The little reed of an officer was that skinny albino.

Dressed in black overalls, Shamara ran around the factory shop chasing "cradles"—metal bins full of spools—up and down the conveyor. She chased one cradle in a fury, as if going to combat with it. Everything in the shop, except for Shamara, was white, and everything wound thread. Synthetic fiber.

She saw Natasha—standing with her back to her, stupid fool, talking with someone—and with all her strength hurled a cradle right at her. The cradle rushed thunderously along at a terrifying speed. Natasha looked around and started to laugh at something, without noticing the cradle.

Time slowed down, then started to flow ever so slowly. For Shamara. But one can outrun time. Shamara runs after the cradle, pushes Natasha, catches the cradle with her hand just as it reaches Natasha's back. The cradle makes a metallic grinding sound, falls, and smashes into smithereens. Then a second, and a third. The conveyor's still turned on. Spools pour out of the cradles.

People dressed in white suddenly appear and bend down over Natasha and Shamara. They're yelling something—can't hear a thing. Only by their lips could you tell they're swearing: *F—ing s—t!*

Shamara asks Natasha something, but you can't hear. She keeps saying the same thing over and over. When they disconnect the conveyor, you can finally hear.

"You alive, Natasha? Are you alive?" she keeps repeating.

Stukalkina and Dolbilkina lift Natasha up. Shamara gets up on her own. And Raya the foreman—her braid coiled like a crown on her head—hits Shamara in the face with all her might. Shamara almost fell over, breaking her fall with her hand. She got up, wiped herself off.

There's a wedding in the dormitory. The pregnant Marina and Pashka are getting married. Pashka's small, shorter than Marina by a head, with hair red as rust.

Above the drunken din, he yells, "Hey, everybody—I'm off the sauce! Ya hear?!"

Downing a glass of mineral water, he gapes, "That's strong fuckin' stuff! Narzan![3] Ya hear?! This ain't no Narzan—it's crap! Some bitter shit, huh? Shout 'Bitter,' you assholes![4] You all came just to chow down, or what?" And he pressed close to Marina's aloof white face. And above the top of his head, Shamara saw Marina's eyes, big and nearsighted, therefore estranged and absent from the wedding.

Shamara was sitting at the table with Ustin—right beside him, as befits a husband and wife. Stukalkina and Dolbilkina had seated Lera between them, and were both catering to him; as if he were a true, fair maiden, they made sure their three plates were laden.[5] Lena and Kolya were sitting together, with his portrait—half the size of the wall—behind him.

Across from Shamara and Ustin sits Natasha.

"You aren't drinking anything?" Ustin asked her. He wanted to pour her some vodka, but she covered the shot glass with her hand.

"Ugh, I can't take it! He's being so formal with her," Shamara says to no one in particular. "Next thing you know, he'll be calling her Miss Natasha! Miss Natasha, what'll you be having, ma'am? Don't you guzzle vodka, ma'am?"

"I don't drink vodka," says Natasha.

"Not like a real Russian girl," says Shamara.

"What about champagne?" asks Ustin.

Before Ustin can even pour the champagne, Lena snatches the bottle from his hand.

"Give it here! Kolya, put a kopek in!"

"What for?"

"Put it in!"

"Hey, what's all this about?" Natasha asks, getting excited.

"When it fills up, we'll get married—it's an omen. Pasha! Where's your bottle of kopeks? You gotta break it! For luck!"

"Marin?" asks Pashka.

"We've got one," Marina answers in embarrassment.

"What d'ya mean? I broke it. Didn't have enough for the hair of the dog."

"I filled up another one. . . ."

"That's a wife for you!" yells Pashka and grabs her breasts. "Look! Everybody, look! My wife, the big milk machine! Bring the bottle, we'll break the friggin' hell out of it!"

Natasha is jotting something down in her notebook.

"What are you writing in there?" Shamara asks her. "What're you writing?"

"About the bottle . . . local customs . . ."

"What d'ya think we are? Papuans?! Miklukho-Maklay![6] Writing, she says!"

"Lay off her," Ustin shouted at her.

Pashka's yelling, "Watch your faces! Watch out! I'm breaking it! For luck! Five, four, three, two, one! Whack!"

And he breaks it against the floor. The golden puddle of kopeks spills out by the doorway. And in the doorway stands Raya. Next to her, an officer—the albino, the very same one.

"And who's this come to join us?" Pashka yells. "Why, it's our workers' conscience. Let's welcome him with applause." He claps.

"Idiot," says Raya and thrusts a crystal vase at him. "This is from me and Max."

"Rayechka! . . ."

They sat down opposite Ustin and Shamara. The albino looked at Ustin, Ustin at the albino. Then Ustin got up and went over to the tape player. The albino didn't recognize Shamara.

Ustin set up the tape player and now is dancing with Natasha. It's disgusting to watch. They're looking at one another as if they're licking each other—just as they did earlier in the bus. Pashka's sitting and talking with the albino. Shamara listens but monitors Ustin and Natasha, without taking her sharp eyes off them.

"If I laid her, Maxim, then as an honest man I should marry her. In general, everyone should marry. Take Lera, for example. Lera, what do they call you? A herm—"

"Hermaphrodite," Lera readily responds.

"Yeah, yeah, that's it," Pashka nods. "Lera's his own man and his own woman, he doesn't have to marry, he's a family in himself, a cell of society. But us, we have to get married. So, tell us, who are you? KGB? Just be honest. . . ."

"Pasha!" says Marina.

Suddenly Shamara notices that Ustin and Natasha are gone. She rushed to the hallway—not there. Into the kitchen—not there. Nowhere to be found. She heard Natasha's quiet laughter. They were in Raya's room. She entered threateningly:

they were standing at the window and laughing. They looked around happily, their faces radiant.

"Listen, you!" she said to Natasha. "I'm a simple woman, you know. I can punch you right in the eye."

"Get out of here!" Ustin commanded.

"Go to hell!" she shouted, and then to Natasha, "Who do you think you are? How'd you even get in the picture? You're being told in plain Russian—this is my husband! This is my husband! This isn't your husband! This is my husband!"

"I'm no husband to you."

"Who are you, then?"

"No one."

"I saved you back then, and now it's 'let's have some fun,' right?" And to Natasha, "Eight of 'em screwed me in the snow. You forgot, huh? I didn't put a single one of 'em in jail. Felt sorry for the vipers."

"I married you then, didn't I? What more d'you want?"

"A softhearted Komsomol member!"[7]

"So why'd you send me to jail afterward? You had a husband, and then you blew it."

"I felt like it, that's why! You gotta drink less. Remember how you used to tie one on!"

"You drive a man to drink!"

"And what about you!"

"Natasha!"

Natasha was looking at them as if they were monsters.

In the silence that followed, they could hear Pashka yelling in the next room. A terrifying yell, as if he were being killed. Shamara rushed in. Pashka was tearing his wedding shirt to pieces. "You don't believe me! You don't believe a wounded soldier! You were making zinc coffins for us here, with see-through holes. Look, you bastard!"

He showed the albino his horrible scars.

"Pasha," Dolbilkina called him quietly. "Marina's in the bathroom, hanging herself."

. . .

"Open up, Marin. Come on, open up," Shamara pleaded with her through the door. Behind the door there was no sound. "You hear me, Marin? Come on, tell me you hear me."

"Marin, here's what I'm gonna say," Pashka whispered into the door. He kept whispering to her, whispering, and she listened as she hid, listened and listened. Then she started to cry. He kept whispering, whispering, and she kept crying, crying. . . .

Shamara left, went into the main room, and asked Stukalkina, "Where's Ustin?"

"He left," Dolbilkina answered in place of Stukalkina.

She collapsed onto the bed and asked, "And Natasha?"

Silence.

Shamara is sitting on the bed, reading something. She glowers at Natasha, who's just come in from her shift. It's daylight. Natasha keeps looking for something, but can't find it.

"Have you seen my notebook?" she finally asks Shamara.

"This one, you mean?"

She hands it to her.

"You write well. Good for you," she praised her. "Especially about Ustin. Oh, the poor, poor guy, how Shamara tortured him. . . ."

"This is despicable." Natasha blushes. "This is . . . how could you . . . how dare you!"

"What are you working yourself up for?" says Shamara. "If you had a reason, all right, but . . ."

Natasha made to put the notebook on the bookshelf. The shelf was empty.

"Where are my books?!"

Shamara doesn't say a word. She watches silently, expressionless.

"Where are my books?"

"On the garbage dump," Shamara says in a neutral voice. "They were dusty."

Natasha jumped out onto the balcony. Shamara dashed out after her. They watch the books burn on the garbage dump.

"They're burning," Shamara says languidly. Then suddenly she grabs Natasha by the shoulder and asks fervently, "You're not afraid of falling off the balcony, are you?"

She looked down.

"It's high. You might break."

Natasha opened the suitcase. The suitcase was empty.

"Where are my things!"

Shamara's lying on the bed, looking at the ceiling. "The same place the books are." She jumped up, unbuttoned her overalls, a pink dress under them. It was the dress Natasha had worn to the wedding. "But this one I saved for myself. May I?"

Natasha doesn't respond.

"So, let's make an exchange: I give you the dress, and you give me the husband. What do you say?"

Natasha doesn't respond.

Shamara speaks as if asking her own advice, "Should I go to the police and report: My husband's been stolen. . . ."

And abruptly she asks point-blank, "You in love with him?"

Natasha gasped in surprise. "Yes!"

For a moment, neither uttered a word.

"A real star turn!" said Shamara and exited.

Shamara wanders around Ustin's yard in her pink dress. Boats are lying around; the yacht is still unfinished.

"Ustin," she called out.

There was a lock on the door. She touched it.

Shamara makes her way to the stage, pushing aside the crowd. Lera's standing there, singing a funky song.

"Ler," she calls him. "Ler!"

Lera makes an announcement. "And now," he says, "a ladies' dance—the *lezginka*."[8]

And he jumps down, joins her . . . wearing a bow tie. They met Stukalkina and Dolbilkina as they squeezed their way out of the dancing mob. The two Galyas were looping around like rabbits; they had their own special dance.

Their faces lit up with joy when they saw Shamara.

A shaven convict was being led out of the dance hall, his arms pinned behind his back. The albino, in uniform, walked behind him, a cop at his side. Shamara looked around. So did he, but they didn't greet each other.

"Who's that?" she asked Lera.

"Mr. Boss Man," said Lera. "Your Ustin's boss."

Shamara boarded the plane—Nesterov's Loop.[9] It was deserted, and it wasn't evening yet.

"Well?" asked Lera.

"What do you think," she asked. "Does he love me?"

"O Lord!" said Lera.

"Go ahead, tell me. You know."

"I thought something happened."

"Something did."

"What?"

"Does he love me?"

Lera connected some wires. "Want to go for a ride? Should I switch it on?"

"Does he love me?"

He pushed the button. "We're off."

She was spun around as if she were on a skewer. Like a shish kebab. She lifted her arms and fell down, as if falling from a cliff into the water.

"He doesn't love you!" Lera shouted as Shamara fell.

"Switch it off!" she shouted from up high.

"He doesn't love you!"

And she fell again.

She no longer knew what was up and what was down. Arms extended, she was floating in weightlessness, straight into the crimson sun, as into blood, and that son of a bitch kept yelling, right into her ears, he yelled, "He doesn't love you!"

He didn't know how to stop the plane. And she was already losing consciousness. He kept jerking the switch and pushing the buttons, then running around the platform, pushing everything.

"Shamara," he pleaded, "hold on!"

The carousels started to move; the boat swings started to rock; some shitty thingamajig began to spin and flop over. There was a hellish squeaking and screeching.

He caught hold of the plane as it descended and pulled Shamara out from the seat belts as the machinery snarled, sparks crackling. He dragged Shamara out and released the plane, which, once set free, twisted into a Deadman's Loop.

He carried her, lifeless—that's how light she was—and, after her stint in the cosmos, weightless too, as if in the other world.

He laid her down on the ground. She looked at him from afar. Then, as if she'd learned the truth there, in the cosmos, she said, "He doesn't love me."

She recovered her breath and sat up. Lera hovered anxiously beside her, eager to say his piece.

"Zina," he said. "Marry me."

She actually recoiled. "What are you talking about!"

He rushed on, "My father will give us a motorcycle as a wedding gift—"

Shamara neighed like a horse. "And are you gonna use your finger to give me babies?"

She keeled over from laughter, face buried in the ground.

"Zina, I'm having an operation this fall."

"And what will you become," Shamara neighed. "A boy or a girl?"

"A boy," Lera answered seriously.

"And what if you become a girl?" She almost died laughing. She neighed and neighed with laughter, then suddenly burst into sobs.

Wishing to calm her down, Lera hugged her.

"I love you," he said.

She removed his arm from her shoulder, got up, and moved off, saying maliciously, "Keep your love to yourself, why don't you!"

She walked past the empty carousels; they kept turning, the empty boats rocked, and some thingamajig whizzed by with a hooting sound. With a roar the plane plummeted like a suicide.

Shamara knocked quietly on the door to Raya's room. Raya was watching television. A color one.

"Raya, I've dropped by for a visit."

"You don't say?"

"Come on, Ray, what d'ya say?"

Raya hesitated. "Maybe I don't have any?"

"Ray!"

"Okay," Raisa said decisively. "Just be quiet about it. Who's around?"

"No one. They're all working their shift."

Raya got a bottle. "I'm turning into a drunk. At least I'm not alone."

Raya grew flushed. Just like a queen.

"You know how much I could make in America? You don't, but I do know. I'd make—"

"How much?"

"A million. Don't interrupt me. I wouldn't be living in this fleabag of a room, understand? I'd live in a villa. I'd have a Mercedes, understand? Go ahead, pour some more."

"And me?"

"Don't interrupt. I have an inexplicable talent, understand? You can't explain it. There, you see my hands?"

Raya stretched out her hands.

"You think these are hands?"

"What else?"

"These aren't hands. They're my brains."

"So what's in your head?"

"In my head I have one kind of brain, and here I got another kind. Understand? I think with my hands. I'm a star worker, right?"

"Right."

"And what do I have to show for it?" Raya waved her hand

around the room. "Certificates—enough to wipe yourself with. Not even rubles. I keep my mouth shut, but I'm smart. You think you're a slave? But you're not a slave. We aren't slaves, because there's no one to buy us. I'd sell myself, but there's no one to buy me. I cost a million, understand?"

"Yeah."

"Let's talk about men," she said suddenly. "I don't have a man."

"What about the white one? The officer? The one who was at the wedding?"

"That's not a man; that's a comrade. He's got an inexplicable talent. His furniture walks."

"What do you mean, 'walks'?"

"On its feet. All by itself, on little wheels. We're sitting, drinking, and it brings us snacks. All white!"

"Who?"

"The furniture. It's white!"

"Raya, Ray . . ."

"Ah?"

"How do you go on living without love?"

"Silently. So what?"

"Ustin doesn't love me."

"Who? Ustin? Doesn't love you? You?" She even sobered up a bit. "So we'll put a love spell on him right now! Why didn't you say something earlier? I know a spell. But think it over! It could put a curse on the guy."

"Put the spell on him!"

They walk around the construction site, stumbling, holding each other up, and giggling. Overhead, the moon's shining.

Raya finds a board. "Stand still. Repeat after me: 'May it come to pass that without me he can neither live, nor exist, nor drink, nor eat, not at dawn, not at dusk, not at midday, like a fish without water, like an infant without his mother's milk, cannot live, so may the servant—' What's his real name?"

"Sergei Vasilyevich Ustinov."

"Like the marshal. There used to be a marshal by that name, Ustinov. A member of the, of the—"

"Ray!"

"Oh, yeah . . . 'he can neither exist, nor drink, nor eat, not at dawn, not at dusk, not during the regular day, not at noon, not on starry nights, not in raging winds, not in the sunlight of day, not in the moonlight of night. O Misery, sink in your teeth, Misery, eat right through the chest to the heart of your servant, Sergei Vasilyevich Ustinov. Grow and spread through all his veins, through all his bones, your aching, yearning thirst in the name of your servant, Zinaida Petrovna Shamarina!'"

As they descended along the bridges, Raya said with confidence, "My mother used this love spell to charm my father. It's a reliable spell, no question about it!"

As they happily made their way back, they suddenly ran into Ustin at the street lamp. It was like a dream. And he was so affectionate.

"Hello, Zina," he says.

Even touched her with his hand for some reason. They greeted him and went on their way, giggling. They weren't in the mood for him.

"It worked," giggled Raya. "He's under the spell."

"It worked," giggled Shamara.

They walked on drunkenly without even looking around.

Natasha opens her eyes in the blackness of the room. Someone is dancing at the window. Conjuring magic above the night table. And there's music, or something like it. Something on the tape player, maybe. . . . It's Shamara, dancing quietly so that no one can hear.

"Shamara!" she called out in a whisper.

Shamara dances, dancing something totally incomprehensible.

"Zin, what are you doing?"

Natasha switched on the light. Shamara looks at her without seeing her; she's so lost in her dance, in her trance. She turns the music up louder: it's a recording of frogs singing a wedding song: *wh-a-a, wh-a-a*. Shamara sings along and dances: *wh-a-a, wh-a-a*. And she keeps turning it louder and louder. The frog chorus sings on.

The girls from the other rooms come running in.

"Turn it off!"

Shamara responds, "Wh-a-a-a!"

"Come on, please!" Dolbilkina asks her.

Shamara switched it off and turned around, still dancing. "I want a man!"

Her eyes are blind, can't see anyone.

"I want a man!"

By now she's shouting.

"Don't yell!"

"I want a man!"

She bangs her fists against the wall, pounds it with her head. Stukalkina and Dolbilkina pull her away. She thrashes in their hands like a fish, shouting, "I want one! I want one! I want one!"

Shamara sits beside Ustin's door, sits banging her fists against the door. "I want you! I want you! Ustin!"

It's quiet. The moon's shining. Sails are drying in the yard. They sigh whenever the wind blows.

Shamara lies down on the porch. She's shivering like a dog.

"Ustin, open up, I'm freezing. . . ."

Her teeth are chattering. She whines plaintively, "Open up, I'm cold. . . ."

She whimpers, "Let me in to warm up. . . ."

She hugs her body to warm herself. She's trembling all over.

"Why's it so cold?" she asks in surprise.

And she bangs on the door. "Ustin, I'm really going to freeze. Ustin!"

The sun was already high. Shamara walked quickly through the forest. Ustin was behind her. He spoke as if he were taking her to her execution.

"Forward march! Look straight ahead!"

She stumbled and looked around sheepishly. Ustin yelled out, "Go on! Faster! *Schnell!* No stopping!"

It was a forest of acacias, so the shadow was delicate, light, transparent. It slid gently across Ustin's harsh face.

"Go on, go on," he shoved her from behind.

They made their way along a dead-birch grove, with its white corpses of trees.

"Where're you taking me?" Shamara asked.

"Walk, don't talk."

He brought her to a forest clearing where there were maple trees and the ground was bare.

"Lie down," he ordered her.

"Where?" She looked around helplessly. The ground was as dry as a rock.

"Lie down!" he shouted.

She lay down right there where she was, frightened and obedient.

"Take your dress off," he ordered.

"What for?" She didn't understand, merely looking up at him from the ground.

"Because!" he shouted. "I've had it with you, you understand?!"

She thought he'd brought her there to kill her.

"What are you planning to do with me?" she asked.

"And what does one do with you, don't you know?"

Ustin started to unbutton his pants. She understood.

"I don't want to!" she yelled and started to crawl away.

"You wanted to last night and now you don't? I don't care if you want to or not! Take off your dress!"

"I don't want to do it like this!" Shamara shouted. She raised herself, wanting to escape. . . .

He caught her, like an animal, with a single movement. Tore off her dress. It tore as if made of paper.

"Why the dress?" she had time to yell.

She fought him, hit him in the face.

"Bastard! Bastard!"

He fought back in dull silence. He took her roughly, as if he hated her.

She kissed his sweaty face:

"My darling . . ."

Cheek to cheek they lay, finding each other's lips, kissing briefly, hardly touching. She caressed his hair.

"My dearest," she kept saying.

Caressing his face as he lay, eyes closed, she said, "Tell me you love me."

He was silent. Then with closed eyes he said, "I love you."

Someone poked into her face. She looked—it was a dog's muzzle. Then from the other side, too. Then another one. She lifted herself up. There were seven dogs standing there looking at her and Ustin. The dogs were Lera's.

Lera was in the bushes on all fours. His eyes flashed amid the bushes.

Still lifting herself up, she called out, "Ustin!" Her call was peremptory, that of a wife summoning her husband.

Ustin opened his eyes and saw Lera. Lera was crawling away on all fours.

"Kill him!" Shamara said to Ustin. "Kill him!"

She pointed her finger at Lera. Her face was burning. And there was such a power in her that Ustin picked up a rock and as if under a spell went after Lera.

They chased him to the water, to the Akhtuba. At first he kept asking, for some reason asking, "What are you doing, guys? Hey, don't!"

Then he fled in silence, something wheezing in his chest. . . .

He collapsed into the water, got up, tripped, fell in again. And not getting up this time, he started swimming, swimming away from them.

They stood on the riverbank watching him. Shamara wore the dress, which was in tatters. They were breathing heavily.

The seven dogs stood on the bank for a while, then got into the water and swam toward Lera, one after another. They caught up to him in the middle of the river and started whirling around near him.

Ustin watched the dogs and Lera. He watched sadly. Gazing at the river, he calmly told Shamara, "I hate you."

She looked at the river as if she hadn't heard him and said, "I hate you too."

She was swimming underwater. Through the water she gazed at the sun, then plunged down to the very bottom. She sat there, her legs crossed, like a human fetus. For a long time she sat, clutching a snag. She wanted to disappear. Then with a decisive movement she pushed off, surfaced, and jumped out up to her waist. The sun blinded her.

The whole sky was filled with sun.

Oh, Lord! She was so sick of it all! The two fools—Dolbilkina and Stukalkina—are sitting in the kitchen and watching television.

Shamara enters with a thud. So that they understand that Shamara's arrived: a worker's got off her shift and wants food. She throws her purse on the table with a thud.

Pashka was sitting at the table, drinking port, his face covered with snot.

"Zinka, my friend . . ."

He turned his head. For some reason, it was totally shaven.

"Zinka," he says. "My friend! Have a seat!"

And he goes into a coughing fit. He scrapes his head against the edge of the table, getting all stained in port. There was a little puddle on the oilcloth.

"You pig!" she says with loathing. "Pig! Drank yourself sick in broad daylight!"

"Zinaida!" Suddenly he yells so terribly that Shamara falls silent.

"Zinaida," he says more quietly. "Sit down."

And, looking sternly into Shamara's eyes, he solemnly says, "Let us drink to God's servant, Maria Pavlovna! To the day of her birth and to the memory of her soul. You don't clink glasses when drinking to the memory of someone's soul, stupid!" he says, stepping away. "Today at seven in the morning she was born, and at seven-ten she passed away. And her life was . . . her life was"—Pashka chokes and adds in a hoarse, disjointed voice—"ten minutes long," and he swallows his port.

Shamara takes a sip.

"Drink it all!" yells Pashka. "Bottoms up! These assholes wouldn't even have anything to drink! Work, they say. What friggin' work, when there's such . . ."

It finally sinks in.

"A daughter, Pash?" Shamara asks joyously. She understands. "It's still early, isn't it? Why, of course it is! Pasha!"

She drinks the whole glass the way people drink water when they are thirsty.

"She's rotten!" Pashka yells for some reason. "Ya hear? The doctors say she's rotten inside! Her liver, her heart, her kidneys—everything in her is rotten. She should never have given birth. Rotten to the core!"

"Why, she's healthy, Pasha!" Shamara's yelling too. "They're all lying!"

"Rot! Everything's rotten inside, understand? They're pushing for her to go on disability, there's rot, they say. You'll never give birth again! You've had it!" He let out a high-pitched howl and began scratching himself on the edge of the table in such a frenzy that it started to shake. "I won't dump her, Zin, I'll never dump her! I'd be a bastard. . . ."

Suddenly Shamara got angry: everyone loves someone, she's the only one unloved, and she heatedly spat out, "You're gonna dump her! Like you'd dump a dog! You're lying, you'll dump her!"

"I won't!"

"You're all pigs," she says tiredly. "You've already started with the drinking. You'll mess about with the disabled, then dump her!"

"She made a man out of me!"

Shamara knew all too well that he wouldn't dump her. She glanced around and saw the girls. They were sitting, watching soccer on TV, as if they knew shit about soccer. She hissed at them, "Get outta here, will you? You couldn't even have a drink with the man." And they disappeared, as if they'd been waiting only for her to hiss at them.

"Pash," she says. "Don't you listen to me. It's such a crying shame. Let's drink: to Marinka, Pash, to Mashenka. May all guys be just like you. . . ."

"Zin, she was born and only took two breaths, like a kitten. . . ."

"Pash, don't. . . . Pasha?"

"Huh?"

"Why'd you shave your head, huh?"

"Marinka was afraid that the baby'd be born with red hair, so I . . ." Pasha laughs quietly, then immediately starts sobbing.

"You little fool, Pasha, you're still such a little fool. . . ."

They sit, for some reason cuddled up to each other like children, and speak in a whisper.

"Pash, don't worry, you'll get a little child from the orphanage and raise him so he'll be good, good as good can be, and then everything in your life will be good . . . so good . . ."

"Zin," Pashka whispers, looking around. "Zin, know what? Marinka's gonna go blind soon; the doctors give her half a year. We knew a long time ago. We're thinking, We'll have a baby, it'll work out somehow. Ya hear, Zin?"

And Shamara gets all choked up and cries, "How come this happens? What for? Why are we so unhappy, Pasha?"

They cried quietly.

"How do we go on, Pash?"

"Don't worry, Zin. Somehow we will." Pashka comforted her.

. . .

They're chopping meat at the butcher's.

Wha-a-ck! Bloody splinters fly from the frozen carcass. *Wha-a-ck!* A robust guy is hewing the carcass of a whale. The whale smiles with one-tenth of its mouth. The guy piles up the red chunks on a serving platter and yells, "Whale meat!"

"What meat?"

"Whale! You deaf? Take what you're given! Don't paw it! Don't paw it! What do you think you are—royalty?"

The line said, "Pretty soon we'll be eatin' crocodile."

Shamara's standing in line. The line goes right out into the street. The police let in one person at a time. But the line is still very anxious, all very sweaty and disheveled.

A fellow with bug eyes was crowding Shamara.

"Why're you shoving?" Shamara asked politely. Then ever so gently she shoves her elbow into his ribs: *one-two!* She knew that trick. If she hadn't stopped him short, he'd push ahead.

Bug-eyes doubles up. "Little bitch!"

"Little bitch yourself," she answered with dignity.

The salesman yells at an old woman, "Give me the coupon!"

"I gave it to you, sonny," she says obsequiously, as if talking to God.

God stands there with the ax. "No, you didn't!"

"I did too!"

"Like the saying goes, 'Sittin' on that bench I used to do it with everybody.'[10] . . . Listen, Granny, you gave me the coupon for butter. You gotta give me one for meat." He checked through all the coupons he had stuck on the nail.

Granny digs around in her purse; it's not there.

"Get going!" the salesman shouts. "Don't hold up the line!"

The line pressed forward, but Granny had a firm grip on the counter, and there was no budging her.

"What's your problem?" The salesman is surprised at the pesky woman. "What is it, huh?"

"Give it to me without the coupon," declares the woman. "That stuff there isn't meat!"

"So, what is it?" he shakes the bloody chunks of meat. "Candy?"

"Fish!" Granny says. "In the Scriptures it says 'fish-whale.'"

"Christ!" shouts the salesman. "Next!"

The line pushed forward, squeezing the old woman out. Shamara was next—sweaty, frightening.

"Two kilos!"

And she put her coupon on the scales.

"That piece over there. Right next to it, next to it, you're getting warmer. . . . No! I'm telling you, the one on the left!"

"This one?"

"Over there, under that one, yeah, no, put it back, show me the one over there. . . ."

"Don't be so choosy. This ain't no bazaar." The god got angry.

"Don't be a show-off! You've picked the wrong girl for it. Understand?" Shamara immediately got all wound up. It didn't take much. "Weigh it! Weigh it, already!"

"Daughter . . ." A wave flung the old woman into Shamara.

"And weigh some for Grandma!" yells Shamara.

"Take it and choke on it!" He practically tossed the meat in Shamara's face.

"Sonny!"

"There's no meat left in the whole country, Granny!"

And Shamara fervently voiced her dream: "They should chop you up into meat, you bloody bastard. Then there'd be enough for the whole country!"

At the table, Shamara uses the store's long knife to cut off a piece from her own chunk for the old woman. She weighs it out on the scales used for monitoring weight.

"Grandma, is four hundred grams all right with you? Okay, I'll cut off another hundred."

She cuts, her hair falling into her eyes. She raised her head to fling the bangs off her face—and there, outside the window, Ustin and Natasha are walking in the heat. They're holding hands and walking in the golden summer.

Shamara tossed the meat into her string bag and set off, set off after them as if enchanted.

The line made way for her: Shamara had a knife as long as a sword in her hands.

As she walked along, she couldn't recognize them: Ustin, her husband, walked along happily, unlike himself, and Natasha, too, walked along happily. Their very backs were happy. They walked, eternally in love with each other, their hands touching, their eyes touching, their breath and words touching. Laughing together about something.

Traces from Natasha's heels remained in the softened asphalt. Shamara followed them. She left her own trail—the meat was dripping.

She trudged along after them as if in a dream. They turned into the park. She followed them down the tree-lined walk.

Suddenly: "Daughter!"

Granny was running after her, untying her handkerchief with her one remaining tooth.

"Take the money. . . ."

Shamara turned around and stared madly at the old woman.

"What money . . ."

"Eighty-four kopeks for four hundred grams . . ."

Five-kopek pieces bounced from her handkerchief onto the asphalt. They rolled around in all directions and sparkled in the sun like gold. She rushed to pick them up—the knife in her hand. Granny cautiously took the knife out of her hand.

"Come on, give me the little knife or you'll cut yourself. I'll take it back, or else they'll curse you out."

Shamara looked at her hands: they were all bloody.

"That's from the meat," said the old woman and gave her the handkerchief to wipe it off.

"From the meat," Shamara repeated. She thought hard about something. Then she wiped her hands with the handkerchief, finger by finger.

She rose from the bench. She'd made a decision about something. Off she went.

"Daughter!"

Granny again.

"What?"

"What about the money?"

Shamara came back. Like a hoodlum, she brought her face up close, her eyes narrowed, and with hatred said to the old woman, "Beat it, old lady! Get!"

Granny's eyes were as blue as drops of water. She told Shamara a secret. "The thing is, I had a coupon for meat. But the Lord said that whale is fish."

Touched in the head.

Shamara ran down the path. They were nowhere to be found. She started rushing around like a caged tiger.

There they are, drinking kvass. Drinking from a single mug. They had their drink, then left. Now it's her turn to get a drink. She went up to the stand, where a pale, plump saleswoman in a *kokoshnik* sat behind the window, watching the world through porcelain eyes.[11] She was swelling out of her clothes like kneaded dough rising out of its bowl.

"One cup," said Shamara. She started looking for her money. The saleswoman poured some kvass, kvass so cold that the sides of the mug misted over, and she placed it in front of Shamara. But Shamara can't find any money.

"Could I have lost it?" she confided woefully to the saleswoman.

The saleswoman took the mug and poured the kvass into the sink for washing the mugs. She washed the mug, then sat down to watch the world, looking right through Shamara.

It was hot.

"You're really something . . . !"

Ustin had totally lost his mind: he's picked this Natasha up in his arms and is walking along. People are looking, after all!

And she howls, hugging his warm neck and giggling as if someone's tickling her. He's simply carrying her Nowhere. Shamara walks behind them and listens as Ustin tells Natasha: "My father told me, 'If you have my grandson, I'll give you a Zhiguli.'[12] Are we gonna give him a grandson, Natash?"

Why, that's what he told them, Ustin and Shamara!

"We are." Natasha laughs. She laughed, then fell silent: Shamara is staring her straight in the face, only half a meter between them.

Ustin doesn't realize a thing. Still happy, he continues, "I'll be released in a month, and we'll take off, I'll show you to my parents. Did you put in for a discharge, Natasha? Are you listening?"

Natasha is silent, watching Shamara.

"I'm listening, I'm listening," Shamara says to Ustin.

He turns around, Natasha in his arms.

"You?!!"

He starts setting Natasha down on her feet.

"You?!"

Shamara begins to twitch: it's unclear whether she's going to start crying or burst out laughing. Her face trembles violently. She manages to get herself under control. With a nervous laugh she said, "Loan me six kopeks until payday. I want some kvass."

Ustin put Natasha down on the ground. "Wait just a minute. . . ."

His face wore an ugly look.

"Oh, Mama!" Shamara said, and squatted down, her arms covering her head. She suddenly felt frightened.

Speaking to the crown of her head, he says, "Get out! Get out of town!"

She retreated from him. "Good luck in making me do it!"

"Think so?"

"Yeah!"

"Fine." He thought for a minute. "Then I'll leave." And he turned to Natasha. "Natash, will you go away with me for good?"

. . .

Shamara trudges after them at the train station, stumbling over other people's bundles, stepping over suitcases. "Ustin, you've only a month left. . . . This'll be an escape. . . . Ustin, they'll catch you anyway. . . . I'm calling the police right now!"

A cop appeared, like a genie out of a bottle. He glances at their holy trinity. They freeze, holding their breath. They stood in silence, and after he left Shamara said, "The angel's passed." Then she started up again, "Ustin . . ."

They went out onto the platform. Night had fallen.

People were sleeping on the warm asphalt.

"The train's running late." The words emerged from the darkness.

But something with eyes is approaching.

"What's that? The last commuter train?"

"The last one already came through. This one's unscheduled, from the chemical plant."

Ustin pulls Natasha toward the commuter train. "Let's go. . . ."

"Ustin," says Shamara. "Take me with you."

Ustin looked around helplessly: Shamara stands there, looking utterly pitiful.

"Will you take me?"

Ustin hesitated, was on the point of taking her, then remembered, "But it's you I'm running away from . . ."

"Well, then, kiss me goodbye," Shamara says humbly.

And Ustin gives in. As he kisses her, Shamara embraces him tightly, so he can't break free, and sobs on his chest, "Ustin, they'll give you a new sentence!"

"Don't jinx me!"

"If they put you back in jail you'll be mine again! Natashka won't wait. Will you, Natash? Say you won't!"

"Let go."

"I won't! You're not going anywhere!"

And the commuter train speaks in a hoarse bass, "The train's not going any farther! Please exit the cars! The train's now going to the depot at Svinoe Zaimishche!"[13]

Now Shamara also laughs hoarsely, but on Ustin's chest. "See, I told you you're not going anywhere!"

"Witch!" Ustin says. "Devil!"

"So what," says Shamara. And she let Ustin go—there was no point in holding him back now.

In a thunderous voice the commuter train announces to the whole world, "You're being told in plain Russian: the train is going to the depot! Where? . . . To your friggin' mother, that's where! Understand?"

Shamara celebrates her victory, but Ustin tears apart the commuter train's door as if it were the hide of a bull. Shamara looked and saw only the edge of Natasha's dress caught in the door. Quickly, quickly, like a snake, it slithered away as they pulled in the colorful tail. And they were off in an instant. Shamara ran after them.

She kept running and running for some reason. The last car was entirely without doors, as if after a bomb attack. A guy with a shaved head stood there.

"Go on, jump," he said, "I'll catch you."

She up and jumped. He caught her, but she got dragged down, almost sucked under the wheel. He barely pulled her out. It was like lifting a barbell. All covered in sweat, he pressed her to his wet chest.

"Oh, my sweetie of a boy. . . ."

The car shakes; the train rides on without stopping; the lights suddenly burn bright, then go out completely. The guy asks, "So, how can you tell I'm a convict? I'm even wearing a suit."

"You can just tell," says Shamara.

He laughs ominously. "Well, I'm on my way to a date. I got a woman there."

"Uh-huh," says Shamara. "What do I care."

After a short silence the guy asked, "What's your name?"

"Guess."

"Olia, no? Well, then, Tania. Ira? Liudmila, probably . . ."

Shamara shakes her head: *No.*

"Natasha?"

Shamara thought a moment—the guy was waiting—and nodded, "You guessed it."

The guy covered his eyes, sat for a while, expelled his breath, and opened his eyes. "So . . ."

When he opened his eyes they were inhuman, like tin. And he looked at her with his tin eyes and took out a knife.

"Did you say your evening prayers, you little slut?"

"What're you doing?" Shamara looks at the knife, incredulous. The knife's handle was beautiful, made of multicolored plastic. "What're you doing?"

He rolled up his sleeve. "Can you read?"

NATASHA is tattooed on his arm. He made a threatening gesture with his fist at the tattoo. "Oooooh!"

"Get ready," he told Shamara.

"For what?" she wailed.

"For death!"

"What for? What did I do to you?!"

He stared with his eyes of tin, and stared and stared.

"Bitch!" he suddenly yelled with all his body and soul. "You promised to wait for me! Didn't you?" He advanced.

"Yes, I did," said Shamara, retreating.

"Couldn't even wait a year! And you're already blowing that friggin' stool pigeon Vaska."

"I . . ."

"You're blowing him! I asked you, didn't I—Natash, just wait for me! I loved you, you bitch! I was an A student. I'd done military and political training! You even wrote me letters! You forgot what you wrote! 'Let's get married,' you wrote! Remember?"

"I remember." Shamara was retreating toward the doors. She was almost there.

"Remember! Remember how they laughed when I came home! You and Vaska would walk past my house laughing! I killed a man because of you!"

"Killed?"

"Don't push me! Don't laugh! He got killed laughing like that!"

Shamara stood at the opening where the doors had been broken off. Outside, freedom was sweeping by, black as the night.

"Your Vaska pissed in his pants, too, when he was a kid! And you laugh at me!"

The tip of the knife was at her heart. It pricked her.

"I'm not laughing."

"Any minute this little knife can . . . and then you'll laugh!"

"I won't!"

"But your Vaska's laughing!"

"Vaska won't, either." Shamara tried to persuade him. For a second, he believed her; the tin left his eyes, and his eyes cleared.

"Why, you're my sweetheart," Shamara whispered. "You're my darling . . ."

She had to jump while the guy was still softened. Shamara probed around with her foot for the opening, then with her hands pushed away from the guy and tumbled into the darkness.

"Natasha!"

She rolled into the darkness: *Ah, ow, dammit!* Then she ran, falling down, and as she fell, she looked back: a huge woman with a sword raced after her—black as death in the searchlights that covered her: *O-o-o!*

She got used to the darkness. She looked: the train was moving on, a distant golden snake carrying Ustin away. She dragged herself forward, heading for a distant bonfire.

Lera was singing by the bonfire. Something strange, in English, in different voices.

There were hippies sitting beside him, really getting into the song. One hippie with an Adam's apple was dancing by himself at the bonfire. Shamara stood and stood and started to cry. These people—she loved them all so much. She felt so warm. She felt so good, the way you feel only when you die.

Then she went up to Lera. Lera wore a hippie jacket with badges on it, all dressed up, the pack of dogs nearby—all seven of them.

"Lera," she said. "Take me home."

As they walked along she said, "I'm going to walk and sleep, and you lead me, okay?"

"Maybe we should go to my place? My mother fried up some whale cutlets. . . ."

"No." She shook her head. "I want to go home, to the dorm. What were you singing, Ler?"

He said something in English.

"What's that?"

"'Jesus Christ Superstar,'" Lera answered.

"Jesus?" she was surprised. "What's this, Ler, you believe in God?" she asked, falling asleep on his shoulder.

She walked, sleeping. Their steps were audible for a long time: *shkh, shkh, shkh.*

A flashlight in her face.

"Get up!"

Shamara is lying on her bed in the dorm, her arm covering her face. Some guy yells, "Get up!"

"Get that light out of my face!" she finally says. She could make out the face: Max, the albino, Ustin's boss. "You idiot! I just fell asleep."

"Get up!"

"You gonna turn it off?! Okay, go ahead and look." Shamara threw off the sheet and lay naked.

He turned it off. Dolbilkina and Stukalkina switch on the light, walking around like two Ophelias in their nightgowns and curlers. They're not afraid of Max. "What are you doing here?"

Shamara turned to the wall and covered herself as if she were sleeping.

"Where's your husband?" Max asks Shamara. Shamara sleeps, snuffling.

"You mean Ustin?" asks Dolbilkina. "He never comes here."

"Zinaida Petrovna, I'm asking you officially," says Maxim. "Where's your husband?"

Shamara can't take it.

"Where? You go ask her where! Where, where . . ." Shamara beats Natasha's bed with her fist. "Go ahead and ask her where she went with him. Under what bush?! You're not looking in the right place, boss!"

"Come with me," says Max. "We need your help."

"What? My help? For you? You want Shamara's help? A stool pigeon whore you want! You scumbag!"

"Prokhorov!" Max called.

Prokhorov came in, grabbing Stukalkina by the tit.

"Scram, you sluts," he said when they started squealing.

He wrapped Shamara in the blanket. "Into the car, Max Sanych?"

Raya glanced into the room. "Not asleep?"

Prokhorov threw Shamara over his shoulder, holding her tightly by the hair. "Just try to fidget or show off, just try!"

Max asks Raya, "Ray, you got any?" And he holds up two fingers. Ray nodded her head, holding up one finger. She brought out a small bottle wrapped in newspaper. The paper showed shots of the prison bosses. At the door she asks, "Max, do you want some cutlets? Whale cutlets?"

"It's better for you raw," Prokhorov said as he went down the stairs.

"Huh?"

"Raw meat, I'm telling you, is better for you."

In the car he asked, "Where do I take her?"

"To my place," said Max.

Max's apartment is white. The furniture's albino too. They put Shamara down on a white carpet. Max sat at a white table.

"Come here, let's have a drink, you fool," he says.

"Give me something to wear," says Shamara.

Max pushed a button—he had a remote control on the table—and some sort of thing rolled in through the door. There were shirts on it. Shamara chose a light blue one and sat down across from Max.

"You look good," says Max. "You all need a good washing, a good cleaning—so you'll pass for real people."

"So, what's that make us now?" asks Shamara.

"Cattle," says Max. "Well, let's get going!"

He raised a shot glass, his eyes signaling the clinking of glasses.

Shamara says, "I'm not drinking."

"Fine." He drank up, sat awhile, closed his eyes, and tilted his head. "So, what were you doing at the train station today, huh?"

"Where?"

"We saw you. Who were you seeing off, huh?"

"Who?"

"That's what I'm asking you—who!"

"Nobody. Don't shout!"

"What were you doing there?"

"Going for a walk."

"Answer me!"

"Going for a walk!"

"Prokhorov saw you at the station!"

"I was going for a walk!"

He slaps her face—there!—she asked for it. He wipes his hand on a handkerchief.

"You asked for it."

Shamara sits, the blood drained from her face.

"Sorry," says Max. "Sorry, Zin . . ."

He scared her to death with his apologies. He got down on his knees.

"Forgive me . . ."

"What's with you?" Shamara backs away. "And now he's apologizing. Big deal, it's not the first time. . . ."

Max whispers something into her bare knees. She frees herself. Something glitters on the wall.

"Max, what's that?"

As soon as he'd knelt before her, she felt in charge of the situation. "What's that?" she chirped.

Handcuffs hung, gleaming, from a nail.

"Come on," says Max, "give me your hands."

And—snap! Right on her wrists.

"These are special bracelets for little girls. A new design. I invented them. You like them?"

And he guffaws soundlessly. Even his laugh is colorless!

"If you turn this little round knob right here, then—"

"Ow!" Shamara yells.

"That's right, it's going to hurt," Max agrees. "A one-of-a-kind design. An experimental model. You're the first to test it. You're like Gagarin. Like Belka and Strelka.[14] You remember Belka and Strelka? Let me put you on a chain, it'll be more relaxed that way."

Max chained Shamara to the table with her handcuffs.

"You don't need your hands, do you, since you're not drinking."

And again, "So, then, what were you doing at the train station? Try to remember."

He put a photograph right under her nose.

"Didn't see this guy at the station, did you? A psycho. Kills women. Why? We don't know. He escaped from the prison psycho ward."

Shamara looked, and didn't say a word.

"That's right, go ahead and keep quiet. . . . He's right to be killing you. You all should be destroyed."

Her eyes kept sticking together. Shamara would prop her chin up with her hand; her sleepy face would slide off it and hit the table. She'd raise it, holding it up, and look at Max. He kept on talking and talking. He drank and talked. Whenever she woke up, she was frightened to see him, like a corpse sitting at the same table with her, twisting its lips.

"If you only knew whom you're sitting with! I'm the son of an academician. That's right. I lived in Moscow on Kutuzovsky.[15] That's right. I graduated from the academy. That's right. And from the military graduate school. Do you know what the military graduate school is?"

Shamara shook her head: *No.*

"You ignoramus. It's for the best minds. I'm an outstanding mind. Sure, I drank, and I didn't hide it. That's why they exiled me to this wasteland. But I drink here too. So, one may ask, why did they exile me? I drank, drink, and will drink.[16] They're just afraid of my mind. I can invent anything! I can invent the guillotine, the electric chair, the electric gallows. . . ." He pushed a button on the remote control. Things on wheels started rolling into the room.

"Things," Max said, "are better than people. They're more obedient. Watch!"

His things were dancing.

"Do you know the difference between the Butyrka and the Taganka prisons? You don't, you ignoramus. You people here don't know anything. I'll explain. The Taganka was built according to an American model: five floors, cells along the walls, and an open space in the center with an iron staircase. A stifling prison, understand? And Butyrka? Butyrka was built according to Kazakov's plans. Do you know who Kazakov was? He built Moscow University and the Butyrka prison. The Butyrka prison is an outstanding monument of architecture and construction, understand? Everything in it is thoroughly thought out! If they'd given me the chance, I'd have built a prison just like it! Right down to the very latest in technology. Hear me?!"

"Let Ustin go!" Shamara said suddenly.

"What?"

"Give Ustin back!"

"It seems I haven't caught him yet. And you, it seems, haven't had a drink."

"If I tell you where he is, will you let him go? You can say that you sent him there to get bricks, or paint, or shit!"

"And what do I get for doing that?"

"I'll inform on the psycho in exchange. I know where he is."

"What do I need a psycho for? He's not ours, he's from the psycho ward. We're trying to catch him just for the fun of it."

They looked at each other like two intelligent animals.

"Do you love Ustin?" asked Max.

"Yes," she answered after a brief silence.

"Can I get some ass, too?" asked Max and touched her knees. Shamara moved her knees away and thought about it.

Max made his move again. "If I get some, I'll let him go."

"If you let him go, I'll give you some," Shamara bargained.

"You give—I let him go," said Max. "Word of an officer."

"It's a deal," said Shamara and offered him her handcuffed hands. "Take them off."

"It may be interesting to try it with them on." He nodded at the handcuffs.

"No," said Shamara firmly. "That wasn't part of the deal."

In the morning she got up, pulled on Max's jogging suit, and went to the door. In the doorway some revolting thing on wheels began to stir, move, block her path, and called out as if it were alive. She approached the window: the windows had bars. She sat down on the ottoman. Max was asleep, all skin and bones, his hands crossed over his chest. The handcuffs were lying on the carpet. She took the handcuffs and Max's hands and—*snap*. Let him sleep in handcuffs. She went out into the corridor, kicked the revolting thing aside with her foot, opened the door, and left.

The conveyor is working, and the cradles with their spools flow right along. Shamara looks fixedly at them for a long, long time, as if from another world. She looks intently, as if wanting to understand: What is this? Where's it going? What's it for?

Raya stands in front of the factory. Near the huge portrait of her. She's admiring it. Shamara walks up, and in embarrassment to be caught beside the portrait, Raya says, "That's a real fright they drew. Do I really look like that?"

Shamara glanced at her as if from distance: Who is this?

Raya says, "Say, how about going to the Comrades' Court? They're trying this thief—she stole from every single member of her work team, can you imagine? There's a show trial at the Palace of Culture."

Young girls are riding the tram and showing each other a photo.

"They're looking for a murderer. He kills anyone dressed in red."

"With what?" asks Raya.

"He has a special little awl. . . ."

"Only girls . . ."

"His fiancée didn't wait for him to get out of the army, so he's taking revenge on all women."

"He'd have done better to just knock off his fiancée. . . ."

"And, girls, he's so good-looking!"

Shamara opened her eyes and glanced at the photograph. It stung her eyes, and she looked away.

On the stage stands a red-haired girl wearing a white blouse with a Komsomol badge and shouting to the audience, "What, you think I have any use for your rings? I don't need anything! It's my hands that do all the stealing, not me."

Raya, the judge, interrupted her.

"You, Pavlova, don't railroad the proceedings. Let the plaintiff speak."

The plaintiff jumped onto the stage, "Zhanna, I trusted you! I never had a better friend, comrades. You were like my own sister to me!"

"The facts," says Raya.

"I'm telling you a fact . . . the fact is that once, in front of her, I put my gold ring into a seashell. Then I took off my earrings and put them in, too. Then I went to the bathroom! When I came out, there was no gold and no Zhanna. Zhanna, why do you steal from friends? To steal from strangers is one thing, but why from friends? Comrades! She was such a friend to me—we were inseparable. She taught me how to salt mushrooms and make sewing patterns. She's such an interesting person! Zhanna! Comrades!"

Red-haired Zhanna is mad. "Why are you lying right to my face? Liar! Here you are, take it, please. . . ."

"Bring in the stolen items," says Raya from the stage.

To the accompaniment of music they brought in a rug, a fake fur, crystal vases, and a tape player.

Shamara headed for the exit.

"How'd you manage the rug? It's pretty heavy, isn't it?" The audience felt sorry for Zhanna.

"I could barely drag it away," complained red-haired Zhanna. "Almost broke my backbone."

The audience howled with pleased laughter.

Shamara walked along the street—she was sick and tired of sidewalks. The cars honked—*oo-oo,* the horny dogs! A dump truck was driving toward her, then made a U-turn and stopped beside her—*prr—ru!*

Pashka: "Zin!"

She climbed into the passenger seat of the truck.

"Zin!" he says. "I've been looking for you all over the city. They've caught Ustin! Max sent me to find you."

Shamara suddenly came to life, like a flower after the rain.

"Pashechka." She kissed him.

Pashka was radiant.

"What'd you kiss me for?"

"Did you see him?"

"No."

"Is Natashka with him?"

"I don't know."

"What about the psycho?"

"What psycho?"

"Pa-ashechka!" she kissed him.

They both laughed. It started raining, first a light sun

shower, then a downpour. The sun went on shining. The dump truck flew along on the sunny wings of water sprites.

She went into Max's office, happy, all covered in raindrops.

"Hello!"

Max was speaking with someone and frowning. He saw Shamara, said something to the man, and the man left.

"Here you are." He grimaced. He snagged something from the table with his finger and lifted it—the handcuffs.

"Nifty," he said. "One–zero in your favor."

"Where's Ustin?" she asked.

Max stiffened, and his face grew dim. He put the handcuffs on the table and drew himself erect.

"Zinaida Petrovna, we have asked you here to verify the corpse of your husband, Sergei Vasilyevich Ustinov, who was killed while attempting to escape."

Shamara stared and stared. Max became nervous.

"And, by the way, why is it that your last names are different: Shamarina, Ustinov?"

"We forgot to ask you," said Shamara. Her eyes kept staring.

They went to the morgue. They walked along. Something was dripping. Shamara kept looking under her feet. She walked behind Max. There were puddles under their feet. Leakage after the downpour. They walked up to the body. It was covered with a sheet. They uncovered the face. It wasn't Ustin. Someone else. She started to cry. The person's arm was outflung, with "Natasha" tattooed on it.

She looked at Max. Max said, "One–one, a tie game."

And he started laughing soundlessly and couldn't stop. He craned his neck.

And all the while something was dripping and dripping: *drip, drip.*

She came home, went into her room—Natasha was lying on the bed. Like an old woman, Shamara sat down beside her.

"Where is he?"

She's silent. Only the water in the kitchen goes *drip, drip*.

"Just tell me, is he alive, at least?"

Natasha turned around and looked at her.

"He's on Green Island," she said.

Shamara is sailing down the Volga in a motorboat. To protect her head from the wind, she's tied a kerchief around it. Her face kisses the wind.

There are oaks growing on Green Island. Shamara walks among the oaks.

"Ustin!" she shouts. "Ustin!"

There's nobody there.

"Ustin!"

From up an oak Ustin asks, "Why're you shouting? You alone?"

Shamara gets some food out of the basket: potatoes, tomatoes, eggs. "Eat, go on, eat."

"How'd you find out I was here?"

"Natasha . . ."

"She ratted on me?"

"Only to me. She's in bed. Did you hurt her feelings, Ustin?"

He requested: "Just drop it."

He swallowed the bread in chunks.

"Ustin, I made a deal with your boss that this wouldn't be counted as an escape. . . ."

"You don't say! What is it, then?"

"An expedition . . ."

"Fine . . . and where did you make this deal for me?"

She yelled, "What business is that of yours? What business of yours is it what I do! All you can do is make fun of me! All anyone can do is make fun of me. . . ."

"What's your problem?" He touched her. "You are my wife. I can ask, can't I?"

She fell silent.

"I got him to do it for a bottle," she said.

They were riding in the motorboat. Ustin looks into the distance. Shamara can't stop looking at him.

They went up the mountain. There's a church standing on the mountain, a poor one made of planks. The paint covering it is cheap, light blue and green, the sort used on cemetery fences.

Shamara requested, "Let's go inside, Ustin."

Ustin keeps walking and shakes his head: *No!*

"What's there to do inside?" he asks.

"Let's just look around," she cajoles. "Please, Ustin!"

An old woman was washing the church floors. She was finishing up. It was the granny from the line.

"Hello, Grandma," Shamara said to her.

Granny looked, but didn't recognize her. "Hello, children."

She wrung out the rag and put it on the threshold. "Just remember to wipe your feet, children. All us old ladies here wash the floor ourselves; we take turns."

It was light inside the church; sunbeams poured in from everywhere. The floor was still wet, amber, sunlit. Shamara took Ustin's hand. They stood in a shaft of sunlight.

Shamara said to the sunbeam, "We're husband and wife! We're husband and wife!"

She turned to the icon of the Mother of God with the little child and crossed herself awkwardly. Ustin tugged at her hand.

"Have you totally lost it, or what . . . ?"

There's a ringing of tin in the service area of the factory cafeteria. The workers are banging their tin plates with spoons.

"Open up the mess hall! It's time!"

Shamara takes five glasses of tomato juice. Nothing else.

At the table Raya asks, "Are you sure it's Max's?"

"Shh, quiet! I'm sure."

"I'm looking at you, and your eyes have got so . . . pregnant . . ."

"Ray, help me! Ustin and I've already bought the tickets. . . ."

"For when?"

"We're leaving in three days. I just have to get him away from that Natasha, no matter where. . . . If he finds out that Max and I . . . that Max made me—"

"I know of a sure method. My grandmother taught my mother, and my mother taught me," Raya says and suddenly asks: "So, Zin, what's he like as a man. Not bad?"

"Who?"

"Max."

Shamara sits on the balcony, holding her stomach. It hurts. Down below, in the distance, she saw Ustin walking along the path and Natasha going toward him. They stopped. They talk. Ustin pulled Natasha by the arm. Natasha tore her arm free.

Shamara clamped her teeth onto the railing—it hurt. She couldn't stand it—she ran into the bathroom. Natasha ran toward her.

Shamara said to her, "Natasha, help me!"

In the bathroom she ordered, "Make the water hotter! Add the manganese! Give me the towel!"

Natasha glanced into the bathtub: half a tub of blood. Up to Shamara's knees. Water pours out of the faucet. She started to feel sick.

"Don't look! Turn around!" she shouted at Natasha. "You're not allowed to look."

Then she said, "Give me the newspaper."

She wrapped something up.

"Throw it in the garbage."

She gave Natasha the little bundle. The paper showed shots of the prison bosses.

· · ·

Natasha opened the garbage chute and stuck the little bundle through. She looked into the fetid maw, then closed it.

Shamara lay down for a little bit, and now she's already walking around the room. She's looking for her clothes. Natasha tells her, "Zina, you should lie down. After all, if you want to call a spade a spade, this was an operation."

Shamara walks around, angry and happy at the same time. "A Soviet woman's not afraid of abortions! Abortions make a Soviet woman even more beautiful!"

She started to leave.

"Where are you going?" Natasha asks.

On the threshold Shamara looks around, smiling unhappily, "So, where'd he go?"

"Zina!"

"We're leaving tomorrow. People are coming to see us off. And he's not here. Mind if I go?" she asked Natasha.

She swayed, supported herself with her hand against the wall, and listened to her heart—then set off, using the wall as her support.

Everyone gathered to see them off. The table in the big room was set. But Shamara and Ustin weren't there.

People sat in the kitchen, chewing sunflower seeds. They tossed the shells on the floor.

"Go ahead and throw them on the floor," said Lena, who had come back from vacation. "Tomorrow's cleaning day, anyway."

Stukalkina and Dolbilkina were jostling with each other by Shamara's tape player, recording funny folk ditties for her.[17] "Sing this one, Gal. . . ."

"You must be kidding! That one's nothing but obscenities!"

"Come on, sing it!"

Then they turned on the tape player, listened to their own songs, and howled with laughter.

They'd bury they faces in their laps.

"Ah, I can't take it!"

It sounded as if someone was outside the door. There was a rustling, as of some person or some animal rubbing itself against the door and whimpering. They listened closely.

Natasha went to the door. She opened it. It was Shamara, whimpering.

When Natasha opened the door, Shamara lifted her face, her beautiful face, now beaten and bloody, and for a second their eyes met, Shamara's eyes, always triumphant and crazy, now full of intelligence and pain, immense human intelligence and immense pain. It was just an instant, like an exhalation. She fell flat on her face in the hallway, mumbling something senseless, drunken, and terrifying.

"Shamara!" shouted Natasha, and the girls stuck their heads out of the kitchen, saw Zinka lying on the floor, and immediately started screeching in unison.

Dolbilkina and Stukalkina rushed to Zinka's side and carried her to the bed, silently and sternly. At their side Lena kept chirping:

"Oh Lord, my blouse, who gave you permission to take my blouse, you got it all dirty, oh Lord, that's what happens when you give your things to someone, it's all bloody!"

They chased her away from Zinka, from Shamara, as if she were a ferocious dog ready to pounce, but in their fright the Galyas laid Shamara down on Lena's bed under the portrait of Kolya-the-Groom, and Lena parked herself near Zinka's pillow, got down on her knees, and started lamenting over her now-ruined bed.

"On my sheet, my white sheet, why did you put her, when she's all dirty, on my sheet?" she wailed.

"Who did this to you?" . . . "Who did this to you?" the two Galyas asked Shamara in turn; leaning over her, Dolbilkina and Stukalkina kept hammering like woodpeckers: "Who did this to you? Who did this to you?"[18]

Shamara mumbled something, staring vacantly and senselessly.

Lena looked spitefully at Natasha, "You ask her, you're practically family, after all. Or I'll call the police! She could easily croak on my bed! I just get back from vacation—and here you go!"

Natasha leaned down right to her face.

"Do you hear me, Zina, do you hear me? Who beat you up? Who?"

Outside Lera burst into song:

> "When she was just a kid, still a gal,
> But branded with a nickname foul,
> He had his fun, then dumped the 'whore,'
> And married a 'nice girl,' who suited him more."

"Zina! Who beat you?"

Suddenly Shamara looked straight into her own heart and breathed out:

"Ustin . . ."

She turned away.

Lena shouts, "I'm going to call the police. At the health resort I got out of the habit of this dog's life. Let the police deal with them, with her and her criminal . . ."

"Stop her, we don't need any fuss," Dolbilkina says to Natasha. "Our apartment's a model of maintenance. Lenka, don't call them! She'll come to any second. Come on, Shamara! Maybe we should call an ambulance, girls?"

"We don't need an ambulance," says Raya. She takes a bottle off the table and goes into the kitchen. "She'll recover."

Kolya, Lenka's fiancé, came in. Kolya pushes everyone aside.

"Get back, so there won't be any mistakes!" And he sniffs Shamara's face. "She's drunk," he announces importantly. "You can call the police."

Shamara opened her eyes. Her face grew wrinkled, and her lips trembled.

"Mama!" she says. "Mama, dearest!" she says fervently in a sobbing tone. "Why did you leave me, why did you abandon your very own little girl, Mama! You see what they're doing to me, you see how they torture me, Mama!"

Tears flow down Shamara's face, foam forms in the corner of her mouth, and her voice grows stronger:

"Mama! Don't leave me. They've trampled me down, torn me to pieces, Mama! Your hand, give me your hand, Mama. . . ."

Shamara raises herself up on the bed and looks at everybody with unseeing eyes.

"Mama, give me your hand, where are you?! Have pity on me, Mama!"

Dolbilkina holds out her hand to her, Stukalkina strokes her head, and both bawl openly and freely. Shamara lies back down, smiles blissfully, bright tears flowing down her face.

Kolya shrugs his shoulders and says, uncertainly, "Still, maybe we should call the ambulance?"

But Dolbilkina and Stukalkina chase him and Lena away, then go into the kitchen, and howl together in a single loud voice. Natasha sits near Shamara, holding her hand, almost crying herself.

"Mama," Zinka whispers to her, pressing her hand. "My mama." And suddenly she looks at Natasha with intelligent, sober eyes, still wet from tears, and, with a wink, whispers, "They believed it, eh? Stupid country hicks. Call the police, they have to call the police right away, the vipers, they feel closer to the police than to their own grandmother. It's Ustin they should've taken to the police. You know why he beat me? He beat me 'cause of you. He doesn't want to go with me. He loves you. 'She's clean,' he says. You're the clean one. But me, I . . . you take care of him . . . I'm giving him away. He's yours now. You gonna take care of him?"

She looks at Natasha and suddenly bursts out sobbing, "He's mine! Mine! I won't give him away, won't give him to you, let him beat me, let him even kill me. He's mine!"

She cries. Natasha goes to the door; Lena's standing in the doorway. Natasha tries to push Lena out with her body, but Lena grabs hold of the doorjamb. "It's good at least that all this happened before cleaning day. Tomorrow we'll chuck her out, so everything can be clean!"

Natasha goes to the kitchen. Dolbilkina and Stukalkina are in there, crying, and Raya, drunk, sits leaning over the tape player, listening to the funny ditties and silently shaking with laughter.

At the pier Lera and his dogs are seeing Shamara off.

Above the pier are written the words "Terminator City."

"You go on, why don't you," Shamara tries to persuade Lera. "The boat's late."

"So, where will you go?" Lera tries to find out.

Shamara stands with her little suitcase, shrugging her shoulders.

"Oh, somewhere. Where there are no bosses." She smiles.

She jumped into the boat. Sat down. As they turned around Lera waved.

She smiled at him—already from a distance, she smiled from inside an already different self.

They set sail toward the sun. Beside them sailed barges with watermelons.

On the riverbank she saw Ustin's cottage with the unfinished yacht. She looked and looked at it, until it disappeared from view.

1990

· · ·

Translators' Notes

Title: "Shamara" comes from *shamra,* a word from the Caspian region that refers to a violent windstorm from the sea.

1. In Russian slang, "light blue" (*goluboy*) refers to male gays, "pink" (*rozovaya*) to lesbians.

2. This is an ironic recasting of the cliché of Soviet pseudohospitality, "You must visit more often."

3. Narzan is a popular brand of Soviet mineral water.

4. At Russian weddings, guests traditionally drink the wedding toast, then shout "Bitter!" ("*Gor'ko!*") to the bride and groom, whereupon the couple kisses, "to sweeten the brew."

5. This pseudofolkloric rhyming line alludes to the Soviet custom of "three on a bottle"—when three drunks would purchase and consume a bottle of vodka, often in a doorway, because none could afford to buy it alone.

6. Miklukho-Maklay is a famous nineteenth-century Russian explorer.

7. The Komsomol was the Communist Youth League.

8. The *lezginka* is a fast, bravura folk dance popular in the Caucasus.

9. The reference is to the famous acrobatic loop performed by the prerevolutionary pilot Pyotr Nesterov (1887–1914), which the Funland ride presumably imitates. (Thank you, Sasha Prokhorov.)

10. The line is from a type of ditty (*chastushka*) called *rifmylovushki,* in which the first, suggestive couplet becomes diffused by the improvised tongue-in-cheek innocence of the second. (Thank you, Georgii Levinton.)

11. A *kokoshnik* is a decorative headpiece worn by Russian women as part of folk attire.

12. "Zhiguli" is the brand name of a popular Russian car.

13. "Svinoe Zaimishche" translates literally as "pig marsh."

14. Yuri Gagarin was the first Soviet man in space, a national hero. Belka and Strelka were two of the first dogs launched into space by the Soviets.

15. During Soviet times, Kutuzovsky was a main thoroughfare in one of the central and most prestigious areas of the city.

16. The phrase ironically evokes the ideological cliché "Lenin lived, lives, and will live."

17. "Folk ditties" is *chastushki* in the original Russian. Based on works of oral folk poetry, *chastushki* contain humorous and topical subjects, often treated bawdily and set to simple tunes.

18. The Russian involves an untranslatable pun based on the two Galyas' surnames: "Stukalkina" (from *stukat',* or "to knock") conjures up the slang expression for "stool pigeon" (*stukach*), while "Dolbilkina" (from *dolbit',* or "to keep hammering away") evokes the repeated action and sound of a woodpecker.

■ □ ■ □ ■

PIGGY

Translated by Andrew Bromfield

I HATED THE PIG FROM THE VERY FIRST DAY. I ALREADY HATED IT AT the station, when I hugged and kissed my mother. Her faded cotton dress gave off a sharp, unpleasant smell that made me wince.

"Haven't you slaughtered it yet?" I asked.

"No. Why, do I smell?" My mother began to sniff in fright at her shoulders, turning her head from side to side, putting her nose to the cloth, and taking several quick, short sniffs.

"I don't notice it," she said in guilty embarrassment. "I've gotten used to it." And she stood stock-still for a moment.

She often used to freeze like that, like a bird: she stood there—tall, bony, and plain, with her sunburned collarbones protruding (she liked dresses with a wide neck), ungainly, with birdlike eyelids that made her small eyes look closed; she froze motionless, as though she had forgotten where she was and who she was, and then yawned affectedly (after one of these affected yawns she usually said something that was important to her, something she didn't want to say, but she overcame her hesitation and said it anyway, after a yawn, as if it were nothing special, and I disliked this little trick of hers, because I knew that it was something important to her). "That's what the girls at work keep saying, 'Slaughter it. What's it good for,' they say. 'You smell of that pig of yours,' they say. I never seem to do anything but wash, wash, wash."

She gave me a frightened glance, and once again I was overcome by a wave of shame and pity. I know these "girls" she works with: fat, and proud of it, white skinned, self-satisfied, with the singsong hypocritical voices of the wives of bosses—directors of shops and cafés, warehouse managers. I remember very well how we bought her a pair of gold-plated earrings for ten rubles because they were exactly the same as Ifteeva's gold ones that cost two hundred—they had exactly the same little lilac stones set in them as the ones that belonged to Ifteeva, the wife of the city gas supply manager. I remember very well how happy she was and how long it was before they noticed her new earrings, and Mother sat there tense and straight, stock-still, and her ears, which had been specially pierced for the first time in her life—at fifty-four—turned bright red and looked as though they were stretching with the weight of the earrings, as though the earrings weighed a kilogram apiece. And then they noticed! They cackled in joy and fluttered their plump hands, with rings on them, the rings with stones and the plain bands, but the expression in their eyes was cold, hostile, and cautious. "Masha? Where would you get them? Our Masha?" And Mother's face thawed, thawed the way icicles do, and her lips stretched out into a smile of inane happiness, and she was so happy sitting there. . . . And they touched Mother's ears with their short, fat fingers, and it hurt, but Mother didn't show it; they took off her earrings as though to admire them, but they started avidly searching for the hallmark—and when they didn't find one, they glanced at one another in triumph, and now their eyes were as glad as the expression on their faces and their triumphant voices. "Well, now, Maria Stepanovna, you nearly fooled us, for a moment we actually thought . . ." They weren't being hypocritical now; they were genuinely glad as they forgave Maria Stepanovna her little trick. But Mother tried to convince them, in an unnaturally high voice, that the earrings were silver. "They put a hallmark on silver, too, Maria Stepanovna, but there's nothing on these." Ifteeva herself fastened the earrings back on Mother's ears with her very own gold-laden hands. And Mother gradually hunched over and then froze motionless, and her face froze, and from the small eyes that looked as though they were closed, the tears flowed down over her face and onto the lips that were set in a broad, pitiful smile.

"Let's go then, shall we?" Somehow my words came out a bit harsh.

"Why don't we take the bus?" Mother asked.

I had a sudden vision of people wrinkling up their noses and turning away from my mother, who smells of pig manure—the men who smell of wine and eau de cologne, and their sweet-scented wives, and their children who smell of oranges—and I winced momentarily in pain, as though it had actually happened. I wouldn't let anyone, not anyone, turn their backs on my mother!

"We can walk. We're not that old yet!" I quickly bent over the suitcases so that Mother wouldn't notice my grimace.

It was as though I were running away from her with the two heavy suitcases. (Don't help me, I can manage, it's balanced like this.) And the heavier the suitcases became, and the more cramped my fingers were, the faster I ran, with short little steps, my feet and the suitcases raising dust from the goosefoot and heather that half covered the narrow asphalt pavement; almost nobody ever walked along it. I could hear Mother's rapid breaths growing shorter and jerkier, and for an instant I had the unpleasant feeling that a dog was chasing me, and I ran still faster, without looking where I put my feet and expecting to stumble and fall at any moment.

"Daughter." I heard my mother's call and stopped in surprise. Nobody had called me that for a whole year. "Let's have a rest."

I put down the suitcases, which fell over and bounced gently on the heather. I turned around. Mother was running toward me, her red face empty of all expression except the single desire to catch up with me; her hair was tousled, and her dress had crept up above her knees from running; her legs were a dead white.

That's my mother, I suddenly thought, and once again there was that wave of pity for her—for my mother—and resentment for what someone had done to her and despair that I couldn't change anything or punish anyone for the fact that my beautiful mother had become this woman. But when she ran up, breathing fast and jerkily, the same sharp, unpleasant smell stung my nose, even sharper now, mixed with a smell of sweat that made it quite intolerable.

"You!" I cried, and I realized that I had only run so fast in order to shout out the word, in order to run as far away from other people as possible and yell out what I felt, in order to run away from this pity and shame and despair and love for her, in order to be free of her by crying out, "You! You're an engineer, and just look at yourself! I'm ashamed to look at you, I'm ashamed to be seen with you! You keep a pig! You smell of pig! I'm going to slaughter that pig of yours! You farm laborer! Are you short of money? Then I'll go to work, do you hear? You go around the garbage dumps collecting scraps for swill!"

(While my heroine carries on shouting, I'll explain why she's doing it, why she's in such a furious rage. She has come to spend her college holidays in a garrison town. The civilian population here lives in small Finnish-style houses, and the others live in five-story blocks. The town, which is the real thing, with squares, monuments, and parks, has its own laws. In this town it is forbidden to keep chickens, rabbits, and other filthy beasts. But the civilians in the Finnish houses keep them, anyway. From time to time, the population is fined for such unsanitary habits, and the chickens and the rabbits are temporarily evacuated from the town. And then people start keeping them again. And my heroine's mother has begun to keep a pig. Now do you understand?

(What is this, then, some kind of revolt? No. It's simply that my heroine's mother is poor. All on her own, without a husband, she has to clothe her daughter and pay for her education as an engineer: the town despises people without a higher education. The town has its own laws. And the daughter knows them well. Her mother has to feed and clothe a grandson, who will appear in the story later. The town despises those who have a child without a husband. The daughter knows this, but the child is there to be cared for, and without a husband. These things happen.

(My heroine's mother is poor. But poor with a special kind of poverty. Alongside the wives of officers, the children of officers, the grandchildren of officers, where there is no place to hide yourself and your poverty. In this town you and your poverty are like a gaping hole in an officer's overcoat; you can be spotted for miles around. In her internal monologue my heroine will even use the words "majors' and colonels' wives." She is afraid to actually say them; she is afraid of betraying some military secret. She will never say how she entered this town, but she will enter it through the checkpoint; her mother will get a pass for her. She won't dare talk about it. She is a daughter of this taciturn town, and she honors its laws and secrets. She is prepared to be poor, as long as her poverty is proud and pure. Her mother has taken in a pig, and her poverty has become shameful. I won't interfere from now on. I won't say anymore. I am also a daughter of this town.)

I went on shouting for a long time, repeating the same things over and over again; it was all the same to me what I shouted, as long as I shouted at her, at this pitiful woman in the patched shoes, at this hateful woman in the faded dress, at my stupid mother, whom I loved more than anyone else on earth, with a broken, pitiful, stupid love. I saw her grow upset, hunch over, draw her head into her shoulders, as though I were beating her about the head, and then suddenly straighten up, her face taking on a bored expression, and she froze stock-still, with a bored face, and she seemed to close her eyes, as though she weren't listening to me. She was asleep and having a boring dream.

I stopped shouting, because I didn't understand what was wrong with her. And when I stopped, she gave an affected yawn and said in a bored voice, "You're only shouting because you don't understand a thing. Me and Vaska had to get through the winter, and you know what kind of a winter it was. And as for the scraps that I collected from the garbage, only me and Vaska know about that. And I kept him warm by the stove; he was only a piglet. But you should see him now. And it's only the scraps . . . I couldn't slaughter him now, not after we lived through the winter together. I feel sorry for him."

She stopped speaking. She looked at me with offended pride.

"But what are you keeping him for," I asked in astonishment, "if you're not going to slaughter him? Are you training him or something?"

"I will slaughter him when it's the right time for pigs to be slaughtered, in November. He's no worse than any other pig, is he? It's not the right time now, is it?" asked my mother, as if amazed that I didn't know such a simple thing.

"No, it isn't," I said.

"There you are, then," said my mother, and she drew herself up straight and proud as could be.

Caught out by her idiotic logic, I whispered, "You're crazy"—and immediately realized that she wasn't crazy, and her logic wasn't idiotic, and I couldn't accuse her, judge her, or even forgive her, because I hadn't lived with her for a long time, and she lived with Vaska the pig and the rabbits and the dog, Fenya, with a chicken who didn't lay, with the cherry trees, the apple trees, and the currant bushes—and they had their own special logic, and they understood one another completely, and Vaska meant more to her than all the girls at work, and this Vaska that she looked after and fed meant more to her now than even I did, because all this was her life now. I understood it all. And from that moment I hated Vaska.

We turned onto our street, and it was as though someone had opened the oven door of a stove: at the end of the street the sun was burning down. It blazed orange, like glowing anthracite, not sinking behind the horizon the way it is supposed to but flaking into burning lumps and lying there on its own blazing fragments, slowly disintegrating, as though it had been stirred with a poker. This was my sun, this was my sunset, so unlike the pink, modest northern sunsets, this was my street, where everything was familiar and dear to me— the old silver-torsoed poplars bearing aloft their thick, dense green foliage and the young cherry trees with their branches almost bare (it had been a good harvest) that were planted here instead of the white and pink acacias that the frost had killed off in a cold year, and the potatoes, with their simple little white florets, growing in front of every one of the Finnish houses, outside the yard, between the pavement and the asphalt roadway, instead of the heather, which, one summer when there was cholera around, had been painstakingly scythed down by the neighbors we now met, whose names I had learned to pronounce with my very first words, the neighbors who never went away anywhere or grew old (only the children changed; they shot up at a tremendous rate, like the poplars, and the ones that were riding about on tricycles last year were fixing motors to their bicycles this year and roaring off on their improvised mopeds as far as the withered maple, which was as far as they were allowed to go; the place where since the beginning of time they played hopscotch and the little kids rode around on the hopscotch squares on their tricycles). The sunset, the street, and the people seemed eternal. I knew what the neighbors would ask and what I would answer. I recognized the nasty, evasive look in their eyes when they spoke about the other neighbors. I seemed to know everything in advance, and I greeted the most startling pieces of news—that Uncle Volodya had died of cancer a month after his wife's death, that Uncle Grisha had hanged himself, and Auntie Raya had left Uncle Victor after living with him for thirteen years—with a counterfeit astonishment and a counterfeit sorrow to match their own, as though it were old, familiar news that wouldn't affect the life of our street, just as it hadn't been affected by the cold winter or the cholera that summer.

Step by step, meeting by meeting, I worked my way onto our street the way a screw threads its way in, glad to feel the familiar captivity tighten at every turn.

And when I saw my neighbor Ira running down the other side of the street with an empty milk can, I shouted to her in my pleasure at the fact that everyone knew me and I could shout out loud for all the street to hear, "Ira, save a place for me in the milk line!" And she waved her hand in greeting as she ran and shouted, "Right!" She shouted it as simply as if I had lived there for the last hundred years without ever going away.

And there was my three-year-old son zigzagging toward us at a run, his arms thrust out in imitation of an airplane, the way children run to their mothers who have just come home from work.

I went into my very own yard and smiled at the sweetish smell of my son's urine by the doorway, I dodged Fenka's long, heavy tail as he wagged it in greeting, I grabbed him by the mane, and said, "So you know me, you crocodile!" and he gently took my hands into his jaws. I took off my shoes and went into the garden, and through the grass my heels could feel the cinders that my mother had scattered on the path in the winter. Next came the boards that the rain had turned gray, and without looking down I instinctively stepped over the place where the point of a nail had always stuck up. I turned around to look: the nail was still sticking up. I stood silently in front of the apple tree withered from old age and remembered the word "damn."

"Damn," my mother had written in one of her letters. "Our best apple tree has withered. But we'll wait a bit yet."

A young cherry tree had withered, too, the one that had competed with the poplars, shooting way up above the television aerial. At first the blossoms had withered—it had blossomed for the first time in five years—they had been caught by the frost at that height and withered, and then no leaves had appeared for a long time. And now, in July, it was obvious that the cherry tree had withered altogether.

"It's your own fault," I reproached it, "you lanky brute!"

I was caught by a breath of wind and enveloped in a sharp, unpleasant smell, and I froze, as though while I stood there, in my own garden, I had been sluiced down with slops from the windows of my own house. And the slops kept pouring down. The wind had no intention of changing its direction, the stench grew thicker, and I felt an intense fury welling up inside me. My orchard! Where I knew everything, where every nail and every smell was fixed in my memory, and now everything (even my mother!) was polluted with this vile alien stench that had killed the delicate flowers of the cherry tree that had blossomed for the first time in five years. I was sure now that it wasn't the cold that had killed it. It had spent five years growing before it blossomed, and then because of this . . .

I went over to it with my head lowered, cutting through the dense wave of the stench with my head and breathing it in deeply, in order to hate this pig even more, in case it should turn out to be likable and good-natured. I breathed in the smell in the naive hope that the air would pass through my lungs as through a filter and once again begin to smell of overripe apples and dill, to smell the way the grass does in the evening or the tar and dusty boards of the shed after the sun has been warming them all day long. Yes, better if it smelled of dust. It stood up to its belly in mud, looking at me. One eye was brown, with a fixed, malicious stare, the other was blue and half covered by short white eyelashes: this pig seemed to be winking at me! Its snout was long and predatory, somehow not like a pig's, without any fat cheeks, and caked in mud. The whole of its long thin body had a hungry and predatory look. It began to urinate as it stood there, and the taut transparent stream seemed to flow for an unnaturally long time. I knew that the pig was being raised to be shared—half for Mother and half for Auntie Galya, who brought a bucket of slops each day—and I mentally chopped the pig's head in two halves, one with the blue, winking eye, and one with the malicious, intelligent one.

"That's the way," I said.

And suddenly the pig put its forefeet into the wooden trough filled with filthy swill and growled. It actually growled, but the threat was helpless, like the growling of a wild beast held in a cage when someone approaches it. The eyelid with the short lashes, over the blue left eye, lifted, and the red pupil glared balefully at me. Then it began to chew the trough in hopeless fury, and its fangs were the same rich yellow as the timber they exposed.

"He's hungry," I heard my mother say. "Hang on, Vaska, I'll feed you in a moment."

Mother began to drive the pig out of the trough with a branch, and it screwed up its eyes and made stupid attempts to dodge the blows; then it staggered awkwardly, and the trough tipped over; Mother leaned over the fencing and righted the trough with the round wooden lid of a barrel, flung the lid under the pig's feet, and poured a bucketful of slops into the trough. The pig immediately stood in it again, stuck its long snout into the slops up to its eyes, and breathed out in the water with a gurgling sound; the slops heaved and bubbled; the pig raised its snout with a pale green strip of boiled onion dangling from it like a strand of spittle. It chewed the melon skins crookedly, chomping wetly as though it had no teeth. It sucked in the air with noisy relish, as though it were something edible, and plunged back into the slops. Its hind legs slipped and skidded around on the circle of wood, it tensed its leg muscles in an effort to hold its legs steady, and its back trembled slightly from the tension.

Somebody nudged me in the side, and I turned around. My son was clambering up the fence to look at the pig. He suddenly leaned sharply forward, and, afraid that he would fall headfirst, I swept him off the fence with my arm, and then, even more alarmed, I grabbed him and showered kisses on his wailing mouth, which was stretched so wide that I could see his moist pink throat. I kissed his wet eyes and his arms, as though I were checking with my lips to make sure that they were not broken, and over his choking sobs I shouted at my mother, "Pigs like that eat children! It's got to be slaughtered!" And I grabbed my son and ran into the house, carrying him off the way some female animal would carry off her cub, kissing him constantly as though I were licking him clean—carrying him well away from danger.

And as I ran along the wooden boards, the nail stuck into my foot, right through to the bone, and, blinded by the pain, I yelled, "Slaughter it!"

Vaska was slaughtered a month later. Four people joined in: Mother, Auntie Galya—a small, rotund woman who chattered ceaselessly, like a dry poppyhead rattling in the wind—me, and Uncle Kolya. Uncle Kolya killed all the animals on our street. He punched rabbits in the forehead; he beheaded chickens and cocks; he shot sick or thieving dogs. There was only one pig on the street, the first pig Uncle Kolya ever had to kill. He was dressed in all the gear he always wore for this kind of work. The checked shirt stained all over with blood, which he never washed, was unbuttoned to reveal his smooth chest, sunburned almost brown. His skinny white legs in the galoshes protruded from crumpled, faded jeans rolled up to his knees, and the mud caked on them made them look as though they were made of clay. He tested a long, gleaming knife on his forelock, which was coarse and white as a pig's bristles, and gave a nervous laugh.

"Have you got the rope ready, Maria Stepanovna?" he asked.

"Rope, what rope? Oh, yes, the rope." Mother fussed, without moving her feet from the spot. Then she ran over to the withered apple tree to take down the clothesline. Uncle Kolya wound it several times around his palms, tugged on it sharply a few times, and it snapped without even stretching. "Rotten." Uncle Kolya spat, and the gob of spittle landed exactly on the end of the snapped rope. "I told you, Masha!" Mother began to fuss again, plunged into the shed, and rummaged around confusedly in there, stumbling over ringing metal basins, and when there was the clanking sound of bottles spilling across the floor, Uncle Kolya spat again. "Crazy damned woman! And she's going to slaughter it!"

Mother halted uncertainly in the door of the shed, holding out a piece of wire with a guilty look, as though she were afraid that it would be rejected, too, and she asked in a frightened voice, "Will this do, Kolya?"

He twisted up his mouth disdainfully, looked at the wire, and nodded his head curtly. "It'll do. Hold it!" And he hacked at the wire as hard as he could with the knife. There was a sound of scraping metal; the knife slipped. Uncle Kolya was unable to contain himself any longer, and he yelled, "Hold it tighter, can't you? You'll damage the knife! You and your pigs!" And without finishing what he was saying, he struck viciously at the wire again with his knife and spat in satisfaction. "That's it."

We decided to drive the pig out from behind the fencing and get it down where the ground was clean. But Vaska wouldn't come out of his little wooden sty. He retreated into a corner and growled menacingly. He didn't even come out when Mother poured him some slops.

"He can feel it," said Mother happily. "Maybe we should wash him, Kolya?"

"We'll wash him all right," chuckled Uncle Kolya. "With fire."

He handed Mother the knife, moved aside the fencing, and began wading, up to his knees in foul-smelling wash, toward the sty. Pulling his feet out with a loud squelching sound, he muttered angrily, "You need waders in this bog. Some slaughterers."

Uncle Kolya beat the pig's growling snout until it turned its hindquarters toward him, and then he quickly tied a knot on its leg and began to tug at the wire. The pig shifted its feet, but it didn't move. He tugged harder. The pig hopped awkwardly and began to edge backward slowly, then it turned around and stopped, gazing at us dully. Its brown eye, usually lively and intelligently malicious, had a sleepy, doomed look. It growled again, but briefly, as if only half awake.

Uncle Kolya beat it on the sides, on the hindquarters, between the eyes, but all it did was shudder where it was beaten, grunting after each blow without moving, bracing its front legs with all its might against the wooden barrel lid, which sank deeper and deeper into the mud. There was a gleam of hopeless despair in its red eye, and the redness in it swelled and expanded, covering the blue, until it stared with a senseless, bloody look.

Suddenly the pig made a dash toward us, and we started back in surprise. It got about three yards, the length of the wire, until Uncle Kolya pulled it up with a hand that had turned blue, and it fell over on its side, squealing in pain and terror in a way that set our ears ringing.

We all set on it at once, bracing our legs against the ground. Holding a basin to collect the blood, I crept along its body to the throat, feeling the rippling of its tensed muscles and the desire of its every cell to live and the squealing that rang inside its body. A few times it gathered its final strength and almost threw us off, and Uncle Kolya yelled above its squealing in a terrible voice, "Where's the knife? Where's the knife?" And Mother waved the long knife in front of us stupidly; she was also struggling to hold the pig, and she didn't notice the knife in her own hand.

"Mother! The knife!" I shouted, and I couldn't hear my voice over the squealing. But on my lips Uncle Kolya read what I was shouting, and he turned around, lifting one shoulder and pressing the pig down to the ground even more heavily with the other, grabbed the knife from my panic-stricken mother's hand, stuck it into the pig's neck, and twisted it. The piercing squeal turned into a squelching and gurgling, the flesh parted gently under the knife, forming a semicircle that looked like a smile on the throat, and the dark red blood flowed out of it, steaming, into the basin I had set in place. The pig's eyes, at first wide open, closed very gently, and I comforted the pig. "There, now, that's all, see how quick it is. It's almost over."

Its body shuddered occasionally. In twenty seconds it was all over. I poured the blood, which was already curdling, into a clean jar and closed it with a plastic lid.

Vaska lay there quite different from the pig I had grown used to seeing. No maliciously intelligent right eye, nor screwed up left eye; its eyes were calmly closed.

I looked at it for a long time. But there were things to be done.

Uncle Kolya scorched the pig's side with a blowtorch. The mud and the bristles curled up into black shavings, and we scraped them off with knives to expose the white skin. The blowtorch went back over the same place, and the white skin turned a glossy yellow, darkened, and began to bake a red color. We turned the pig over on its side, and its belly was so dirty that Mother decided to wipe it down with a rag. And when the dirty water ran off down its sides, we suddenly saw defenseless pink nipples protruding in pitiful naïveté from the soft, white belly. It was a she and not a Vaska at all; I'd never even thought of it—it was always just Vaska. She had thirteen nipples, seven on one side and six on the other. All the nipples were paired off opposite each other, and the odd one out was covered by the bristles on her breast. We scorched the belly and scraped the skin clumsily, and the nipples bled. Then we scorched the head, and it became like thousands of others that are sold in markets and ships—an appetizingly stupid head.

My son was standing beside Uncle Kolya. He'd been hanging around for a long time, since the very beginning, but I'd had no chance to send him away. And there was the vague idea, not even an idea but a feeling, that my son must not be like my effeminate contemporaries, who felt sick at the sight of a severed cock's head. He must be a man who could slaughter a pig himself or shoot a sick dog and punch a rabbit in the forehead, like Uncle Kolya. So I didn't send him away.

We slit open the belly. And my son froze as he watched the pearly intestines tumbling out of the cavity, the dark red, trembling liver, the white stomach, slippery and taut, with its lilac-colored veins, and he kept repeating calmly, or so I thought, "They've killed piggy, they've killed piggy. . . ." (How was I to know then that he would remember this for a whole year, repeating perplexedly, "They've killed piggy," that he would dream of this slaughtered pig for the whole year, maybe all his life?)

I was irritated that he was so calm. I was irritated that I was so calm. And when I saw the trough filled to the brim with the innards, I had the sudden thought that these innards probably weighed more than the meat, and we would have been better off to sell the pig for live weight to the slaughterhouse than go to all this trouble. The fact that I could have such a thought at such a moment horrified me, and my calmness, a certain spiritual inertia, began to depress me. I could recall very well how my godfather, a veterinary surgeon, had slaughtered a pig on a farm, on a pig farm, how it had squealed, hanging on the rope on the pillar with the cross beam, how I had squealed with it, how they had slit its throat, and the blood had gushed out, flowing over its belly, how it had gone limp and hung there as though it had been crucified. I remembered its bloody head with the flayed skin, with the white eyeballs that had tumbled out, and which had turned lilac when we got home. After that I had begun to hate my godfather.

So why was I so calm now?

I saw them hack Vaska in half. They chopped the head in two. I wrangled with the female neighbors who had come running to buy the meat, and sold pieces for four rubles a kilogram, and not for three-fifty, as they wanted—it was freshly killed meat, after all!

I came to an agreement with one of the neighbors. For washing the intestines, we would give her half of them.

I gave the rabbits their feed; they were usually gluttonous, but for some reason they wouldn't come out today. I glanced in at them. They were sitting three-deep against the back wall, panting and shuddering. Even they had sensed death!

I did everything I had to, but my calmness nagged at me and stopped me from doing what I had to do calmly.

I sat down beside what had once been Vaska. The jar of blood stood on the rabbit hutch, and the blood had already completely coagulated and gleamed like dark red jelly in the sun.

Large green bluebottles hung like clusters of poisonous berries on the blood-splattered goosefoot. In the trough the dark red liver trembled as though it were alive.

And suddenly I saw the pig again, with a smile that seemed to be asking my forgiveness for some offense that I had actually committed against it.

A sharp, unpleasant smell reached me. It was the wind blowing from Vaska's pen, and it was as though Vaska were still alive. Vaska was dead, but the smell would live on for a long time yet.

I felt someone watching me, following my every glance, my every movement. Perhaps that was why my calmness irritated me so much—someone else could see it, too. I raised my head and saw my son. He was standing by the shed. He was examining me, his brow wrinkled, struggling painfully to understand something. His gaze was entirely adult and unfamiliar. His blue eyes watched me with intent malice.

"Come here," I said to him.

He didn't move. I stood up. He began to back away. His eyes were filled with terror. His back was pressing against the wall of the shed, but he went on trying to back away, squeezing himself against the gray planks, on his tiptoes. I wanted to take a step toward him but I was afraid to. I took a step. He began to sidle away from me, his back rubbing against the gray boards. He had no shirt on, just his shorts, and I dashed toward him, afraid that he would get splinters in his back. The planks came to an end, and with nothing to support him, he leaned helplessly backward, but he kept his footing, turned around, and ran, constantly glancing behind him (and looking at me with the same hunted look).

I called his name. He kept running away from me. And still not knowing why, I ran after him.

We ran along the broad asphalt road, along our street at first. I almost caught up with him, but I was out of breath. My breathing was short and fast as I ran behind him, he must have heard it, and it almost certainly startled him. At first I saw astonishment in his eyes when he glanced around, but then something in their expression changed—ever so slightly—and now he was looking at me the way people look at a mad dog, and he ran even faster.

He turned into another street. I was falling behind. A car could shoot around the corner at any moment.

"Wait!" I shouted. I was short of breath, and it came out hoarse and weak. He kept running.

"Son!" I called, gasping for breath. "Son!" I implored him.

He stopped. He turned around and waited for me. My hair was all tousled, a coarse strand of it was prickling my lips, and I bit it; my face was sweaty, and I had only one thought pounding in my head: to get to him quickly. My mother's old boots—the wrong size—were cutting into my skin, the dung-wash was slopping around inside them; my mother's cotton dress had ridden up and gotten tangled between my legs.

And when there were no more than two steps to go, I stopped. I was stopped by his gaze—the cold, hateful gaze of my son. His blue eyes had paled from hatred and seemed like a complete stranger's. I stood there, breathing heavily, not daring to approach him. I smelled of a sharp, unpleasant mixture of sweat and pig manure.

"You!" said my son, and I could tell that his throat was dry from hatred. "You killed piggy!" His dry lips twisted convulsively in anger. Then the corners of his lips slowly crept downward, very slowly, as though it were very painful, and he gasped out, "Mommy!"

And we rushed toward each other.

"Mommy!" he cried desperately, sobbing. "Don't kill piggy."

And I silently pressed his struggling body closer to my own, and I could feel my heart's blood rising through my throat and scalding it, so that I couldn't breathe out, until it gushed in hot streams into my head, melting my brain, transforming it into molten lava.

"Don't kill piggy!"

The truth, the truth . . . you mustn't spare him . . . he has to know the truth—this idea of mine seemed to be written in large crooked letters on a piece of paper in my head; it was still there among the molten lava; it was all I could read, and in a dry, hot voice, because my throat had been scorched, I said to my son, "We have to, we have to kill him, that's the way life is!"

And he began to struggle again ("Don't kill him, don't"), but now it was as though a stranger's body were struggling in my arms, wriggling in an attempt to slip free, and my squeezing it tighter and tighter was pointless—it belonged to a stranger. And suddenly I saw that the lava in my head had reached the sheet of paper—the truth, nothing but the truth, don't spare him—and it burst into flames and was transformed into a big black sheet of ash, which rustled gently as it crumbled, and I understood, with all my body I understood, that my son was right, we mustn't, we mustn't! I saw that someone irrefutably logical, someone immeasurably more intelligent than all of us put together, who knew all the causes and the consequences, the beginnings and the ends of things, who controlled life and death and was therefore callous, merciless, and unjust, not good or evil, but simply a bookkeeper indifferent to everything, with blank eyes and a gray face, was drawing up his balance, and to make up some credits or some debits this faceless person was taking away my son, my mother, and me and sadly repeating this standard truth, "We have to, that's the way life is," and together with my son I shouted, "Don't! Don't"—and I felt that as long as I kept on shouting that, and I would keep shouting all my life, then nothing would happen to my son or my mother. That person wouldn't dare to take them away from me, they wouldn't die, as long as I kept on shouting.

We held each other tightly and cried. I got blood on my son's forehead (my hands were bloody) and tried to rub it off with spittle and only smeared more on him, and I kissed his forehead, and my lips became salty. I felt my heart pounding and my son's heart beating along with it. I saw his moist eyes, and his eyes loved me, and I loved them, and I knew that we would never be so happy again. And I held his heart, which was choking and longing to dash away, tighter to me. The cars honked as they slowly and cautiously drove around us. They didn't know that nothing could happen to us and that we would never be so happy again.

A large, ungainly blue bird was running toward us. I looked closely. It was my mother. She was shouting something; her mouth was opening and closing; the veins on her neck were swelling up. But I couldn't hear what she was shouting; somehow I could only hear the loud beating of her heart.

1991

■ □ ■ □ ■

THE GOPHER

Translated by Helena Goscilo

IN SPRING, WE, THE PIONEERS FROM THE SMALL MILITARY town of Yargrad, would set off for the steppe to drive the gophers out of their burrows. A spray machine filled with chlorinated water quietly crawled behind us. Its round sides were wet, like the flanks of an animal.

We'd pour the water from buckets into the black burrow deep in the earth, and it disappeared forever in a soundless stream. And we poured again, and it disappeared again, quickly and of its own accord, as if it had an important, urgent task. And the childishly round, open mouth of the earth would gape blackly once again. Forgetting the gopher and abandoning all hope that he'd ever jump out of the ground (and, if he did, it would be in America, fearfully gazing around among the skyscrapers—so very deep was the burrow), we continued to pour the water for its own sake, then with cheerful recklessness, making fun of ourselves and this hole that went no place. Then with anger and despair at the mystery that mocked us Pioneers, we flooded the throat of its opening without letting it breathe, poured and poured without remembering why we were pouring.

When our spite and hatred, which hovered over the burrow, became enormous, silent, and dense, like the bleached water pouring in a dense, heavy stream, when the air grew thick with this communal spite and started to smell distinctly of chlorine and sweat, suddenly . . . a gopher crawled out of a neighboring hole. Wet and trembling, he crawled out into the light—tiny, as if born from the earth's womb before our eyes—and froze, spellbound.

God's world was intact and gazed at him.

What did he imagine there, in his winding earthen darkness, along which his childlike soul, howling in terror, rushed about, overtaken from all directions by our human, chlorinated spite, our icy hatred seeping through each nook and shelter?

The Flood? The End of the World?

But the world was intact. The world was safe and sound. It was even better than the one before. The sun, which hadn't been destroyed, shone brighter than the usual one. The sky, which hadn't been destroyed, was bluer, and in this saved world the wormwood tinkled with a clearer, more silvery tone.

Raising his soul on his hind legs, he folded his paws on his chest as if praying, and, head lifted, squinting blissfully and shortsightedly, he looked at the sun.

The world was intact.

He quietly made his supplication.

Only then did he look at us, the humans huddled over him.

He gave us a loving look at first, happy that we, too, were alive and safe, unharmed and dry after such a deluge.

Then he looked at us again, this time differently: scanning the scene in a businesslike manner, he realized that there was no escape. Aware of his impending doom, he lay down, as if saying, *Take me. The most important thing is that the world is intact.* And he closed his eyes.

That day we, the Pioneers from class B in the sixth grade, flooded out twenty-two gophers and won first place in collecting the largest number of pelts.

1991

■ □ ■ □ ■

GOING AFTER GOAT ANTELOPES

Translated by Elisabeth Jezierski

I'D SEEN HIM SOMEWHERE—THIS GUY WITH THE LONG, ALMOST lipless mouth—and just recently, I think. He stared at me as only people with colorless, transparent eyes can stare, for in such eyes the pupils are the most important thing. If you were to put this guy at the bottom of a river and bend over the water, the staring, unyielding black ice at the bottom would make you shiver; it would feel as if there were no water, as if you were alone face-to-face with just those pupils. It's better not to look. And so I didn't look in his direction, but I desperately wanted to turn around and bow to him in jest (and in my mind I repeated this turning around and bowing so many times that my neck muscles actually began to hurt). I couldn't remember at all where I'd seen him. (But I *had* seen him before! I'd seen him somewhere! *The Man Who Laughs?*[1] Maybe that's where? No, I'd seen him in person some time or other—precisely that mouth, that long gash called a mouth, that mouth at once pathetic and mockingly disdainful, you couldn't tell if he was laughing or crying.) My head burned with impatience to remember, and I kept gently shaking my head as if jiggling a kaleidoscope, helping my brain cells shift, so that, wandering around and running into one another, they'd fall happily into place and resurrect not only the light and the smell but also the tiny pebble in my hand, unneeded but resurrected nonetheless. After all, it had existed and made my palm sweat (everything would be resurrected, but now it was eluding resurrection), and then suddenly—yes, that was it—the attic, dust that had settled and hardened, in which there were no traces; it dissolved noiselessly under my bare feet; the pigeon nest and two dead fledglings, their unnaturally long blue necks hanging over the edge of the nest, something terrifyingly lilac colored between the cartilage, the sad long beaky mouths, and their naked deep blue bodies (the dark color just recently surfaced), and the coldness of those bodies, a coldness unlike anything else, unlike either the coldness of a living being or the coldness of matter forever dead. This was the coldness of death, of something that had been alive and was now dead but not yet in a state of decomposition, of putrefaction. (Decomposition and putrefaction bring new warmth, as the beginning of a new form of nonlife.) Yes, I was holding death in my hands: it was defenseless, it had a thin blue skin, and if you pressed down on that skin with your finger, a dent would remain, and this dent would remain just like that, as if it had always been there, and it would be cold, not actually all that cold, but your fingers would fear this coldness, as if they had a premonition, as if they were trying to touch themselves—some number of years from now—when they would die.

There was still a third fledgling in the nest. He was alive. Having hung his neck, like his siblings, over the edge of the nest, he was preparing to die. But he stared at me, opening his long beak of a mouth wide, at once pathetic and disdainful; he was almost as cold as his dead siblings, but life kept on throbbing there, under the thin film of his skin, and my life rejoiced in his life and rushed to save it.

I fed the fledgling milk. He slept, wrapped in rabbit fur, yet grew colder and colder: after all, he'd lain for a long time with his dead siblings and had caught their coldness. I tucked him in my armpit and fell asleep. Of course, I wanted to do my best for him, and, to be sure, he did get warm, but when I awoke there was no fledgling. There were only his squeezed-out intestines, his empty, naked skinlet, and his bitterly mocking long beak of a mouth. I'd smothered him.

I remembered all this: unhappily, I found what I'd been looking for: that's where I'd seen that mouth and nowhere else. But there was something, something else in my memory, like that pebble in my sweaty hand, and here's what it was: there, back in the attic, I realized that the fledgling resembled someone, that I had already seen that beaky mouth before. The circle was closing but couldn't be closed all the way. I got tired. Finally I found the answer: he looked like the fledgling. What else can be said? Finally, we were sitting in a restaurant. And I had calmed down.

Irina and I were sitting in a restaurant, the dining room huge but empty: it was a weeknight. It was the end of a difficult day, a day of solar eclipse; people said there had been a lot of deaths that day. Four small adjoining tables were occupied; everybody seemed to huddle together, trying not to glance at the huge empty space of the dining room, at the patches of light on the empty tables, which suggested that the people who should have been sitting there that day hadn't been able to come because they'd died. We sat in semidarkness, the fans above us whirring like bats that had gotten tipsy and lost the ability to tune into one another's signals. . . . Turning clumsily, the bat-fans cast the shadow of their hideous wings on the floor.

It was quiet and depressing in the restaurant, and for some reason we all talked in whispers.

The window was closed, and outside, in the stark emptiness of the extinct world, swayed an elm desiccated by the heat. You couldn't hear the noise of the wind, and the elm seemed to be swaying on its own in the motionless expanse, shaking itself loose in order to free itself of the now useless earth and to fall down to the ground, to die right then and there without waiting for the dew. The elm swayed rhythmically, the way people sway in grief—a grief that couldn't be cried away through its curled-up black leaves, which were tired of living. In its dull sense of doom, the elm somehow resembled a beached whale.

I looked at the elm for a long time, and it became motionless, and we were the ones who swayed, with our small tables, our food, and our drinks, and I had the sensation that all of humankind consisted just of us—ten men and two women—and that we were afraid of losing one another. We had escaped, and we gazed avidly into one another's eyes because we had a long journey ahead of us; yet, try as we might, we couldn't move away from the motionless elm. . . .

But that's not how it really was. Four customers paid and left, and another four arrived in their place: three extremely young lieutenants in battle fatigues and a major who was far from old; his little stars were very new and shone happily and proudly in the semidarkness of his epaulets. These four evidently knew absolutely nothing about our ark, about the Flood and the solar eclipse: during the day they'd slept on the sweaty couchettes of their train compartment; they'd taken turns going to the slimy toilet that reeked strongly and permanently of urine; first singly, then in a group, they'd ganged up to badger the loudmouthed woman conductor (singing "Oh, conductress, conductress, silken-lashed seductress");[2] and they'd swigged hard liquor Siberian style (only swallowing after they'd first swished it around in their mouths). Then they dropped off their suitcases in their hotel room, and now they'd come to drink some more, intent on blowing their daily expense account as fast as possible—and in general they hadn't noticed that humanity had become extinct. On the contrary, as far as they were concerned, there were too many humans: railroad carriages and buses were bursting at the seams with humans, the sidewalks were too narrow for them, humanity spilled over into the street, and no one died— they merely prevented the bus from driving on smoothly at a normal speed. Humanity crowded into the hotels, either not finding lodgings—or not wanting to find them in the rest of the empty world. The male half of humanity in our small little town protected the other half of humanity from visitors who arrived on official business. These visitors went to the empty restaurant to drink away their loneliness, hoping to leave the place no longer alone.

And the game for the sake of which we'd come to the restaurant—hiding the fact from one another and from ourselves—was already beginning. Or, rather, the game had begun much earlier, when the waitress with the tired, indifferent smile of a professional who knows all the rules of the game, with a glance full of sorrowful omniscience and the disdain of a person aloof from it all—organizing but not participating in the game—led us to the table under the only lit chandelier in the dining room. This way everyone had to look at us, whether they wanted to or not. The waitress was like a teacher, and I suddenly began feeling embarrassed in her presence, just like a child. I felt embarrassed about my dress, although it was beautiful and suited me. But my feelings were always terribly dependent on my clothes. Low-cut dresses made me tremble: I felt the invisible work of the skin cells constantly reproducing themselves on my arms, legs, neck, and chest; my arms, legs, neck, and chest seemed separate entities, independent and existing apart from me, having their own thoughts and desires, which didn't coincide with mine. Helplessly and defenselessly exposed, my arms, legs, neck, and chest aroused a confused pity in me for the futility of their life, which wasn't united with mine, and a dim awareness that their life—their irrepressible striving for renewal and beauty, like the striving for renewal and beauty in all of nature—was more important and significant than my life. That's why whenever my arms, legs, neck, and chest were exposed they controlled me, and I was afraid of them. And that's why I suppressed my flesh with sweaters that came up to my chin, why I wore pants—and my sheathed flesh remained mute, only rarely crying out. But here I was sitting in my dress, its snakelike green silk now become my skin, and my dress felt like my body, as yet timid and confused but gradually comprehending and sensing that its day had come, the holiday of the body, the celebration of the body. And cautiously, with difficulty, I was getting used to this feeling and this thought.

The officers looked us over with painstaking thoroughness, the way experts scrutinize a coin, with the detachment of the ordained. They didn't want to get taken in by a counterfeit product, and, with the impatience of true collectors, they were ready to bite into the coin to test whether it was gold or imitation. Was it worth getting involved or not?

Then we heard the major's order: "The skinny one's yours. I want the chubbier one. Get going!"

And "my" lieutenant, quickly leaning forward and emptying his glass, breathed "Yes, sir!" into the major's face and, all black and elastic, got up (like a bent rubber toy straightening up, suddenly and imperceptibly) and made for our table, his eyes staring into the distance.

He strode as if on parade, pointing the tips of his boots outward, but it didn't seem funny because he had beautiful legs and he knew it and loved them: he knew that he was executing an order and felt sure that this was precisely the way to execute such a gaily solemn and unusual order—with a gay solemnity, pointing the tips of his boots outward in this unusual fashion. And suddenly I was struck by how inevitably, with the ceremoniousness of a parade, IT was approaching, that IT which the body had been contemplating in its sweater-covered darkness and futility.

He walked past us.

Irina and I expelled our breath simultaneously and—as if we didn't know a thing, as if we'd heard nothing, as if we'd not seen a soul—began talking and laughing without listening to each other. Yet the chaos of empty words and uncalled-for laughter wasn't chaos; it was solid and spherical. At the center of this sphere was a shared feeling of relief, as if an avalanche had been shed, and this feeling attracted words as trifling as iron filings. Irina and I didn't notice anybody now; we were like "things in themselves," like "coins in themselves," and I loved Irina because whenever she laughed the little dimple under her lip kept getting smeared with lipstick and I had to keep watching that dimple constantly and wiping it with her napkin and laughing with her because she was feeling ticklish, and my entire being seemed absorbed in worrying about keeping Irina's chin clean. Yet all the while I was talking and laughing I could hear his steps moving away at a measured pace, I could hear him clattering with the window latch, the windows opening wide, and the wind starting to blow as if it had been turned on, like a radio. I felt the warm air insinuatingly envelop the silk of my dress, the silk growing warm and alive, and it was no longer clear which was sweating, my dress or my body. And with my back I felt him, "my" lieutenant, approaching.

What followed, though, was very natural, possibly because outside, on the street, you could suddenly hear a song by Celentano,[3] and his voice, unrestrained and hoarse, communicated to the three of us a Western ease and lack of restraint, or else because after the discomfort, the awkwardness, and the tension, there inevitably had to follow a sense of ease and naturalness, and according to the rules of the game the heavy tension had a purpose, and the greater it had been, the easier and more natural things would be later.

His name was Vladimir, and we changed his name, which was awkward to pronounce, to the easy and natural Vova.[4] He was from Siberia.

"From which town?"

"That's a military secret!"

"Ah, so you're Mal'chish-Kibal'chish!"[5]

"I haven't served long enough. Kibal'chish only had one star, but it was a big one. Our major over there's got one. Want me to get him for you?"

The major had red hair. His name was Pyotr. We didn't change it: it was more comical to stay with Pyotr.[6] He brought over a carafe of vodka, and we toasted our acquaintance. Everything was already settled. There was no more need to ask or answer, just to laugh. No matter what I said, no matter what Irina said, no matter what Pyotr and Vova said—none of it had the slightest significance. The "coin in itself" had gotten larger, engulfing Pyotr and Vova, so as to disintegrate later into two "things in themselves": Vova looked at me, Pyotr at Irina—so as to disintegrate later into four parts—this time for good. And this didn't resemble the rules of a game people had thought up but rather an educational film about the life of amoebas: here the amoeba is feeding and growing, here the nucleus is stretching, and here two small halves of a nucleus are separating; there's a pulling apart, the division of the cytoplasm, two new amoebas—and the caption: "In the course of twenty-four hours the division may be repeated several times"—and that's why our conversation had a meaning as ancient as the stretching of the nucleus prior to its division, and that's why the conversation flowed of its own accord.

Vova talked about what people eat in Siberia: namely, venison, bear meat, trout, and other delicacies. I was astonished at how easily and beautifully he spoke. Articulate people have always amazed me, and I can watch them speak for hours on end, rooted to the spot, without analyzing the meaning. This feeling of fascination has to do with my sense of my own lack of eloquence, mixed with admiration. It was with this complex feeling that I looked at beautiful faces, at flashing streetcars, racing swiftly into the night, at the languid flowing movements of cats and the amazing color of blacks' skin. I found speaking difficult and rehearsed each sentence in my head, honing it inside me, which is why my sentences were slow to emerge and sounded wooden. Yet at times I could speak well, without understanding how it happened, without even knowing exactly what I was saying. I'd hear my own sentences as if they were someone else's, and afterward I'd repeat to myself the sentences I'd uttered and be surprised at their content, surprised that the thought I'd expressed had never occurred to me, which means it was totally independent of me.

And, spellbound, I observed how easily words flew from Vova's lips, as if he exhaled them instead of air, and how they'd bubble up on his lips and burst. And I laughed when it was appropriate and when it wasn't (something remote and funny would cross my mind), and laughter bubbled on my lips. So we sat there, emitting bubbles. The nucleus kept stretching and would soon divide, and although I was laughing just as before, I suddenly felt that I was looking at Vova in a different way. My eyes grew hot, they were burning, and I placed the backs of my hands up against them, and my skin felt a warmth that was greater than its own. Earlier, when my cornea had been cold, no warmer than the rest of my body, and much colder than the stuffy air in the dining room, objects and people had appeared indistinct and blurred to me, haloed with a haze, as if the cornea were glass that had misted over. Now, however, objects and people were in focus, not as on a photograph but rather as on an X ray in reverse: the skull appearing black, the flesh white, the frame exposed. Reality had acquired an angular perfection (the perfection of the skeleton); instead of the flesh that fills out and adheres to the frame, there was the emptiness of shining white space. It was as if I'd suddenly stepped out into the frosty air where even the smoke from the chimney stacks gravitated to solid graphic expressiveness and the houses to a fragile transparency—that's how it was then. My eyes grew hotter and hotter, and the warmth generated in the course of the day by the sun and people felt cold to them. I suddenly saw the cozy dining room, the damply perspiring customers in the frosty bright light (and, as before, I felt the stuffiness and the heat with my skin and my breath, as they did), and the cold spotlighted those things that would remain forever: the chair, its form, will be eternal; the form of the table will be eternal; the cold gleam of knives and forks will be eternal; and the human skeleton will be eternal. So what if thoughts and passions change—the skeleton remains eternal, whereas the warmth enveloping us, the warmth of our flesh, blood, passions, laughter, and thoughts, was vanishing into the smokestacks of eternity. The coldly sparkling crystal carafe of vodka served as a model for this eternal world, and one shone through the other: through the glass I could see the immured warm liquid, and through the liquid I could see the cold glass. My hot eyes, immured in the cold of the hot world, were also a model of the world and were exhausted by the simplicity and triviality of the world that was revealed to them. I saw the eternal form of the blinding sheen of the major's wiry hair (he had a child-like smile); I saw the lieutenant's dark skull; I saw the guy's lipless, mockingly disdainful grin, and Irina's swaying warm body. Everything was both of this moment and eternal, and their smiles, tanned skin, disdain, and swaying flesh—all those crucial things which they possessed at that moment (and many, many crucial things that weren't there then)—all that had to vanish into a crystal bottomlessness, into a face-less, concentrated heat, leaving for all eternity things of theirs that weren't crucial: wiry hair, a skull, an exposed skull, and pelvic bones. And this vanishing wasn't a simple disappear-ance but a ritual, a dance in which I, despite my visionary powers, inevitably had to participate. My visionary powers were the equivalent of blindness, and my mind was indignant, but my indignation was fruitless, useless, anticipated, woven a long time ago into the overall pattern of the ritual dance. I longed to see nothing and not to feel my mind, and several times I turned my head sharply left and right. As we all know, during a frost the wind burns your eyes and forces out tears, and by turning my head back and forth in this way, I gener-ated wind and began to cry. My tears cooled my eyes, and they no longer saw as they'd seen earlier, and they no longer con-tained the knowledge and stupid intelligence that can never help anyone preserve what's crucial.

I slowly began my dance, which my lieutenant had doubt-less been expecting from me for so long: I began to gaze at him the way whores do, intently, with an inviting tenderness, as though no one else were any longer there and we were alone, only the table was getting in the way, but what's a table for, if not something for us to get around? And my eyes were shining and cold, like freshly washed berries.

"Vova," I said, although there was no longer any need to say anything, and that's precisely why I had to say something.

Something suddenly banged behind me. I turned around.

There, by the window, stood the guy with the lipless mouth, shortish, bony, his loose white shirt and the white blind beside him billowing out like sails and then sagging as the hot wind flapped around in them. The guy's face was flushed and angry: he stared at me as if he were looking into a void, his wide beaky mouth twisted in bitter disdain. He was squeezing the glass necks of the heavy dark champagne bottles with which he took aim at the empty space outdoors. Foam spurted out of the choking bottle necks into his drunken friends' cupped hands.

"Salute!" he shouted to me, and his voice was so thin and piercing that it hung in the air, trembling like a cobweb about to break, glittering and stretched tight; his lips twitched as if they wanted to cry. "It's a gun salute!"

"Hurrah!" I said softly, mechanically, and then thought: That's right. If it's a salute, then it's okay to say "hurrah."

And suddenly I sensed that this guy had understood everything. He understood what I'd discovered; he understood why my eyes had become like wet berries. His mind, lagging behind mine, was indignant and protested against the immemorial dance. But his bitter protest looked so ridiculous that his lips twisted in bitter derision, as if they were keeping abreast and understood everything.

This guy didn't know that there was one thing I felt in myself which my mind, blinded by what it had seen, had never known or felt. He didn't know that besides the icy eternity of forms and the warm eternity that strikes your nose with the strong concentrated scent of billions of armpits and groins, there's a third eternity. And I felt this eternity in my thoughts and my characters, in my face and eyes, in my smile and my gait. Within me I preserved my ancestors; I felt them within me, and I carried them inside me cautiously, like an eternal fetus; they lived within me as in a dormitory, each one in his tiny cubbyhole. They were often estranged and hostile to one another, like a mother-in-law with her daughter-in-law, but I felt close to them all, the way a mother-in-law is to her grandmother, or a daughter-in-law is to her own mother, and I was in charge of this dormitory, where all the inhabitants were related. I knew all their flaws and weaknesses, and I disapproved of the unruly behavior of one, the craftiness of another, the weakness for alcohol of a third, yet I loved them, not with an administrator's love but the way one loves close relatives. I loved them without showing it, I loved them the way I love my son, and I was like a mother to those who had given birth to me, and I was already conceived in my son (no, I loved my son more intensely, after all, since I didn't know whether he and I would meet again in someone else—whether we would meet in my grandson—or whether we would vanish into a common accumulation of warmth. Our love was therefore more intense, as if it were a last love). And whenever I'd emit a cry of rage it wasn't clear whether this cry was mine or that of my Tartar-Mongolian ancestress, and whenever I sang I did so in the voice of my great-aunt (that's a fact; I could hear it myself). And whenever they squeezed my temples with their fingers, the way they squeezed my mother's with an iron band during her imprisonment, I became quiet and apathetic, just as she had. I knew how to speak in a strange, incomprehensible language in which I nonetheless felt at home: in me spoke one of my luckless ancestors, whom none of my other ancestors could understand and who talked to himself, reciting poetry in his language; and I hated those who were well fed, and I loved the rhythm of a hard fate that coincided with the rhythm of hard work, performed by all my ancestors. I remembered everything, not with my memory but with my whole being, and I lived as if I both existed and at the same time didn't exist, and it was unclear what was mine and what wasn't; there wasn't enough of me for me to achieve self-understanding because I didn't exist by myself alone. It was complicated to live like that, but it wasn't lonely, and I couldn't understand other people who also carried eternity within themselves yet didn't understand that fact and therefore thought of themselves as lonely. They didn't understand that by killing themselves or someone else they were killing at one go thousands of live people who'd been prepared to live forever and whose dying was external. It was a sacrifice to those absurd eternities—to the warm and the cold, to the cold world that gobbled up the warmth yet could never get warm. These people, they didn't understand that death, natural death, was only a ruse devised by everything that was alive so as to deceive absurd dead matter and to preserve the life of what's most crucial. Life pretended to be submissive to fate.

Nor did this guy know that this eternity, pretending to be fatalistic, was fatally unpredictable. This guy didn't know that the person sitting there with the shining moist gaze of a whore wasn't me but some brazen remote ancestress of mine living in furnished rooms or my great-grandmother from St. Petersburg playing this brazen creature on the stage, and I was capable of staring just as brazenly, but it was unclear what that would lead to: either everything would go exactly according to the script, either it was fatally predicted, or else the unpredictable would burst into the furnished rooms where everything seemed forecast; an ancestor of mine having nothing to do with rooms designated for a specific purpose, or with theaters, would burst in, brandishing a truncheon or wearing a black skullcap.

"Some guy, huh?" shouted Vova, and I noticed the large whites of his eyes and his gray irises, retreating into the depths of his pupils. His eyes seemed to pant with rapture, like the sweating flanks of a tired gray horse. "I like this guy, don't you?"

And I realized that I liked the guy, too. Yes, Vova, I'm very taken with him. And, fatally and unpredictably, the guy was already coming toward our table, shaking the bottles in a ridiculous manner, stopping them up with his thumbs, while a dark green foam formed inside.

I waited, half turned to him, and knew all along what he'd say when he reached us. And he said precisely the words I'd been expecting: "Let's have a drink!" he shouted. But he shouted so loudly and shrilly—which none of us had expected—that we all winced. Even he winced and began to shout nonstop, even louder and more shrilly, so that we'd get used to his voice and wouldn't find it strange. "Let's have a drink! Come on let's do it! There's more where this came from! There's some left! To your being here! After all, you made it here. . . . I'll order more. You did make it, after all. Let's drink to our meeting!" But it was no more possible to get used to his voice than to get used to a squeaky door hinge or look placidly at someone drowning if that person was shrilly calling for help. We seized our glasses feverishly without noticing that they were vodka glasses and too small for champagne. We held them out so he'd stop talking and get on with it. We wanted to save those pathetic, panic-stricken pupils, racing as if they were the relatives of the person drowning and shouting shrilly as they raced helplessly along the bank.

His hand shook as he poured the champagne into my glass. Without gauging the size of the glass and the weight of the bottle, he overfilled my glass, and the liquid spilled over the edge and ran down my raised arm into my armpit, then along my ribs, separating the silk from my skin. But he kept pouring.

"That's enough," I said quietly, because, after the shrill shout, sounds started emerging again one after another in the resounding, deafening silence, like objects in the dark once you get used to it, and I didn't want my words to destroy the quiet aftermath of that recovered silence, which had taken the form of an indistinct buzz until his shout. "That's enough," I said quietly.

And the guy abruptly righted the bottle, so abruptly that its heavier lower part bumped against my glass. I instantly heard a shrill "Sorry!" and, deafened, almost hating the guy, I rushed to pick up from the floor the shards of glass and silence. He was senselessly trampling around on the shards, and they crunched under his feet, which for some reason were encased in heavy army boots that looked out from under his wide trousers. I picked up the shards with one hand, pressing them into my palm with my thumb, and with the other I waved away the guy, brushing against his face and his hands as I tried to get rid of him. But I couldn't get rid of his shrill voice, which had drilled through my ears. I wanted to hit him on the lips, on his lipless mouth, from which his voice poured nonstop in an unbroken stream: "Leave it, I'll do it. . . . It's my fault, after all. . . . That repulsive bottle. . . . Let me do it. . . ." I straightened up so as to hit him but found myself looking down right at his head and saw his thin hair, white as ivory, and the bright baby-pink skin mingled in my wail-like cry: "Be quiet!"

The guy backed off slowly and sat down at an empty table nearby. He looked on guiltily as I tried to dig out the glass from the parquet floor at the risk of cutting myself. The glass had been ground into the wood by his boots.

Silence wearily reestablished itself once again, re-creating itself, as it was supposed to, slowly and steadily, the way a photographic image emerges.

Irina's laughing body was swaying serenely, her chin thickly smeared with red. For an instant I felt an involuntary pang of fear for her, connecting the sharp pieces of glass in my hand with the red stain on her chin as cause and effect. Pyotr was also laughing, looking at Irina, and wiping his chin on the spot where Irina's chin was smeared, and it wasn't clear whether they saw or heard us.

Vova looked on placidly, as if he were the master of the house, and kept pointing out to me whatever shards of glass caught his eye. He kept tapping his glass against his knee, bending his head first to one side, then to the other, so that the glittering edges of the shards would be more visible, and each time I found another piece he'd say with satisfaction, "Vova's eyes are as keen as a hawk's. There's another one—no, not there, right in front of you. Maybe we'd better get the waitress to use a broom, it's taking you forever. . . ."

But I knew that he liked the fact that it was precisely me picking up the shards—acting like a housewife—and I, too, liked my lowly housewife role. What's more, it seemed that Vova would have liked to break his glass as well, the way hussars do, but he couldn't make up his mind; it would have looked absurd at that domestic moment and would have come between us. At last I finished picking up all the shards. There were a lot of them, but they were all tiny and fit into the palm of one hand. I carried them behind the partition that separated the dining room from the serving counter and the kitchen.

There, behind the partition, the waitress sat watching television. The TV was on the gas range, a range that had no burners and had evidently been discarded and replaced by a modern electric range. You could tell that the waitress was bored watching TV, yet she watched it with rapt attention, secretly rejoicing that, instead of ticking by in vain, her boring hours on the job were of some use to her and her spiritual development. From here you could hear everything that was going on in the restaurant, and you could be sure she'd heard the guy's exclamation, followed by mine, and the sound of breaking glass. Peeved that someone would come now to ask her to remove the broken dishes, she was staring at the TV screen with rapt attention, putting off the moment when she'd have to get up. She winced when I came in but didn't turn around; instead, she glued her eyes even more peevishly to the screen, absorbing the last few images. Judging by the distressed, restrained way she kept shaking her head, it looked to me as if she wanted to speed up the images in order to increase the amount of time compressed in them—time that she could enjoy free of us.

"Here," I said, holding out my hand with the shards and looking not at her but at the television. "It was a glass."

"That's all? There was such a racket!" she said, without turning around, and I felt her relax and her sense of time recover its previous slow rhythm.

"Where can I throw this?"

"Over there," she indicated, without taking her eyes off the television. Resentfully I thought that I ought to write a complaint about the waitress and her TV.

As I got rid of the broken glass, a shard stuck to my finger. I tried to brush it off with my other hand, but the piece was deeply embedded in my finger, and I stood for a while looking down at it, quietly waiting for a feeling of fear and curiosity to overcome me, knowing and foreseeing what would happen next. Then I shook the piece of glass loose and pulled it out as I would a stinger, quickly and carefully. My finger started to bleed. And the more it bled, the stronger became the feeling of horror I'd had as a child for something I should never have seen, of pity for the finger that was growing numb and had to die because all its blood was pouring out. I felt secretly triumphant that this uncontrollable red life was flowing out of me and not out of someone else, that such beautiful, powerful blood was living in me all on its own. I felt that I should hide it and show it only to my friends, who were crowding around like a herd that dimly sensed danger, and that I should run away in tears, howling in self-pity and in terror of dying, and that I should call out triumphantly to my mother, "Look! Blood! I'm bleeding!" If I didn't pay close attention to myself, none of this remained in my adult life, except for the words I now uttered with outward calm but with inward triumph because this minor misfortune would tear the waitress away from her TV, and for a fraction of a moment my bleeding would bring us closer.

"I'm bleeding," I said.

"Cut yourself, did you?" she asked me with perfunctory sympathy. And she didn't turn around.

I began to whimper quietly, licking the blood off my fingers. For some reason it was sour-sweet, like champagne. Why in the world should the woman turn around and look at me? Why in the world should she want to get closer to me because of some dumb finger, when maybe every day she saw smashed and bloody snouts and had to tear herself away from her TV show because of them to call the police? Maybe the sight of blood made her sick, and if there was no need to call the police, then she wouldn't have to look at someone else's intoxicated blood that was being flaunted; and right now there was no need for the police. . . .

I couldn't tell what made her suddenly tear herself away from the TV and come over to me. She took my hand and said, without looking at me, "Broads really get me! They have their period every month, but just let them cut a finger, and they start bawling." These coarse words, probably normal for a waitress, didn't go with her stern schoolmarm face.

She opened the oven: its maw was unexpectedly white, and she took a bandage out of it and bent over my finger. As if taking the relay baton from her, I stared stupidly over her head at the TV, as if it were impossible to leave without keeping an eye on the images on the screen rushing by with the speed of time.

"I'll get them! I'll ask! Champagne glasses! Five of them, there are five of us! Champagne!" We heard the piercing voice and, for the first time, the waitress and I looked at each other. Not that I got any closer to her—my cut was too slight for that, no doubt—yet something gave way, enabling me to ask, "Do you know that guy?"

"No," she said, "I don't, but I've seen him somewhere before."

He came into our sanctuary, muttering and screaming ("Five tall wineglasses and a bottle"), and here, in the neat, almost homelike little room, removed from the excited, lustful dining room, I thought his voice was a disaster. It made you wrinkle your nose, as would the smell of unwashed socks, and the guy was drunk while I was overly sober. Guessing what I was thinking, he started to whisper, his lips twisting painfully as he reined in his recalcitrant voice, hissing sharply where the sounds *s* and *sh* occurred in a word. "Mi-ss, s-some ch-ampagne, plea-s-e, and five tall gla-ss-e-s. Four plu-s one ek-ss-tra, five in all." The waitress left. He suddenly saw my bandaged finger and made a move toward me. He took one step, and his body continued to fall forward, as if it hadn't realized that his legs had stopped, and I put my hand behind my back, as if by doing so I could stop his body from falling . . . and it did stop, and righted itself. His body swayed back and forth, with the abrupt, resilient movement of a spring fastened to the floor.

"Let me ss-ee," he hissed, and I proudly showed him my beautiful snow-white finger. His face froze instantly, imperceptibly, and turned into a mask of grief and horror, and in this frozen mask the gash of his mouth, the protrusion of the nose, the gashes of the eyes, and the protrusions of the brows all lost their concrete designation; in the split second of convulsion that transformed his face into a mask, they resembled the dissolving and elusive movement of waves. I felt instinctively sorry for him, instantly experiencing the pain of his cut finger, forgetting that it was my finger that had been cut.

And he stood there, swaying, as if he were crying with his whole body, just as the elm outside had swayed earlier.

"My fault again, it was me. See—it was because of me again . . . ," he muttered in a squeaky rush of words, and I remembered that it was my finger that was hurt.

"It's all right, don't worry," I said, and went over to stand right beside him, so as to curb the angle of his swaying.

"Let's go," he said suddenly. "Let's make a break for it, come on, while they're waiting in there"—he glanced around—"for the wineglasses. We'll go to the restrooms. Then we'll run for it. Let them have the champagne. . . ."

"No," I said, and for some reason added, "Later, maybe later."

We followed the waitress into the dining room, and Vova's cynical comment ("Died a hero's death, did it?") regarding my finger, which was swathed like a mummy, for some reason seemed dearer to me than the grimace of pain on the guy's face. I couldn't quite manage the "wet berry" stare, but I knew it was essential for me to do so to put things right. I had one drink and then another, and "my" lieutenant drank with me and gazed at me absently. I saw the caressingly moist whites of his eyes, darkly tinged with blue, like hens' eggs stripped of their shells. And my whole being was completely transformed into body, so shameless and thirsty that it shivered with fever. . . . My brain attempted to resist all this, but it had already become alien to me, and my body, greedily resolving it, as if it were an abscess threatening it with destruction, gradually changed from its state of enervated sensuality to one of dull awareness, like the gaze of a wild beast. My body grew conscious of itself, and, because it still did not believe what was happening, it observed intently and with difficulty the desire forming within—a desire that you could touch and smell, that was sweet, tormenting, and obscure. The body dimly remembered that this was precisely how it had felt billions of years earlier when it was a cell that had only just emerged from inanimate matter, in precisely this way the cell had felt exhausted from solitude, and prepared simultaneously for death and for happiness, it had torn itself in half, remembering that instant forever and making a gift of this memory to my body. But, strangely enough, although my body wanted to stay with Vova (Vova was tan, while the guy's white skin, which didn't tan, seemed to me—as it would to anyone who had grown up on the sandy shores of a big river—somehow indecent and alien), yet I longed to go off with the guy. Maybe it was because with Vova everything seemed obvious and depressing, like jogging in place, whereas with this other one, whose name I didn't even know, everything was uncertain, including how and where our flight would end. I simply had to run off with him.

(Read on carefully: somewhere around here lies will start cropping up—exactly where, I myself don't know.)

I glanced at him, and he understood everything. We understood each other like dumb beasts. I would have to leave my handbag behind. Slowly, so they'd make no noise, I pulled open the zippers of my bag, muffling their rasping voices with my fingers. I had to find out whether my papers were in the bag (Irina had the money). My bag contained a children's book—

Dr. Ouch—powder, and lipstick. Remembering my papers and money was automatic and instinctive; my movements were precise; my body was knowing without knowledge. Having sighted the goal, it tensed and braced itself like the knowing body of a wild animal, and everything was accomplished independently of me, the way it happens in dreams. And as in a dream I noticed that Vova was observing me out of the corner of his eyes, but I didn't acknowledge that. Instead, I retreated into myself and started to tug back and forth at the zippers, as if I were doing it for no particular reason. I found myself wishing the zippers would break because it seemed a pity to leave behind a new handbag, whereas if the zippers were broken, it wouldn't be such a pity to lose it for good.

The guy had also noticed Vova's glance and the fact that I'd retreated into myself, but he probably thought that I'd resigned myself and decided to stay. I was moving the zippers altogether too mechanically, which is why everything seemed irrevocable. The zippers produced a rhythmic rumbling sound, like the louder and louder purr of a cat falling asleep. No doubt that was why, alarmed by my yearning and submissive body, he attempted to stem the irrevocable quickening rhythm of my fall, which was inevitable, the way the dance of primitive peoples is inevitable once the rhythm of the tom-toms quickens. So he exclaimed, "Hey! I've some boiled crayfish! A whole case of them! Let's eat them! They're cold, but we can have them like that, they were caught today! Do have some!"

He started tossing them on the table, and they fell with a dry thud, like reddish-orange coffins[7] equipped with claws so as to bury their own dead within themselves. Their black eyes seemed squeezed out of their sockets. They had a sweetish smell made even more loathsome and nauseating by the added smell of spices. They reeked of decomposition and decay, of putrefying flesh boiled with dill. I couldn't watch the others break their red shells into pieces, I couldn't stand it; it was as if they were devouring my stinking flesh with their staring dead pupils. And my ears couldn't stand the choking, hissing, asphyxiating whisper that penetrated the obediently open pores of my body. There was a hissing in the dark pores like the draft in a tunnel caused by an oncoming train, and this hissing reverberated against the bones of my skeleton, then receded, echoing back along the same tunnel into space. My whole being was like a sponge that had absorbed this hissing: "You don't care whom you do it with . . . go on, then, get outside, I'll be there in a minute, wait for me outside. . . . I've still got some more . . . you don't care whom you do it with. I've been waiting all evening, all my life . . . whereas he . . . you don't care, he doesn't either, but I . . . go on, get going. . . ."

I got up and, very quickly and stiffly, afraid of spilling the nausea that had welled up in me, carrying myself like a slop bucket, walked across the parquet floor. I walked across the parquet floor and headed for the stairs, past the carpet on the stairs, past the marble in the lobby, past the metal grill at the entrance (sliding my hands across the wood of the double doors), and went through the doors into the darkness. I turned a corner and went along the asphalt (my burning cheeks brushing against the bristly bark of the elm), turned another corner, and scrambled along the ground up a little hill, my hands and feet clinging to the warm earth, and I grabbed at a wooden pipe because the hill wasn't a hill at all but a storehouse of earthen goods. As little kids we used to sled downhill from this storehouse, from this hill, which in winter was covered with ice. We used planks yanked off wooden packing crates, and we'd fly on them incredibly far, and as we flew downhill, the boys would squeeze us. While squeezing us, they'd kiss us with foam-covered lips like those of horses; their saliva was fresh and clean, as if it were our own, and we'd lick their saliva off our lips and again go stumbling up the hill to do the whole thing over again.

I saw him right away, but I didn't believe my eyes because it was dark. I peered into the darkness for a long time, until my eyes were ready to believe anything. He was standing under the elm, in the light coming from the window, and was whirling around in place, like a white bird that had fallen out of a tree in its sleep.

"Hey!" I said, and he scrambled up the hill, using his hands. His white shirt was dangling loosely down his back like a broken, useless wing, and I felt a vague fear of something until it dawned on me that I was afraid that the crazy evening wind would return and carry him off, lifting him by his drooping wing. He caught hold of the pipe and wanted to say something, but I covered his mouth firmly with my hand because just then three people jumped out of the darkness onto the wide lit path. Clutching their heads with one hand, like caricatures, they ran around the elm, reluctant to cross the boundary between light and dark, as if the path had glass walls. (One of them had my handbag dangling from his side, like a flat pancake; it banged against his hip and made a sound like a tambourine because it contained copper coins.) Then, having had their fill of light, all three of them plunged as one into the darkness, from which they emerged still clutching their heads with one hand, just as before. I could barely hear the coins rattling in my bag now, the sound growing more and more infrequent and doleful, as if the bag were a live creature being forcibly taken away from me while it tried to draw my attention with its voice. When my bag could no longer be heard, I realized that the officers had been holding on to their caps as they ran, and I started laughing and removed my hand from the guy's lips, as if giving him permission to laugh, too. But he didn't laugh, and as I continued laughing, I felt that my hand, which had been covering his mouth, wasn't participating in my laughter either, but seemed to be siding with the guy, and his narrow, half-open beak of a mouth, his front teeth, and his childlike pointed chin had left an imprint on my palm, on which the lines of fate had been melted by his hot breath and now replaced with traces of his mouth, his teeth, and his chin. I furtively wiped my palm on the rough wooden pipe, just as if I were scraping off a drawing, but it didn't help.

"Well?" I said. I was alarmed, and his long silence frightened me.

"Let's go," he said.

And we started making our careful way downhill. I held on to his shoulder, trying all the time to put as little weight on it as possible so that he'd think I was light, and this made my hand suffused with heaviness. As soon as we reached the bottom, he abruptly lurched forward. I almost fell, and grabbed at his arm, hooking it through mine, but it was very awkward; his elbow pushed against my stomach, my elbow knocked against his side, and the skin at the crooks of our elbows stuck tightly together. We set off like that, and I asked him:

"Are you from around here?"

And he answered:

"Yes."

We fell silent, walking along like two strangers, and our intertwined arms were alien to us, as if some unknown entity were waddling between us, knocking against us.

The darkness was impenetrable. You seemed to be looking not out of yourself but into yourself, as if you were inhaling and exhaling inside yourself, living and breathing inside yourself, which is why it grew oppressive. I closed my eyes, intending to get some sleep because I didn't feel the space around me or my own movements. My body was motionless, enclosed in the stuffiness of a dark blanket. But as soon as I shut my eyes, I realized where we were going. Smells began to emerge out of the darkness; they seemed to emerge from my memory, and I might have doubted the actual existence of their source, except that one such source was walking right beside me: the guy reeked of overcrowded railroad cars, and to doubt his existence was difficult. The skin at the crook of my elbow was burning, the way bedsores probably burn, and that's why my memory conjured up, out of the smell of damp wood, steam, clean flesh, bundles of birch twigs, the pinkish building of the municipal baths.[8] This ephemeral building constructed in my mind was an exact duplicate of the building we were passing.

We went past a boiler house (the smell of coal dust) and a bakery (that needs no elaboration); then memory in its building fever outstripped the smells, and, therefore, as I was mentally constructing a shining white building devoid of smells, it promptly was flooded by a hospital smell. And only then did the building become complete, the way an empty room becomes occupied. A real building is merely an abstract sign, but a smell is music more concrete than matter itself. So we went on, breathing in the music of the buildings, and the farther we went, the quicker, more familiar, and disquieting this music became. I could already name each note: a smell of strawberries (the Kalitins' yard—their whole yard is full of strawberries), the smell of chlorine (the Muraviovs' yard—the back of their outhouse faces the street), the smell of a doghouse (the Gribovs' yard, where Treasure is kept chained), a faint smell of kerosene (the Bobkovs' yard—their house was built on the site of a kerosene store that had been torn down), a rabbity smell mixed with the smell of roses (the yards of the merchants Ivashkin, Nesse, Khalmuratov, Drozdov—they sell roses and gladiolus in the summer and rabbits in the fall). If we'd walked along this side street, then a symphony of smells from my own street, which I'd known since childhood, would have burst forth. But we stopped: the smell of dried fish—the Sinitsyns' yard (old Boria was a fisherman, a poacher, but a harmless one; he poached black caviar only for his own use, not for sale; as members of the Blue Patrol, we children had waged war against him).[9]

The guy's skin peeled off mine like a Band-Aid, and he moved away from me and started fiddling around with the lock on the garage door. I asked, "You live in this house?"

"Yes," he said firmly. But I knew that wasn't true; I knew very well who lived in that house and whose jeep was in the garage, and he smelled too strongly of overcrowded railroad trains for me to trust him.

I went off and stood under the cherry tree. The trunk of the tree was in the yard, but the branches cascaded with their whole weight over the fence and flowed all the way down to the ground. I stuck my hand through the planks of the fence (it was impossible just to stand there idly when something awful was going on there, near the garage), and my hand touched the tree trunk. For some reason my hand shook as I feverishly explored the cherry tree; its bark was rough and defenselessly virtuous under my hand, which felt around with masculine boldness. Ashamed of my marauding hand, engaged in something depraved and illicit, I closed my eyes, and the pitch darkness stopped being darkness and was transformed into a pain that my eyes shared with the cherry tree. I tore beads of rosin off its skin and stuffed them into my mouth and furiously chewed and chewed the slippery, sweetish substance, and my mouth filled with saliva. It was as if I were gnawing a thread that I couldn't tear off and gnaw through, the thread that tied me to this guy who was a stranger to me, the thread that wouldn't allow me to run away or cry out. By the way the thread trembled, I could feel how his hands were shaking and couldn't turn the key in the lock. And I kept chewing the rosin because I felt awful. As I observed myself from the side, it struck me as desperately funny how my body was posing for someone; my pathetic body was standing there quietly, avoiding unnecessary gestures, always watching me and afraid of superfluous movements, fully aware that they weren't superfluous at all, that they stripped me naked, to my essence. My body was never one with me; in its immobility was something of Egyptian statues, whose outward immobility conceals the fusion of all existing rhythms. Think what you want.

But today my body knew I'd have to become one with it, and all my thoughts and the thoughts of those who could see me inevitably fused with my body's desire and its immobility. I stood under the cherry tree, seemingly independent, on my own, apart from the guy, and seemingly prepared for flight and dazed submissiveness. And it also could look as if it had been raining and I'd run to take shelter under the cherry tree (I knew absolutely nothing about the guy standing a few feet away from me), and also that we were a couple: I was the lady, and he, my beau, had moved off to answer nature's call, and I was standing to the side, trying not to hear the indecent sound of the stream hitting the ground. Think what you want.

The garage door gave an unexpected creak, and the guy unexpectedly started to speak, squeakily, like an ungreased hinge—evidently something was wrong with his vocal cords—I suddenly saw them, rusty, like waterpipes, there in the pink moistness of his throat, and I wanted to clear my throat in his stead.

"Are you there? Get in."

And I obediently trudged over to him and got into the *gazik*[10]—everybody called this make Billy Goat—an ugly old jeep in which Sinitsyn had returned from the front. The jeep smelled of fish, and it was cold inside, the way it must be in the belly of a fish. As I was crawling past the guy's knees (he was already at the wheel but hadn't opened the other door), I fell against him accidentally on purpose, and for a second I felt his warm body before I tore myself away from him. I couldn't think about a thing. I began to feel deathly cold after I tore myself away from him, and I started shivering. This wasn't the tremor of desire; I was simply cold, and I had to warm myself against his body, nothing more. But we backed out of the garage; I couldn't fathom why we did, and why I should have to wait, when I had to get warm right away.

Suddenly he honked, and immediately all the dogs in all the yards started barking and the cocks started crowing, and we drove in the barking darkness that rattled its chains and crowed at us, a darkness we bisected with our headlights. We drove past my house, but the smell of fish and the cold made me utterly incapable of remembering, and I just glanced mechanically in the direction of my house. At that moment the guy looked at me; in the faint light his face was yellow and radiated light and warmth, and more than anything I wanted to press my cold lips against his hot yellow ones, to unbutton his silly shirt and to get warm, just to get warm. . . .

I was glad he was there, the only human being I'd met in the loathsome fish belly where I was getting frozen to the marrow; and we couldn't possibly part because each of us would have died there alone.

I asked him where we were going; now only words would hide what the body was in no condition to hide. And so words came to the body's aid, clear and simple words, full of falsehood and deceit, however; everything in me was full of falsehood and deceit because I didn't give a damn where we were going and why. Everything within me tried to hide my true self, and I didn't know why I was hiding like that within myself, as if I were hiding God knows what and not just the simple thought of getting warm, warm, just getting warm.

"After goat antelopes," said the guy.

I'd been expecting the usual deceitful answer: "Down to the creek" or "Just driving around a bit," and that's why what he said didn't sink in right away. Staring ahead dully, I thought about those words for a long time. We were driving across the roadless steppe, along the bright corridor (from the headlights) that dead-ended in a black wall. We were racing toward the wall without getting any closer; it kept receding, slowly moving back yet not disappearing: the dead end remained there, ahead of us. And in the same way the words "after goat antelopes" kept receding from my consciousness until I got used to them by endlessly repeating them to myself without thinking about their meaning because I was cold and wanted only one thing: to get warm. And my shivering merged with my incessant repetition of the meaningless words, and my longing for warmth took on the form of "going after goat antelopes." My longing found a name. The words stopped being irrelevant and didn't prevent me from waiting for the moment when I would finally unbutton his shirt and cling to him with my whole body. The anticipation was agonizing because this scene had been spinning around obsessively in my head till I was dizzy, but precisely because of its obsessiveness it had become concrete, and the anticipation became joyful: it was as if I'd glimpsed the guy there, in the distance, and we were drawing closer to each other, and the anticipation was realized, just as the fact that the jeep was rushing madly ahead was realized. The road stretched between us, and we rushed toward each other like madmen, our speed shortening the distance and the anticipation.

The jeep stopped as abruptly as if—after walking toward each other—we'd unexpectedly collided in the dark.

We sat without stirring, as distant from each other as before. I waited. Then he turned away from me toward the window and asked in a squeaky voice:

"So what are we going to do next?"

This banal question was familiar to me, and I felt disgusted that we were now going to exchange banalities, that there was no way of avoiding them, and that there was no way of avoiding what he was going to do with me, when all I wanted was to get warm, but it was impossible just to get warm without this embarrassing thing that he was going to do with me.

"Oh, that!" I said. "That's just what we're going to do!"

The more brazen, the better. I crawled into the back of the jeep and brushed my knee against his. He twitched and pulled away, and I felt disgusted again: first he drives off with me, and now he pulls away.

There were dry nets and sacks in the back of the jeep. I sat down on them and said sharply "Come over here!" and frowned at my own words. He didn't budge and said nothing.

"Tell me your name, at least," I said.

"Who cares?" he said after a short pause. "It's all the same to you, surely."

"You're crude," I said. I kept frowning, feeling revolted at uttering hypocrisies when I was so very, very cold.

"People are always crude when they talk," he said slowly.

"'Talk to me a little, Mama,'"[11] I said. "Come over here."

"No," he said quietly.

"Why?" I got up and my head touched the roof of the jeep.

"That's how it's going to be," he said, and I could feel him smiling.

"So why in hell, why the hell, did you drive off with me?"
I shouted.

"Just . . . ," he said. "So they . . . so they wouldn't . . . ," he
stammered.

"So nobody could," I prompted. "Is that it?"

"You've got a son," he said in a whisper. "And a husband."

"Found out, did you? And here I didn't know!" I shouted
and sat down again on the sacks. I felt like crying. Damn! I
felt deathly cold; I didn't want anything except to get warm. I
wanted no more falsehoods and said very softly, "I'm freezing, d'you hear, freezing . . . ," and I was surprised that my
breath wasn't visible.

"I know," he said wearily.

"I'm freezing," I said. "Come over here."

"No," he said. "You mustn't."

And suddenly I either saw or recalled his eyes, with their
whites and pupils, the eyes of a righteous man.

"A savior," I said, feeling slightly nauseated, as if from
hunger. We didn't understand each other, and if he had come
to me now, I'd have hit him. "How I hate saviors."

I got up, swaying. I had to get out of the freezing vehicle.
I moved past him, leaning against his chest, and my numb
fingers didn't feel the warmth of his body. By now I was so
cold that he couldn't have warmed me anyway. I opened the
door and choked at the dry heat that rushed violently at me.
I collapsed as if I'd been shot, as if I'd never learned to stand
or walk, as if my frozen feet had suddenly melted. I fell on
the steppe and inhaled the burning, bitter scent of wormwood, inhaling it endlessly without exhaling. The void of my
body filled with wormwood bitterness, and I slowly began to
thaw. Something hot seared all the way through my back; the
crushed wormwood sprang upright again and shot through
me. I writhed in pain and turned my face to the sky—to be
blinded—the hot stars blinded me; they burned like the sun,
like thousands of white-hot shards of sun, which had splintered there in the black sky, and from there, from the sky,

along with the heat, came a fresh and penetrating scent: the stars smelled of wormwood. And everything turned upside down: I was lying on the black steppe of the sky, and stars were shooting through me, and from the earth came the heady scent of wormwood. The whole world was round, huge, black, and hot. The whole world was drenched in the scent of wormwood; the world was destroying me and was sprouting through my useless thawing body, so that my body could merge with it, as snakes and gophers and lizards do, and I protected my eyes, without knowing why yet.

I shielded my eyes with my hand, and my yielding body, with fish scales sticking to it, narrowed and lengthened and slowly began to coil into rings, sparing my head—my eyes! my eyes!—and the coils acquired weight and springiness. It was as though I were being born anew out of earth and wormwood, slowly and with difficulty recognizing my ties with the earth and my separateness from it and my superiority over the unseeing world, for I had eyes. Undulating slowly, my head stretched upward from the coils, but I couldn't tear myself completely away from the earth; I couldn't shoot through the sky, which was swiftly receding from my approaching eyes while the stars kept getting smaller and smaller. All I could do was pursue the sky the way our jeep had pursued the black wall, which kept slipping away, the way people on ships give pursuit in the void . . . all the while seeing the black dead end ahead slipping away. And it's possible by turning upside down and distancing yourself from the earth to shoot through the earth and see the black dead end ahead slipping away, and seeing the dead end along the horizontal and the vertical axes and realizing that it can't be reached, yet race ahead anyway. And this optical illusion became the only salvation in this cunning, slippery, unseeing world, and that's why I'd protected my eyes. But I didn't want salvation. There was no salvation. At each and every turn there was only a dead end, and I didn't have to race ahead to reach it. I didn't give a damn about the dead end of the stupid, unseeing world or about eternity—warm, cold, and pulsating eternity. All my reflections were falsehood and deceit; I really didn't give a damn about my ancestors and descendants, whom I'd never seen; I was simply saving myself from myself and the world. But I didn't want salvation. What I wanted was for this guy and me simply to understand each other; if we couldn't do that, what use were eternity and ancestors to me? What's the use of all that to me if the guy's sitting in the jeep, freezing to death, alive, while I'm over here looking at some stars or other.

I got up slowly. My eyes would have been level with the guy's had he been standing there. Now I knew why I needed my eyes. I suddenly longed to see my son and my mother, who were sleeping sprawled on the floor because of the sweltering heat that buzzed over them like a mosquito. There was no forgiving anything in this deadly game. Like all blind creatures, the world had very good hearing and didn't miss a single word, even when it was spoken inwardly.

Since the guy was lying with his chest on the steering wheel and his arms clasped around it, I crawled into the jeep over his back. At that moment I loved him very much, the way I loved my brother, who'd died at birth. My brother was born one month premature. He drew one breath . . . and died without ever exhaling. His name was Vova; they chose the name before he was born. In my mind's eye I'd often see how he took one swallow of air but couldn't expel it again; it hurt so much. They slapped him on the back, but the air got stuck like a stone in his throat, and he couldn't even cry. It wasn't a question of atrophied lungs; something frightened him so terribly that he could neither breathe out nor cry. What did he see? What frightened him? What did he think about in that one minute, that single second? He had blue eyes and black hair. He kept on growing inside me and beside me, and he would have been twenty now. Maybe, just like this guy, he would have dragged me out of the restaurant, would have made me cool off in the steppe, would have reminded me that I had a husband and a son.

"Let's go," I said.

The guy made no sound; you couldn't even hear him breathe. I got scared, and my head started to spin from fear. I hit him on the back, hit him hard, and the jeep responded with an infant's wail, honking weakly and spluttering.

The guy stirred.

"What's wrong with you? Whatever's wrong with you?" I yelled.

"Nothing. Just thinking," said the guy. What could he have been thinking about?

"Let's go," he said. "Want to go home?"

"Yes," I answered.

We were strangers, as before.

And again we raced on, as if standing still, with the steppe before us, nothing but the steppe.

They appeared suddenly. Something changed in the corridor of light along which we were driving. It filled up with golden dust; the dust grew more dense . . . and suddenly was transformed into the outlines of some absurd golden animals. For a moment we glimpsed their powerful, bobtailed hindquarters and their lowered heads, which were turned back toward us. They ran very fast, one after another; the noise of the motor had probably startled them quite some time ago. It was strange to see them running so swiftly—faster than our jeep—as if they were golden-reared store models, running one after another in a row. They disappeared immediately.

"Goat antelopes!" shouted the guy and stepped on the gas.

The beam of the headlights once again picked the antelopes out of the darkness but this time illuminated all of them together. There were seven. One took a lumbering, clumsy jump toward us, then stopped, and another one collided with it, and they both dropped into the darkness; yet another, which had its head lowered to the ground, like the other, kept looking around blankly as it started moving away slowly and indecisively, as if just then it didn't care whether it ran off or not. It stayed in sight. A fourth leaped up and hung vertically in the night, and for an instant the stars flickered between its lyrelike horns; the rest dashed about as if the end of the world had come, but the last one, its head thrown back, flew like an unseeing mass straight at our jeep.

"Stop!" I yelled and yanked at some lever. The guy hit me in the face with his elbow; with a screech, the jeep jerked to a stop. But it was too late. Leaving the headlights on, we jumped out of the jeep and saw the goat antelopes flocked together. They stood there briefly, looking around meekly and timidly, then suddenly started to disappear in complete silence, one after another, as if the darkness were herding them, one by one, through a wicket gate.

It was dying. The goat antelope was a kid, its muzzle covered with blood. As it inhaled, the skin on its trunklike nose wrinkled all the way to its eyes: the air it noisily exhaled was mixed with blood. With its hair still dark and curly, it looked like an ugly humpbacked lamb. Its yellow eyes looked at us trustingly, full of pain, and in fear that we'd go off and leave it alone with that terrible and important thing that was happening to it.

The guy got out his jackknife. Seeing the blade, the baby kid continued to look at us just as before, trustingly and gratefully, but bleated softly as if asking: Why? And far away on the steppe its mother's voice answered. I turned away.

Afterward we sat leaning against a tire. He cried with effort, making coughing sounds, spitting up some words.

"Me again. . . . Always me. . . . Why?"

I cried because he was crying, yet I couldn't even touch him or calm him: the dead kid antelope lay between us. It wasn't hard for me to cry. We were terribly close to each other yet painfully far apart. As we sat crying on the steppe, the blood of the kid antelope drew us together and separated us forever—this was the last time we'd be sitting like that crying. Because the whole thing was my fault. I was guilty of many deaths. That was my fate, that was my cross, but I won't tell anyone about it; I won't confess. I'll bear myself; I won't unload it onto someone else—I don't want to save myself. He might have become close to me, that guy, if only I'd said a single word, but I didn't want to save myself, and that's why he'll be a stranger to me forever. I'll get off quietly with my tears.

We drove along an old road that nobody used anymore.

"We can't go any farther," I said. "There's a gully over there."

He swung the jeep around.

We drove back to my house in silence and parted in silence. I stood behind the back door and listened, waiting for him to leave. He didn't leave for a long time. Then I heard his steps, something falling on the porch, steps again, then the sound of a motor. That was it. In the early twilight I saw the blood-covered goat antelope lying on the porch.

In the morning I dreamed of cutlets. I woke up, and the house was filled with the smell of cutlets: Mama was frying them before going to work. The smell was odd, as if the cutlets were being fried in rancid butter. But there was no time to think about that. Actually, I didn't wake up of my own accord; someone woke me. It was Liuba. She was retarded, which is why people called her Liuba the Dummy. She was already twenty-five, but her face—dull and vacant—remained forever that of a fifteen-year-old. Her flesh, unwanted by anyone, was ready to explode. As children we used to play together with her; then we started school and began to make fun of her. She stayed behind with the preschoolers, and every year she got ready to go to school with some normal little seven-year-old, but that girl went off to grow wiser, while Liuba stayed behind on the bench by her house and waited for next September. She kept waiting to start first grade until she turned twenty. The time came when her girlfriends began to get married and have children, and we would make fun of her by talking in mock seriousness with her about her fiancés. We discovered, to our surprise, that what she dreamed about aloud, excitedly and naively, was what we harbored in our own hearts. Whenever I came home from school, I'd notice that her face grew sadder with each year; she'd no doubt realized what her problem was, or else someone had explained it to her. She wasn't stupid; it was simply that she stayed exactly as we'd all been in childhood.

"Get up! Get up!" she shouted. "A car wrecked in the dump. The police are there! They came with their sirens howling: *ooh, ooh!* Like at a fire."

I ran, keeping my eyes fixed on the ground: I was wearing rubber flip-flops, and it was easy to trip in them. That was why, when we reached the dump, as soon as I raised my eyes, I immediately saw him. They were already covering him with a sheet, and I saw only his blood-stained shirt, his bitterly smiling long mouth, and his pale eyelashes against his bluish-white face. They covered him with the snow-white sheet, ordering, "Move along, move along." The jeep was in the gully, its wheels in the air, and Sinitsyn, scarlet faced, was there with a policeman, Liuba standing next to him, while people reluctantly dispersed.

I turned back. Liuba caught up with me and blurted out, "It's Sasha Ladoshkin."

The earth tilted. I remembered: the white morning world splintered and whirled about me.

"What?"

"Sasha Ladoshkin. Remember?"

I always remembered him. I loved him and can't think of anyone I ever loved as much later on. I was six. But that didn't matter. I remembered how I went to his house on his birthday; he was four months younger than me. I set out alone in the evening, and it got dark quickly. I lost my way in our small town and didn't recognize the club or the movie theater. I was picked up by the woman who delivered milk from house to house in a little handcart, which she does to this day. She knew everybody in our small town. We slowly went around her delivery route, selling milk until we got to Sasha's house, which was next door to Sinitsyns'. Now that there was less milk in the cart, the milk woman's piercing shout of "Mi-ilk!" had grown fainter in the darkness. I arrived at Sasha's very late. The guests were already leaving. Sasha and my mother sat at the table. On the table was the birthday cake—uncut. Sasha sat with his arms around the cake, guarding it. He'd been sitting like that for a long time. He was waiting for me. I can't recall the expression on his face.

Why did he drive to the gully?

The porch in kindergarten. Sasha and me behind the porch. We're ducking nap time.

Sasha says, "Want me to teach you how to smoke?"

"Yes," I say.

He lights a match, sticks it in his mouth, and puffs out his cheeks, trying not to breathe. The match goes out in his mouth, and smoke comes out. Then he brings his long narrow lips close to mine, and his lips smell of sulfur. Then it's my turn to "smoke," and we kiss again.

I don't remember anything else. His father went crazy, and Sasha and his mother left town. I only remember that I loved him, and I'm not sure I ever loved anyone as much later on.

Why did he drive to the gully?

Liuba's telling me about Sasha. He used to live in Pskov. Studied at the Technological Institute. Completed his army service. He came back the day before yesterday. Spent the night at the Sinitsyns' and in the morning went to catch crayfish with Sinitsyn. Last night Sasha went somewhere. Sinitsyn gave him the keys to the jeep. He crashed close to morning; it was just getting light. He'd taken the old road, the one nobody uses anymore; there's a gully around the bend. The gully wasn't there before, right?

How could Sasha know about it?

"See. Besides, he came to get married. He told Uncle Boria he had a fiancée here."

"A fiancée? How come?" I said. "He was six when he left here, wasn't he?" *Want me to teach you to smoke?*

"Yes."

"How come?" I said. Nobody knows, of course, that I know the answer.

But Liuba says nothing, and I turn around to see Liuba transformed. Her eyes are full of joy, her face blushing in confusion, like a bride's.

"How come?" I said.

And Liuba starts spouting nonsense: how he'd come in secret every year and promised to marry her and wrote her letters from his unit, but she burned them because she thought he was deceiving her. Then he arrived yesterday, but she didn't show herself.

Letters? But she doesn't know how to read, I think, and suddenly I start to believe her passionate, lisping account. Now a legend was being born. Tomorrow the whole town would be repeating it. The girls would tell one another how a soldier fell in love with Liuba the Dummy, how he loved her from childhood to the grave. And each of them would blush and secretly believe that Sasha loved *her* and had come for her and not for Liuba the Dummy, and he was in such a hurry that he wrecked his car.

Is that why you drove to the gully?

I start to feel mad at Sasha, as if he were alive.

"No," I say to Liuba. "You're not telling the truth. I'll tell you what really happened."

And suddenly her face began to cry. Her vacant eyes cried, as did her fat red cheeks, her low forehead, her flat nose, and her big swollen lips. I was struck by how much Liuba looked like me when I cry. It was as if I were seeing myself in a mirror. But however much she looked like me, she had neither a husband nor a son, and never would have. Whereas I had everything, everything! And Sasha as well! Sasha as well!

"I believe you, Liuba, I really do! Liuba!"

If I were to tell everything that really happened, all the girls in our town would come up to me and one by one would spit in my face. And they'd be right. No one must know everything that really happened, Sasha.

. . .

Want me to teach you how to smoke?

"You know," says Liuba—she's already smiling. "These are goat antelope cutlets. I had some once."

I left the restaurant with Vova.

It was already getting light when someone knocked at the door and asked for me. Mama said I was at a girlfriend's and didn't open the door. Through the glass panes of the porch, she glimpsed a guy in a white shirt. He had a long mouth. Mama had seen him somewhere before. He threw a goat antelope on the stoop and left.

Everything that happened that morning is true.

1982

· · ·

Translator's Notes

1. *L'Homme qui rit* (1869) is a novel by Victor Hugo. Presumably, the reference is to a film version.

2. The line is from a popular song.

3. Adriano Celentano (born 1938 in Milan) is a prolific Italian singer, composer, actor, and filmmaker, well known in Russia.

4. In informal situations, Russians, especially of the younger generations, address one another not by their formal names (which require the use of patronymics) but by a diminutive. Many names have more than one established diminutive. The appropriate one for "Vladimir" here would be "Volodia," not "Vova," which denotes a greater degree of intimacy.

5. Mal'chish-Kibal'chish is the name of a youthful revolutionary hero in a children's story by Arkadii Gaidar (1904–41). For refusing to betray military secrets to the enemy, the boy is decorated with a big golden star, which he wears on his chest.

6. To call the major Pyotr, instead of the diminutive Petia, given the situation, is odd.

7. Red or orange coffin lids are used for official funerals and are propped up next to the church door while the body is on view inside the church.

8. In Russia, birch twigs, with their leaves still attached, are sold on the street outside municipal baths. Customers use these twigs in the sauna or the steam room to stimulate the circulation by lightly tapping their bodies with the twigs. The birch leaves emit a pungent, pleasant odor.

9. Under the Soviet system, boys and girls about nine to fourteen years of age made up the Blue Patrols, a form of junior police, watching and reporting on neighbors.

10. A *gazik,* or GAZ, is a jeep introduced during World War II and subsequently manufactured by the Gorky Motor Works, of which GAZ is an acronym.

11. The line is from a popular sixties song in which a daughter is trying to communicate with her mother, asking her to talk about anything, so long as she speaks to her.

■ □ ■ □ ■

POPLAR, POPLAR'S DAUGHTER

Translated by Helena Goscilo

MY SISTER NAD'KA CONCEIVED BY A POPLAR SEED.

Poplar down was flying then like snow, a hot wind blew from the south, there was heat and a white blizzard, the down would stick to sweat-dampened skin, everything itched, and that southern wind inflated her. The wind inflated Nad'ka, they said, and in the fall her stomach began swelling up like a balloon when it's inflated with a bicycle pump.

And I made my decision.

"Nad'ka, take off your clothes!" I shouted when we were left home alone. I shouted right in her face, even though she was deaf, totally deaf, didn't hear a thing—deaf as a post! "Take off your clothes, you fool!" I yelled, while she kept smiling that foolish smile of hers, which made me want to bury my head in shit and howl.

And I pushed her roughly, kept pushing her toward the door, then dragged her by the hand down the wet autumn garden paths, shoved her into the wooden summer shower, and locked the door on the rusty hook. Inside, it smelled of bast. Nad'ka remembered that she'd showered there in the summer and that she'd had to undress, and she slowly began taking off her clothes and hanging on a nail her green woolen cardigan, maroon flannel housecoat, dark blue knit man's undershirt, and pink felt drawers, and, as I watched, the drawers—large and pink, as if alive—slipped off the nail and fell into the dirt. Bending down, she picked them up, feeling sorry for them, shook them out, and smoothed them, and I watched as she hung up the black sateen men's boxers that she'd inherited from me (I was still attached to them), and it was strange, as if a part of me showed black, crucified on the soft, pink flannel. . . .

She stood, huddled up, looking at the gray square of sky from which the rain was falling, an interminable, fine, cold autumnal rain; behind the gray clouds—with the *craah-craah* of crane calls—invisible birds were flying off, while I kept looking at the huge, round, tanned, leather balloon of her belly, with the patterned imprint from the elastic—that balloon grew bigger and bigger with each day, and I was afraid, really afraid, that the taut skin wouldn't hold out and would burst, but it kept on growing, this balloon, and I secretly started expecting that one day this balloon of hers inside her would lift my sister Nad'ka up there, from where the rain was falling, from where there came the *craah-craah* of cranes, and she would hover above our sad, gray military town and would float in the sky like a blimp or like the sun and, from there, from the sky, would smile her foolish, senseless smile, which made me want to howl. And perhaps then compassion and happiness would begin on earth.

"Get dressed!" I said.

She kept looking up at the rain and didn't hear either me or the birds.

"Get dressed!" I yelled. I patted her on the back, and her shoulder blades protruded from her back like sharp wings, and her skin was covered in goose bumps.

She turned around, and I held out her black sateen boxers, stretching the elastic. She understood and stepped into them.

"Good girl," I told her, as if she could hear. I always expected something from her. Every day, I expect her suddenly to hear me or start speaking or stop being a little fool. I always think that any moment now . . . or tomorrow. . . . It's because I strongly sense Nad'ka's kind, beautiful soul, encased, for some reason, in a stupid, deaf-and-dumb body, as if confined in a prison utterly devoid of sound.

POPLAR, POPLAR'S DAUGHTER

And I also expect Nad'ka to give birth to that beautiful soul of hers—and this soul will be strong, smoothbore, rustling, green, growing up to the sky, like the poplar from whose seed she conceived.

1998

■ □ ■ □ ■

LITTLE FOOL

Translated by Elena V. Prokhorova

A Novel-Vita

PART ONE

I

Creak.
Creak.
Creaky-creak.
Creak.
Creak.
Creaky-creak.
Nad'ka's swinging on a rusty swing: *up-down, creaky-creak.*

I'm standing on the roof, watching.

Nearby, our mom's hanging out wet laundry in the yard: Father's blue polyester undershirt—*creak.* My undershirt, identical to his, but faded—*creak.* Father's black sateen boxer shorts—*creaky-creak.* My boxers, identical but smaller, slips—Nad'ka's and Mom's own. Bra, drawers—a light blue pair, huge as the sky, the other one pink, of soft flannel. . . .

Then she hung up Nad'ka's stockings, one by one. The stockings hung there like Nad'ka's feet: one foot and the other.

Dad tries to start the car with the hand gear. He turned it once—the car wouldn't start—Damn! A second time—Damn it to hell! Third, fourth. . . . He turns it, swearing like an automaton, without respite, silently swearing.

The car's called a *gazik*. Or "goat."[1]

It's fall.

2

A year ago in spring the tulips were blood red. My sister Nad'ka was running along the steppe, collecting them. Stepped on a snake—warming itself—it slithered out and bit Nad'ka, the viper, bit her like a dog, that viper, vermin—*chomp*—gray scum, bit her above the knee, and I began sucking the poison out. Nad'ka peed in her pants. Don't pee right on my head, you fool, I told her. I was sucking it out with my lips, my lips were cracked, I sucked in all the poison, became like a viper, I walked around the hospital and hissed, *A-h-a*—and I kept grabbing Nad'ka by her foot; I'd creep up to her and grab, Nad'ka would pee right on the floor, and I'd crawl away, I had no tail, I wished there were a tail; Don't pee, I said, this isn't the steppe, it's a hospital, it's not my head for you to pee on; I slowly crept back to the ward; I really missed having a tail. The viper, creeping away, touched the tulips with its tail—*ping-ping*—and the tulips quivered with their bloody heads—*ping*. Afterward we took the tulips to Dad's car, Gagarin had just gone into space, we picked the tulips in his honor, we brought them and placed them at Lenin's feet in Gagarin's honor. There were so many tulips, right up to Lenin's stone knees; he was standing all in tulips up to his knees as if in blood; it was beautiful. But when Nad'ka and I left the hospital, the tulips had already withered, lying there dead. Nad'ka started crying, she felt sorry, me too, but she's a fool, it's fine for her to cry, not for me, *A-h-a*, I said; she peed right in the square in front of Lenin, Father almost died of shame, he was in his military uniform, and he laid into her, but that made it even worse, even more shameful: a reenlisted officer beating up a girl—Is he drunk?—She's his daughter—All the same, he shouldn't hit a child—But she's a fool—What?—A moron—All the same, he shouldn't do that, better put her in an asylum than taunt her—Well, she did pee—Jeez, what a family. . . . Father can't wait until his retirement, let them all croak, these damn people, the cursed military town surrounded by rusty barbed wire; I wish I had a tail and a tooth filled with poison—*a-h-a—bang!*—he hit me in the tooth: Why're you hissing, eh?—red blood started dripping from my lip onto the asphalt, red like tulips, the crack in my lip will never heal!—Daddy!—Why're you hissing, viper's spawn! Nad'ka was wailing at our side, like a red fire engine—*A!*—a red *A* was pouring out of her throat and dripping onto the asphalt. Father grabbed us, kissing us on our red lips, Be quiet, he kept saying, be quiet. We fell silent.

He raised his blue eyes to the sky and said with bloody lips: "*Lord,*" he said. "*Lord!*"

Nad'ka has just appeared in our house.

3

"Don't creak!"

Creak.

"Don't creak!"

Creak. Creak.

"Didn't I tell you not to creak?! Nad'ka! Do you hear me?"

She doesn't hear. Doesn't hear a thing. She's deaf, completely deaf, doesn't hear a thing—deaf as a post!

But Nad'ka smiles up at me with her strange smile, as if she heard me but didn't understand what I'd said; she nods to me, and, her face helping her body to push the swing, she rises closer to me—so as to hear—flying higher and higher. She almost reaches me in her flight, I can touch her face with my hand. And I make a decision.

I lie down on the roof, my stomach on the cold slate, my face turned to Nad'ka.

Higher, I say to her, higher, Nad'ka!

And when her face, crimson with happiness, with crazy bulging eyes, soars off the ground and rushes toward me at terrifying speed, I say:

"Nad'ka!" I say. "Where did you come from, where'd you set out from? What did you come for? After all, we lived without you. Where did you come from, Nad'ka?"

For a second, her confused face is suspended next to mine.

I look into her pupils: very, very close.

I looked at her: *Nad'ka!*

She's silent, but I hear her silently saying, *I'm Ganna.*

The swing was creaking: *up—down.* It creaked louder and louder.

4

In the hot May of 193– a cart creaked rustily as it entered the ancient Astrakhan village of Kapustin Iar. It was hard to make out who was sitting in the cart: a sandstorm occurred at that time, and the occupants of the cart covered their faces either from the sand or out of fear, as if somebody were about to hit them. And all of a sudden our eyes also felt as if someone had thrown sand and dust in them: winds in the Astrakhan steppe are weird, and it would have been better for us to get in that cart and drive and see.

Not because we were in the wrong place at the wrong time, but because it's alive—the horse raises its tail, and from under the tail golden apples will roll to the ground. "You shameless rusty-red, couldn't do it before, right?" the old woman, the one driving, said to the horse. The old woman's name is Kharyta, and she isn't that old: she dresses like an old woman because she's a cripple, can't move her legs.[2]

"Such goodies going to waste," she grumbles, and the girl next to her reveals her face, which looks thirteen years old; she's wearing a dark dress and light kerchief, has the impassive face of an icon. Her name's Ganna. She's always silent, thinking her thoughts.

Kharyta made out some people in the dust, said hello to a man in the dust: he was walking though the dust cloud and stumbled at her greeting and stopped and looked at the woman and the girl senselessly, as if drunk, not understanding; but he wasn't drunk.

And they drove on, and she greeted another man—he, too, stumbled across her word as he ran and froze like a roadside pole and gazed senselessly, waiting for them to pass. And a woman with empty buckets got up and looked on silently; only the sand kept pelting the buckets, and they jingled quietly as they swung. And it grew dark, the sandstorm entered the village with a vengeance, and everything smoked from the white dust: the road, the roofs, the trees. People were running in the dusty smoke as if to a fire, you couldn't stop them; only one man stood at a distance, as if waiting for Kharyta and Ganna, so as to show them the way. They turned in his direction.

They approached, saw dusty stone boots, big boots, inhumanly huge, and they didn't look up, it was scary. Kharyta turns the silly horse—There, there, you little slut—the horse is snorting, it's so hard to turn around; they'd gotten into a flowerbed, the horse was stamping in place, breathing on the flowers, and blowing the dust off them, under the dust there are tulips, their heads are red, live. They drove on a little farther and looked back—the flowerbed was red like blood, in the middle somebody's inhumanly big boots, and above them you couldn't see: it was whiter than white from the dust. And now they were driving as if through milk, and there was nobody for Kharyta to ask where the orphanage was; they're looking for the orphanage, and the village is huge, you can drive day and night and it keeps going on.

When you're fishing at dawn in the mist, and the mist is like milk, so you can see neither the river nor the bank, in this mist all of a sudden—*ding-ding*—a muffled fisherman's bell clangs, meaning a fish has gotten caught in a bottom trap; it was the same here, in this dusty mist: *ding-ding* ahead, and the horse made for that clinking sound and really got going, and it grew brighter and brighter, clearer and clearer, and thank the Lord—there's a really nice boy walking in front, a really fine lad, with fishing rods and fish traps, and silver fish on a twig shine right in their eyes, so that it almost hurts. He's from there, from the orphanage, he'll show them the way, Follow me to the horned school, it's in the horned school, behind the mill. Kharyta's glad to see him, Kharyta complains to him about the inhumane humans, and the boy walks along and says, Yes, the people here are like that, they're exiles, the people are the enemy; all the people in the village up and decided that it would be deaf and dumb; deaf-and-dumb folks, without language, they don't hear anything, don't understand orders, nobody knows what to do with these people. They're the only normal ones here, those in the orphanage, it's good there, you can even go fishing, they let you go.

Ganna looks at the silver fish, they have the sun in them, and they tickle, tickle her eyes; she gives a ringing laugh, like a sonorous bell, and the boy casts her a backward glance. "It's really good at our place!" he tries to convince Ganna. "She doesn't believe me!" And he burst out laughing himself, and Kharyta started laughing, and Ganna laughed so nicely, laughed like a bird. But it's hot. And the boy took off his cap, shook it as if shaking off snow, wiped sweat off his forehead with the cap, and wiped off his laughter together with the sweat, turned around, and set off at a walk. Kharyta stopped laughing: a cross was shaved on the boy's head—one strip from ear to ear, another from his forehead to the back of his head—with one vein throbbing. What's this, lad, who gave you the cross and why? So that we wouldn't run off, Granny, wouldn't run away.

And he walked on. They follow. Follow the live cross, with one vein throbbing.

But Ganna's still laughing, like a wounded bird, she can't stop: it's because the silver fish tickle her eyes. She's a fool, is Ganna, she should close her eyes and not look at those fish;

Kharyta tells her—Don't look, Ganna—but she doesn't understand and keeps laughing like a wounded bird, like a tired bell, until tears come to her eyes: *ding-ding.*

5

They drove up to a temple with four small towers: instead of crosses, each tower had a weather vane. Kharyta crossed herself before God's temple. The boy laughed.

"This is our orphanage. They call it the horned school. Monks used to live here, now children live in the cells. What are you crossing yourself for, Aunt Kharyta? Those aren't crosses, they're horns, with weather vanes to show where the wind's blowing. You're making the sign of the cross to the god of winds."

"God is one!" Kharyta bowed to the horned temple.

A triplet of girls surrounded the boy and started talking, vying with one another.

"Marat! Brother! Did you bring any fish?"

The boy squatted down and started dividing the fish.

"This fish is for you, Vera. This one's for you, Nadezhda. And this one for you, Liubochka." One little fish remained. He looked at Ganna. "And this one's for you, girl."

He took her by the hand and put the fish in her palm. The little silver fish lay there on her little palm. Ganna looked at the fish, raised her eyes, looked at Marat, and smiled.

"Hand over the fish! Hand the fish over to me!" A woman with a red tie suddenly shouted. As she walked she yelled in a voice used to giving orders. "Any fish that's caught must go into the communal pot."

The frightened girls handed their fish over to her.

"We just wanted to see. . . ."

"I know you, the Abramovs! 'To see'! Individualists! You drag everything to your family! You put the family first, over everything else! Your father may have been an enemy of the people, but he used to be a Party activist. And you behave worse than the children of former kulaks![3] You should be ashamed. If I want to, I'll have you sent to different orphanages. You, Vera, I'll send to the north; you, Nadia, to the south; Liuba to the west; and Marat to the east, to Siberia. You'll get it for your family feelings!"

She saw the cart and came up to it.

"What kind of machine-gun cart is this?"

"They brought a new girl," said Marat.

"Traktorina Petrovna. Director of the orphanage," she said sternly, standing in front of Kharyta. "What do you want, old woman?"

"Take the little orphan, Petrovna, take her for Christ's sake. I'll pray to God for you." Kharyta bowed to her. She stood on the ground, on her crutches. She was so small, she looked as if she were bowing to the ground.

Traktorina Petrovna got angry.

"Stop your religious agitation." She shifted her leaden eyes to Ganna. "Who's the orphan here? You?"

Ganna looked at her fish in fear, then at Traktorina Petrovna. She stuffed the fish in her mouth, choking, and swallowed it together with the scales.

She swallowed it and smiled pitifully. The scales stuck to Ganna's lips and made them silver, like the fish.

"She's so wild," Traktorina Petrovna remarked squeamishly in astonishment. "Follow me to the registration. It's okay, we'll reeducate you. We've had much more difficult cases. And you—go to the watchman. The whole family. Ask him for the 'licks of rod porridge.' Ten portions for all of you."

"Traktorina Petrovna!" beseeched Marat. His sisters started crying in unison.

"All right. You've convinced me. Take all the blows yourself; you're a man; you're a knight. I'm so kind today!"

6

In the red calico room there was only a chair and a mirror on the wall. Ganna sat on the chair, looking at herself: she liked what she saw.

"Stay with us as a cleaning woman, Kharitina Savelyevna," proposed Traktorina Petrovna, approaching Ganna with some scissors. "There are only two adults here: me and the guard. We can't manage."

"I need to go home. I've got to take care of my house and my vegetable garden. Once I hand the girl over to you, I'll start for home. As soon as she's registered, I'll—"

"We'll register her in no time," Traktorina Petrovna said, beginning to cut Ganna's hair. "Our haircut is the document. We're no bureaucrats. Close your eyes."

Ganna obediently closed her eyes. As Traktorina Petrovna clipped her hair, she kept asking, "Where are you from, girl? Who are your parents? How'd you become an orphan?"

"She's an orphan from birth, Petrovna." Kharyta answered instead of Ganna. "She came on a raft, down the river, in a crib. She lay there on a crimson pillow, like a doll. I'd brought my horse to the river to drink, and there I see her floating by; I called some of the men; they dragged her out. She was still a little baby; the whole village helped to raise her. . . . We have nothing to feed her now, hunger's everywhere, so I brought her here. . . ."

"Why doesn't she say anything?"

"She never does. She can't talk."

"She's a kulak's daughter!" Traktorina Petrovna said with conviction. "She's playing a sly game. How would a poor man get a crib? And wood logs for the raft. Her father and mother are kulaks. They'd resort to any trick to leave their dirty blood in our squeaky-clean new world!"

"There weren't any kulaks then. The war was on."

"War, eh? Then she's a bourgeois child, for sure! Crimson pillow . . . a White officer's daughter!"

"Don't take sin upon your soul, Petrovna. . . ."

"Don't you worry. We don't keep documents. I keep everything about them right here." Traktorina Petrovna tapped herself on the head. "I execute if I please; I pardon if I please. I don't trust nobody. So, don't be scared, just tell me

whose daughter she is. Some story you've made up—a raft. . . .
Lie if you want to, but know when to stop. C'mon, girl,
tell me. . . ."

"I'm telling you, she can't talk. Something's wrong with
her head. She's weak minded," Kharyta answered.

"Weak minded?" Traktorina Petrovna rejoiced, God knows
why. "That means 'devoid of reason'? That means 'an animal.' Like a monkey. And every monkey can be turned into a
human being. So, let's use her as an experiment."

"She's not a beast. She's a human being!" Kharyta objected.

"What's the difference between a human being and an
animal? The presence of reason! So, she's an animal."

"She has an immortal soul!"

"The soul's simply prejudice. There is no soul."

"Yes, there is!"

"Fine. If there's a soul, then there's God, too. Right? Then
why did your God give her a soul but no reason? Answer that!"

"'God chose what is foolish in the world to shame the
wise'!" Kharyta answered firmly.[4]

"You're a darn sight too religious for a cleaning woman.
Well, all right, girl, open your eyes. Nice, isn't it?"

Ganna looked at herself, cropped close, with a cross shaved
through the stubble. She passed her hand over the back of
her head, rose, took off her shoe, and hit the mirror with it.
The mirror shattered with a tinkling sound.

"You're the daughter of an enemy of the people," Traktorina
Petrovna told Ganna with hatred. "You're an ape, you're scum,
you're an animal. . . ."

Somebody outside suddenly shouted. They turned their
heads. A huge clumsy muzhik was thrashing Marat with a
birch rod. Kharyta gasped, moved her crutches, and crawled
to the door, wanting to get outside. Traktorina stepped over
her and positioned herself at the door like a sentinel.

"Don't waste your effort, old woman, stay where you are."

"He's hurting the child!" Kharyta couldn't understand.
"That beast's beating the boy. How's that? Why?"

"That's not beating, Savelyevna, it's disciplining. . . . Egorych and I are like mother and father to them. Like Mom and Dad. We feed them, we give them water, we whip them—like in a family," Traktorina Petrovna solemnly said. "In our united Soviet family of workers and peasants!" And she added in a strict tone, "Clean up here. And you'll pay for the mirror out of your first salary. After you've paid, you'll go back to your village."

Ganna stood at the window, watching Marat getting beaten. At each blow her whole body shuddered, as if taking those blows upon itself, as if she, and not he, were being beaten.

"*Ga!*" she cried. "*Ga!*"

"Forgive me." Kharyta clasped her hands. "Forgive me, Gannochka, forgive me, daughter, for bringing you here."

Ganna sat down and embraced Kharyta. So they sat, in each other's arms.

7

At night, the children gathered around Ganna in the cell. A red-haired girl, Freckles, burning with curiosity, asked Ganna, "Who are you, girl?"

Ganna made no response. Looked at her with clear eyes.

"What's your name?" Freckles asked impatiently. "Tell me! Is she dumb or deaf?"

Ganna gazed impassively, like an icon.

"I'm gonna tell her a fairy tale," said a skinny boy with the nickname Charlie.

"What for?" A fat boy, Bulkin, shrugged his shoulders. "If she's deaf, she won't hear your tale."

"So we'll check whether she's deaf or not. Listen to the tale, girl. In a house there lived a mother and daughter. They lived and lived, and the time came for the mother to die. . . ."

The three sisters—Vera, Nadia, and Liuba—started crying.

"And before she died she called her daughter and told her: 'I'm asking one thing of you: don't buy a red piano, daughter, don't open its red-red cover, don't play red-red music on its red-red keys. . . .' And so the mother dies, she's buried in a real good cemetery, they put up a tombstone, and the daughter starts living alone. So she lives and lives and forgets her mother's words. One day, she went to a store and there she saw a red piano. And she liked it so much that she bought it. They delivered it to her home. And then night dawned, and the daughter decided to play the piano. She went up to the red piano, opened the red-red cover, and started playing the red-red keys, and the red-red-red blood started flowing. . . . *Give me back my heart, girl!*" The boy suddenly stretched out his hand to Ganna.

Ganna gave a shriek and rushed off down the corridors, as if followed by the Evil One, who was demanding her red heart, and her heart was ready to leap out of her chest; she held it with her hand so that it wouldn't jump out.

"*Ga-a-a-a!*" she cried heavily, like a beast. Children don't cry like that; only animals cry like that from deadly fear. Marat followed her.

Everybody left the cells and also yelled, following her along the gloomy corridors of the monastery.

Ganna stumbled into somebody. She raised her eyes— Traktorina Petrovna stood there like a rock, her arms crossed; above the rock—in her eyes—there was lightning.

The children stood behind Ganna, breathing heavily. Traktorina Petrovna took Ganna by the hand and told everyone: "Outside—march!"

8

Under the moonlight, the children ran in circles around the yard.

Traktorina Petrovna stood in the center, firmly holding Ganna's hand.

"Forward, run! Faster! Faster! I'll show you how to taunt Ganna! Remember: Ganna's mad! She's a fool! Understand? She's not like you! She's like an animal! She's like a dog. How can you torment an animal? Run! Don't hurt her! Ganna's sick! I'm leaving, but you keep on running and thinking; Ganna, you stay here and watch. I'll be back. Forward! Left foot forward! Forward! Left foot forward!" Traktorina Petrovna left at a march, her voice giving orders to herself and her feet.

As he ran in line, Charlie told Marat, "Still, I checked her out! She's not deaf at all! Maybe she's just pretending to be a fool? Let's check!"

"If you don't leave her alone, I'll kill you!" Marat threatened him with a fist.

"What, you've got a crush on her? Are you in love with a fool? Are you?"

They seized each other like puppies and rolled on the ground, growling.

The children kept on running. Marat and Charlie rolled to Ganna's feet like a ball.

Charlie hit Marat in the solar plexus with his head. Ran back in line.

Marat lay at Ganna's feet. Ganna squatted down, stroked Marat's face, and pushed the blood-covered hair off his forehead.

Marat opened his eyes and gazed gratefully at her.

The children continued running. They breathed heavily with exhaustion.

9

In the morning, as she tidied the bright red room, Kharyta pulled an icon out of her bundle and brushed off the dust. It was the Virgin Mary and Child. Kharyta hung it in the red corner and made the sign of the cross.[5]

Nearby she heard, "Take down the icon!" Traktorina Petrovna stood in the doorway.

"I can't."

"Then I'll do it myself." Traktorina Petrovna moved toward the icon.

"You can't." Kharyta blocked her way.

"Why not?"

"Simply—no. Today's Easter, Petrovna. Christ has risen!"

"That's a fairy tale! There was no Christ. And if, in fact, he existed . . . if the authorities executed him, they knew why, understand? Authorities know better. Take down the icon! There's no place for it in a Soviet institution!"

"Where, then?"

"On the garbage dump of history!"

"And where's that dump?"

"Get out!" yelled Traktorina Petrovna, losing her temper. Then, controlling herself, she added, "Clear off, seeing you're a cleaning woman. Mind your own business. Better go feed the children!"

10

Marat and Ganna were walking through the yard.

"Do you want me to show you something?" Marat asked Ganna.

Ganna nodded.

"Marat, where are you two going? Let's go to the cafeteria!" the sisters shouted to their brother as they ran by.

"In a minute. . . ." Marat led Ganna to the watchman's lodge.

They peeked through a crack. The watchman sat in the lodge, eating. He cut a huge slice of bread, spread butter over it, cut off some lard, and put lard on the butter. . . . He took a bite, chewing methodically. Ganna looked back at Marat.

"I know a secret about him . . . ," Marat whispered. "You won't tell anybody?"

Ganna shook her head: *No.*

"Swear!"

Ganna smiled helplessly.

"Okay, I'll tell you anyway," decided Marat and whispered distinctly in her ear, spelling each syllable. "They say that during the famine *he ate children!*"

Ganna looked at Marat in horror. Then she glanced at the watchman: the watchman's jaws worked like millstones. Suddenly, Ganna grabbed her throat, covered her mouth with her hand, and writhed: she was nauseated. Dry spasms shook her body.

"What's wrong with you?" Marat whispered. "Are you sick?" And, not knowing what to do, he patted her on the back as if she had choked.

The watchman came onto the porch: huge, unshaved. He glanced at them. They froze. He gazed at them, frozen in horror, for a long time. He looked them in the eye. Then he unbuttoned his fly and started urinating. Ganna looked down, then raised her eyes. The watchman grinned slightly. Ganna backed away.

Grabbing Ganna by the hand, Marat ran off. When they turned the corner, he asked, "Were you scared? Did you want to throw up? Did you imagine he was eating you?"

In answer to all his words Ganna kept giving little nods.

"Don't be scared. Traktorina Petrovna said he didn't eat just any kids. He was choosy. He only ate kulaks' children. So that society would benefit from it. But you and me aren't kulak children. Don't be scared. . . ."

II

In the cafeteria, Charlie was walking on the tables. He walked with the gait of Charlie Chaplin, whom he resembled. Instead of a cane, a ladle that he twisted dashingly and juggled.

"Charlie, come here! No—here! Here! Here!" the children cried from all sides.

Charlie pulled the cap off Bulkin's head, then jumped onto another table.

"Bulkin! Your hat!" they cried to fat Bulkin.

Bulkin grabbed his head, then ran after Charlie. Falling and tumbling, Charlie got behind Bulkin, hit him in the rear, and, jumping off the table, started slipping away.

"Grab the thief!" Freckles shouted. "Get him!"

The three sisters lined up chairs in Charlie's way. Charlie ran up and cleared them easily—like a swallow—to find himself in Traktorina Petrovna's embrace: he quivered in her arms like a trapped bird. Traktorina placed Charlie at her side and said in a moist, deep voice that summoned like a mother cow calling its calves: "Pioneers! Be ready for the struggle for the cause of the Communist Party of Bolsheviks!"[6]

"Always ready!" the cafeteria resounded.

"Start the song! Only Young Pioneers sing! Now only the left table! Start!"

> "Blue nights, with bonfires soaring high,
> We are Young Pioneers, workers' children,"

sang the left table.

The right table was silent. Charlie was pulling faces behind Traktorina Petrovna's back. He conducted with the ladle. Their faces buried in their hands, the right table was shaking with laughter. Then the left table—the one singing—burst out laughing, too. Now everybody was laughing inaudibly. Only Ganna continued to sing in a strong, clear voice amid the silence, looking somewhere up high above the ceiling:

> "The era of radiant years is approaching
> Always be ready to be a human being!"[7]

Charlie froze, the ladle in his hand. "Folks, l-o-o-k! The mute's singing!"

Marat tugged at Ganna's sleeve.

"Don't sing, Ganna! You're not singing it right! That's not it!"

She didn't notice and sang to the end.

Traktorina Petrovna glanced over at Kharyta, who'd entered with a pot of baked potatoes.

"You said she can't talk. . . ."

"She can't," confirmed Kharyta. "She just sings. Like a heavenly bird."

"You sing well," Traktorina Petrovna told Ganna. "We'll make you a Young Pioneer. I like kids with good voices! I like songs!" She shed a few tears. "Eat your breakfast!" In a fit of emotion, she slammed the door so that lime from the ceiling poured down like snow: white flakes. She left.

Kharyta distributed the hot potatoes.

Ganna stood alone. Her head seemed to be covered with snow.

The snow didn't melt.

12

In a minute, the potatoes were eaten.

"Aunt Kharyta." Verochka snuggled up to her. "Be nice, give me more potatoes."

"There's nothing left, dear."

"Just potato skins, then!"

"There's not even skins left, dear, everything's gone. There's nothing left."

"I'm hungry, too." Nadia started crying.

"Give us eats!" Liuba joined her howling sisters. "I want eats . . . eats. . . ."

Kharyta rushed to them and hugged the crying sisters, trying to calm them down.

"You've got to hold on, my dears. You just ate. . . ."

"We wanna eat," the sisters cried.

"I want grub!" Charlie shrieked, too.

"We're hungry!" the entire cafeteria joined in. "Give us food!"

They banged their spoons on the table.

"Wait a bit, it'll soon be lunch. There's nothing left, you ate everything! Not a thing! Zero!" Kharyta made a helpless gesture.

Then she grew pensive.

"Quiet," Kharyta said. "You'll get your food. Only you'll have to work for it!"

13

The marketplace had a life all its own. On the wooden stalls, gray from the rain, on crates, on the grass, or right on the ground, people were selling what they had, their merchandise sprinkled with white dust and spread on newspapers, bedsheets, and bedspreads.

Mumbling with her toothless mouth, an ancient woman was selling last year's corncob: she held it in her hands as if it were her jaw—with its yellow, shiny, amber teeth that she had removed from her mouth to sell.

A husband and wife were selling potatoes from a cart. Purple potatoes from the May harvest, with pale shoots—for planting—were lying in sacks: two tiny, wrinkled potatoes fell out of the sack onto the ground and gazed upward like the violet eyes of a child.

Dirty brown beet heads were lying on a wooden platform, as if chopped off: a huge man would grab them by their forelocks, shake them in front of the crowd, and throw them back—where they were mixed with carrots, muddy, earthy-rusty in color, large and small, looking like broken and twisted fingers.

Nearby, on an oilcloth, lay bloody slices of meat, dripping blood onto the ground. Green flies crawled at the bottom of the stall, sinking their teeth into the dust that was clotted as if from rain; it was as if they were sucking spicy sweetness from blood-red flowers. . . .

Carp were lying in a pile of live silver: their silent mouths opened in a scream, their eyes round with horror, their strong silver bodies fought for life. A lean, sinewy fisherman in a tattered jersey picked the biggest carp out of the fish trap and with pride lifted the fish in his arms like a baby; the carp—heavy, shining in the sun like a silver bar—froze there, motionless, drawing people's attention. And then, all of a sudden, slowly curving, with all its might it hit the offender— the lean man—on the face with its wet tail, once, twice, and fell, dancing in the dust, to land right at a camel's feet: the camel, big and proud, was also on sale. . . .

Everything at that market seemed the same as at any other market. The same, yet not the same. . . .

The vendors would silently indicate prices with their fingers. Buyers bargaining for lower prices would use gestures to cut off extra fingers. The vendors would nod in agreement.

Only one intractable woman vendor wouldn't give in to a male customer. She kept beating herself on the chest and kissing the blue body of a chicken, apparently showing the buyer how dear that blue chicken was to her heart. The man would roll his eyes, crossing his arms on his chest like a corpse, to tell her in mute language how hard his life was. She'd also roll her eyes: *Everyone's life is hard.* They bargained silently for a long time. Finally, the man got tired of it.

He swore loudly. "Ah, fuck the hell off, you fat face!"

The entire marketplace turned around, looking at them with reproach.

The vendor got frightened, put a finger to her lips—Hush. She silently mouthed the words: *Take it.* Wheezing joyfully, the man took the chicken. He left, pressing the dead little body to his chest.

Everybody turned away.

A quiet, bustling life was going on at that marketplace: some would try on clothes, checking whether they were too small; others would bite down on a ring to check whether it was gold; still others would press a goat's horns to the ground to check whether it was strong. A huge peasant woman was silently inviting customers, shaking pumpkins: her cheeks, like two pumpkins, were round and orange; on her chest hung a necklace of onions, the skins rustling.

Kharyta and the kids entered the market. She had them stand in a line. Examined the people around her. Bowed. Said loudly:

"Christ has risen!"

Everybody froze and turned to Kharyta. And she bowed to the ground again and said loudly, "Christ has risen!"

People surrounded her in a tight circle. And for the third time she bowed to the people. "Good Christians! Christ has risen!"

"Verily, he has risen!" People exhaled the words with their lips. Quietly, silently, mutely, like a general sigh.

A woman's chapped lips silently said: *Verily.* And the lips of the fisherman, covered with carp scales. And the lips of the ancient woman. And the butcher's succulent lips. They exhaled and moved to kiss: the woman kissed the fisherman with her chapped lips, three times. The ancient woman's lips kissed the butcher's lips, three times. The man with the chicken awkwardly kissed the woman vendor, the one at whom he'd just sworn. They kissed each other with tears. Silently. Devoutly. Three times.

14

A young woman was driving a drunken man covered with a bast mat through the marketplace.

"Christ has risen!" Kharyta was telling everyone, kissing everyone.

"Kiss me, too, Granny!" she heard.

She turned around: the drunken man was reaching for her with his wet lips from under the mat, his thin beard thrust forward, seeking to kiss. He wasn't Russian: eyes narrow like chinks, flat nose. With her sleeve Kharyta covered herself from the smell of raw vodka and from the drunk lips, then couldn't restrain herself from asking, "But are you of our faith?"

"I'm a Kalmuck by birth, but an Orthodox Christian by faith," the man answered meekly as he lay in the cart.[8] "From childhood, I've felt great love for Christ in my heart. I got baptized. After seminary, I served as a priest in a local church. . . ."

"As a priest?" Kharyta was surprised.

"He's a devout man," the young woman confirmed. "Father Vasily."

"You're a priest, then?" Kharyta asked again, putting her arms on her hips. "Why, Father, you should be ashamed! You're to lead church service today, wish people joy on Palm Sunday, and you're drunk by morning!" Kharyta scolded him.

"I'm no longer a priest," Father Vasily burst into tears. "They closed the church, broke the crosses, tore out the bell's clapper. . . ."

"And what a bell that was!" the young woman spoke swiftly. "The king of bells! It weighed five hundred and fifty poods.[9] They transported it by ship along three rivers: first on Mother

Volga, then the Akhtuba, then the Podstyopka.[10] I remember as a young girl how all the people went to the pier to greet it, as if it were a tsar. Truly, it was a tsar. The tsar bell![11] And was it powerful! When it rang you couldn't hear a person talking here at the market. You could hear it ringing twenty-five kilometers away: on holidays, in snowstorms, in blizzards, it always rang. . . . And now it's silent without the clapper. They tore it out!"[12]

"Why, the bell's nothing! They seem to have torn out your people's tongues—they're silent, too!" Kharyta said bitterly.

"Now they're silent," the young woman couldn't be restrained. "Tell her, Father Vasily, how they used to sing in church!" And she turned to Kharyta, quickly telling her own story. "They used to sing in the choir, in four voices, led by a precentor, forty people all together! Trebles, altos, tenors, basses—just like a theater—ah, was it beautiful!"

"Beautiful!" confirmed Father Vasily.

"Beautiful!" the young woman repeated like an echo. "And how we celebrated holidays!" She couldn't stop. "During Epiphany, after church service, we'd walk to the River Podstyopka. Our Father Vasily would be at the head with a golden cross, and all the people would follow him. In the middle of the Podstyopka there stood a cross, carved out of ice, sky blue. It shone in the sun. Next to the cross we'd make an ice hole, and people would bathe in the hole. We'd bathe naked in the frost, and nothing ever happened. And those who were sick bathed to be cured. And they were. . . . Because there was faith!"

"And where's your faith now?" Kharyta asked sternly. "Has it disappeared?"

"No, it hasn't," the priest whispered.

"Well, if it hasn't, then celebrate the mass."

"How can I do it without a church?" he asked.

"Now that the church is gone, he's taken to drinking. Before, he abstained," the young woman said.

"Wherever two or three gather in my name—I am among them," Kharyta said, looking searchingly at Father Vasily.

LITTLE FOOL

"Wherever two or three gather, his church is there. Do you understand, Father?"

"Yes, Granny," he replied.

"And don't drink anymore, Father," Kharyta scolded him with motherly sternness. "You're serving here, God himself placed you here," and she whispered something in his ear. Father Vasily's narrow eyes lit with fire.

He listened until she finished, then got out of the cart. "Thank you, Granny. . . ."

"That's how it is, Father," she replied.

She stood on her crutches in the dust.

"Now let's wish each other happy Easter," she said.

Father Vasily kneeled in the dust to be at Kharyta's level.

"Christ has risen!" he said loudly, as in church, so that everybody would hear.

"Verily he has risen!" Kharyta said, smiling.

They looked each other in the eye. Kissed each other. Three times.

"Kiss me too, Auntie!" the young woman asked her.

Kharyta inquired, "What's your name? And how are you related to Father Vasily?"

"I'm from the Bokanev family, we're 'kulaks' accomplices,'" the young woman identified herself. "And Father Vasily's my godfather. . . . My name's Maria."

They kissed each other.

15

Ganna started singing in a clear, strong voice:

> "Christ has risen from the dead,
> Ending death with his own death
> And giving life to the dead. . . ."

Bread and potatoes poured into the children's bags. The huge woman placed her onion garland around Charlie's neck. To the three sisters she handed an enormous pumpkin: they held it together, hugging it as if it were alive, pressing their cheeks to it.

Kharyta stood holding an icon. A line of women formed beside her. They'd approach the icon, fall on their knees, and kiss it. After making the sign of the cross, they'd move off. They gave painted eggs to Kharyta. She put them in a sack: carefully, so as not to break them.

> "This is your Resurrection, Christ the Savior,
> Angels are singing in heaven,
> And with our pure hearts we glorify you on earth. . . ."

Ganna sang, gazing with a smile up at the sky, as if she saw somebody there.

People stood listening and furtively looking at the sky: What did Ganna see there?

"Hey, look!" someone said quietly. "The sun's playing. . . ."

People lifted their heads.

The sky was very blue, as if painted especially for the holiday. And in it, the sun was rolling back and forth like a painted egg on a dish, as if playing.

"Disperse! Disperse, everybody!" they suddenly heard somebody's threatening voice.

Pushing people aside, the Director of the collective farm, a robust man in a semimilitary jacket, made his way toward Kharyta.

"Listening, eh?!" he shouted with joy. "Well, now you're all caught, my deaf-and-dumb comrades, my dear friends. Since you're listening it means you're not deaf. So, you can talk, too! That's exactly what I needed to prove. It's not worked! You're caught red-handed! Now, listen to me! Just try not to hear now! You've been exiled here to be reeducated, and you don't like it here? Playing deaf! What, sand got in your ears? I'll send those who don't like it here up north: they'll clear your ears, they'll rub them with snow until they bleed! Listen, comrade ex-kulaks, to what the Director of your collective farm is gonna say! Tomorrow everybody will go to the field, to the steppe! Buriakov, Popov, Rogozhin," he stabbed his finger at the men, "you'll go to collect tomatoes at the Stasov farm. You understand? I'm asking you: Do you understand?"

The men looked at him silently, without blinking, as if they hadn't heard. Then they turned around and left.

"Koroleva, Zabiriuchenko, Boiko! You'll go to the water-melon field in Pologoe Zaimishche, to plant watermelons. You hear me?" he looked at the women. They looked back at him without blinking, turned around, and disappeared.

"Are you peasants or what?" he yelled, almost crying. "The land will soon turn into stone: you couldn't bite it with your teeth . . . Anna!" He saw the woman selling pumpkins. "Pshenichnaia Anna! Tomorrow you'll take the women to cut sugarcane in the floodlands. This is something new for us, we've got to get the hang of it. . . ."

Pshenichnaia Anna set a pumpkin on her head like a jug, then floated past the Director like an overloaded boat without drawing breath. As if to say, *I neither see you nor hear you.*

"Lastovkin!"[13] He poked his finger at the man with the chicken. The man turned around and left without listening.

"Pyotr!" he called the little man in a tattered jersey. "Rybakov!" Rybakov immediately disappeared. On his shoulders he carried away the basket with fish that looked like silver.

"Bokaneva, you kulak's seed! Driving the priest, eh? Hold it, you mother . . . !" The young woman was quickly walking away, leading the priest by his arm, pushing the empty cart in front of her.

"The Canaries! Do you hear me?"

The Canaries—husband and wife—were carbon copies of each other: yellow hair, pockmarked faces, both drunk. They didn't give a damn about anything, but they couldn't leave: they were selling their camel. The Canaries saw the Director and froze, waited a bit, then set off at a walk, whistling like birds: as if they weren't husband and wife, but two little birds, two canaries; they walked along, swaying and whistling, and didn't hear a thing. The camel sat in the dust, chewing, looking down at the Director contemptuously, like a pasha. Stung to the quick, the Director spat in the dust at the camel's feet.

"Don't look at me like that, you jerk!"

The camel turned its head toward him, its lips slowly chewing, stretched its long neck, and all of a sudden spat at the Director!

The Director stood there, covered with stinking foam.

"Fine!" he said to the camel, wiping off the spit. "That's fine! It's the collective farm for you! The cattle yard! I'll make you respect the authorities!"

He moved off, wiping himself.

The ancient woman rushed over to the Director, shoving a corn cob in his face, her toothless mouth smiling, as if to say: *Buy it!*

"Get away, you old hag," he brushed her off.

She kept on shoving the cob.

"You don't hear me either?" he threatened her.

She moved her ear closer, asked, "What?"

"Get lost, you old hag!" he yelled right in her ear at the top of his voice. "You should all be shot! You kulak trash! Enemies! All of you, all of you should be shot!"

The old woman leaped away from him, threw the cob in the dust, and fled from the Director.

"Your whole greedy clan!" raged the Director. He walked along the counters. "From the youngest to the oldest! Every single one! Like mad dogs! Shot!"

People moved off in a hurry, leaving their goods as they ran away.

"Give me something, for Christ's sake!" Charlie stood next to the counters, begging.

The Director turned around.

"Where are you from? The orphanage? I'll inform Traktorina Petrovna: you're agitating for opium.[14] Get lost!"

Charlie set off running. The other children and Kharyta also left in the cart.

Ganna remained alone on the deserted market square.

"And where are you from?" the Director asked Ganna. "From the orphanage?"

Ganna didn't speak. She looked at him in silence.

"What, are you one of those? One of them deaf and dumb?" the Director asked her mockingly.

> "Holy Easter revealed itself to us,
> New Easter, Holy Easter,
> Mysterious Easter, true Easter,
> Easter Christ the Savior has arrived."

Ganna sang. She sang and sang, gazing upward. Gazing at the heavens.

16

In the cafeteria, a feast was in full swing. Bread, potatoes, lard, onions, flat loaves of bread, fried fish, were lying pell-mell on the plates; a huge pumpkin was slumped in the middle of the table. Next to each plate lay a painted egg.

Kharyta was cutting something resembling a pie, giving everyone a piece. The children would approach her in turn, take their piece, and move off, holding it in the palms of their little hands.

Vera ran up. "What is it? A cake?"

"It's *paskha*, Verochka," answered Kharyta.[15] "A holy dish. Nadia, Liuba, come here!"

Nadia and Liuba didn't hear Kharyta; they were competing with their brother Marat over the painted eggs.

"The one whose egg breaks the other's egg will take it," Marat explained the rules to his sisters.

He hit their yellow eggs with his red one, broke them, and was about to take theirs.

Nadia gave hers.

Liuba shouted, "You weren't fair! You hit the round end with the sharp one! Let's replay!"

They replayed. Liuba cracked the red egg, grabbed it.

"It's mine!" she shouted.

She peeled it quickly and—in a second!—swallowed it. She ran up to Kharyta.

"Give me a piece! I want eats, eats!"

Charlie was telling Bulkin his story, his wet finger tracing the tears on his cheeks. "I started crying and said, 'Give something to the poor, for Christ's sake.' And he answered, 'Begging for opium, eh? Get out of here! Or I'll shoot you!'"

"What's opium?" Bulkin asked.

"You remember that year we ate tons of henbane and walked around like we were drunk. . . ."[16]

"Charlie!" called Kharyta. "This is for you. And this one—the last and the sweetest—for Ganna . . . Ganna!" she called.

"Where's Ganna?"

"She stayed at the market," Freckles said.

"What do you mean?" Kharyta was taken aback.

"I told her: 'Ganna, let's go!'"

"And?"

"She waved her hand at me, meaning for me to go. She hadn't finished her song . . . ," Freckles explained. "I guess she stayed behind to finish it."

"We've got to go get her." Kharyta started getting ready, threw on her shawl, and made for the door. "What if she gets lost. . . ."

She was almost at the door when it suddenly opened by itself—as if knocked out of its frame: Traktorina Petrovna burst into the room with a threatening air. Behind her came the Director and the watchman, who led in Ganna.

"Kharitina Savelyevna," Traktorina Petrovna yelled at Kharyta. "Explain to me what Ganna was doing at the market. The Director of the collective farm brought her here. Was it you who sent her there? What was she doing there?"

"They were begging for food," the Director said. "And this old hag of yours. And this boy," he pointed to Charlie. He turned around. "They were all there. All of them."

"Begging? Pioneers were begging?" Traktorina Petrovna cried.

"Pioneers want to eat, too. Aren't they people, too?" said Kharyta. "Your Pioneers will soon swell from hunger. . . ."

"That's none of your business! Here they get everything their organism needs. Vitamins, protein, calories. Everything they need. You understand?"

"Calories aren't food."

"And what's this?" Traktorina Petrovna suddenly saw the food on the tables.

"People gave it to us."

"No, I mean, what is it?" Traktorina Petrovna picked up an Easter egg with disgust. "Kharitina Savelyevna, I'm asking you!"

"An egg," Kharyta answered concisely.

"I can see it's an egg. But why is it blue?"

"It's painted."

"So why is it painted?"

"Today's a holiday. Aren't you a Christian, Petrovna?"

"Get out!" shouted Traktorina Petrovna. "Never set foot in the orphanage again! Out! Egorych, collect all that unsanitary stuff! A normal egg should be white! White! White!"

Traktorina Petrovna threw the eggs off the table, trampling them with her feet. She kept crying hysterically, "White! White! White!"

The watchman swept the food into a sack: bread, lard, onions, potatoes. He wanted to put the huge pumpkin into the sack, too. The three sisters hugged the pumpkin, refusing to let it go. "This pumpkin's not communal! The pumpkin's ours!"

Silently, the watchman grabbed the pumpkin with his long arm, snatched it from the sisters, and rolled it into the sack.

"White! White!" Traktorina Petrovna continued yelling as she trampled the mess.

Exhausted, she ran out. The watchman and Director followed her.

For a while, the children sat at the empty tables in silence.

Then they got down onto the floor, picking up their squashed eggs.

"Here's mine, the red one. . . ."

"And this one's mine—yellow. . . ."

"And mine's all gone. . . ."

They sat there, scraping the crumbs off the floor and eating them.

"Aunt Kharyta! Why's she like that?" asked Freckles.

"A horned demon has inhabited her and rejoices. He's strong!"

"Are you gonna go away from us?"

"No, I won't leave you alone now, I'll put up a fight. . . ."

17

At night in the cell the children weren't sleeping. Freckles whispered, "Let's play family!"

"Okay," the sisters agreed. "We'll be the children. And Marat will be our father!"

"All right," Freckles agreed. "And I'll be your mother. . . . Children! Sit down and have dinner!"

"And what do we have for dinner?" Liuba wanted to know.

"We've a huge, huge pie with jam, a hundred cutlets, and ice cream. . . ."

"What's ice cream?" Nadia asked.

"It's sweet snow," Freckles was trying to catch something with her lips, as if sweet snow were falling from the sky. "Come on, Marat! Sit at the table like you've just come from work. Put on your coat, as if you just came inside. And then you'll take it off. Get up!"

Freckles wound a scarf around Marat's throat, buttoned him up, and put a cap on his head.

"What a fine husband I've got." She sighed, just like a woman. "I shouldn't let you out of my sight, or else they'll steal you," she said, then grew abashed, blushed, and laughed. "Hurry up and take off your coat! Dinner's getting cold!"

She started unwinding Marat's scarf: she twisted him around like a puppet, turning him this way and that, but only tangled him up.

Marat got angry.

"You can't be the mother of my children!" he said like an adult. "Ganna will be my children's mother."

"Wow! Some wife you've found for yourself!" Freckles was offended. "She's neither fish nor fowl. You've married a fool!"

"But she's pretty!" Marat said, looking meaningfully at Freckles, to see whether she understood what he meant.

Hurt, Freckles sniffed with her pointed little nose.

"Just take a look at yourself! You're ugly!" she whispered.

"A man should be clever and strong. And a woman should be kind and pretty. Then their children will be clever, kind, strong, and pretty. You understand, you shrew?" Marat smugly told her.

He approached Ganna and asked in a self-confident tone, "Ganna, do you want to be my wife?"

Ganna sat on the bed in silence.

Marat gazed into her eyes in alarm. "Ganna, will you be my wife? Yes or no? Tell me! I'll never hurt you! Never lay a finger on you! I'll give you my whole salary! Every last penny!"

Ganna was silent.

"Serves you right," Freckles spitefully rejoiced.

Marat fell on his knees and cried out in despair, as if his fate were indeed being decided.

"Ganna! Be my wife! I'm asking for your hand and heart!"

After some delay, Ganna gave a slight nod, extending her hand to his.

Marat happily led her to the table. "These are our children, Ganna. These are our daughters. This is Verochka. This is Nadia. This is Liuba."

Ganna looked each daughter in the eye, patted each one on the head, kissed each one. She ran and fetched all her treasures from her corner—a comb, a candy, a yo-yo—and laid everything out in front of them. In front of each one she put a bowl of water as if it were borscht.[17] She fed them from a spoon, blowing on the water so that the borscht would cool. The three sisters tried to evade the spoon, didn't want to eat, and giggled. Ganna fed them tenderly and patiently and kissed their hands entreatingly.

"Why are you kissing them!" Freckles couldn't contain herself. "Whip them! Why, they're acting like delinquents!"

"Knock-knock!" Marat knocked on the table. "This is your dad coming home from work."

Like a bird Ganna flew to meet her husband, unbuttoned his coat, unwound his scarf. She placed Marat at the head of the table and, bowing, gave him a bowl of water.

"Phew, I'm beat," Marat told his family. "I signed twenty-two resolutions, fulfilled thirty-three Party assignments. I'm tired!"

"He's sure found a cushy job! Some job, the lazybones," Freckles said with envy. "The office writes, and the money flows in."

Ganna unlaced Marat's shoes. Fetched a basin of water. She washed Marat's feet and wiped them. Then suddenly she lifted the basin and was about to drink the water.

"Don't drink that!" Marat yelled at her. "Don't, the water's dirty. . . ."

"In olden times, wives used to wash their husbands' feet and drink the water," Freckles said. "I read about it."

"But these aren't olden days! Call Charlie and Bulkin!" Freckles ran out.

There was a knock on the door.

Ganna looked at the door like a frightened bird. The three sisters fell silent. Marat asked in a tense, peculiarly wooden voice, "Who's there?"

"Open the door! Or we'll break it!"

They banged on the door.

Marat went to the door and opened it. Charlie and Bulkin burst inside. Vicious, frightening. They overturned the house, looking for something.

"Who're you? And what are you doing in my house?" Marat asked them.

"We're the Black Maria!"[18] the two shouted, showing him a white paper. "And you're an enemy of the people! You're under arrest!" They twisted Marat's arms and dragged him to the door.

The three sisters burst out crying in unison, "Dad! Dad! Daddy! Don't go!"

LITTLE FOOL

The whole ward started crying. They cried for real, covering their heads with blankets.

Only Ganna stood there without crying. She stood, frozen still, as if she weren't there, seeming to think her thoughts. . . . Suddenly, she swooped down on Charlie and Bulkin, threw herself on them, hitting them with all her might, spitting in their faces, biting and scratching them, and hit and hit and hit. . . .

"This is a game!" Charlie screamed, fighting her off. "You fool! We're only playing! It's a make-believe arrest! It's a game! Understand? You've spoiled the whole game!"

But Ganna didn't listen and kept hitting them. Until they ran away.

Ganna hugged Marat, led him to the table, sat him down. She calmed down the three sisters, poured "borscht" in their bowls. Shook her fist threateningly at the door.

She sat down next to Marat.

The family started eating.

From all sides, the children's wet eyes watched them.

18

In the morning Traktorina Petrovna woke everybody up. "Get up!"

The children were sleeping.

"Get up!" Traktorina Petrovna yelled, tearing off their blankets. "You should've slept at night! To the camp line—march! March! March!"

The sleepy children jumped up and reluctantly dressed.

Traktorina Petrovna tore the blanket off Ganna. Ganna was lying there wet: she had wet her bed.

"You piece of trash!" Traktorina Petrovna actually clasped her hands. "Pissed all over the bed! What, you didn't feel like getting up at night? Too lazy to get up?"

Ganna covered her face in shame.

"No, you look!" Traktorina Petrovna removed her hands. "You piss, and I'm supposed to wash it? Well, smell it! What does it smell like? Smell!" She shoved the wet bedclothes in Ganna's face. "Smell it! This is how they teach puppies not to shit. Smell it!" She flew into a rage. "Smell it!"

Marat touched Traktorina Petrovna's arm. Red and sweaty, she glanced at him.

"What do you want?"

"She'll wash it herself. I'll take her to the river. May I? After breakfast?"

Traktorina Petrovna got up, grunting. "All right. Only there'll be no breakfast. You're on a diet today. You'll nibble on apples. Vitamins!" She moved to the door, then stopped. "Only watch out! You're not to wash it! She's got to do it herself! Herself! I'll know the truth by your eyes!"

Traktorina Petrovna left. Practically a second later the door opened. From the threshold, without entering, the watchman poured apples out of a sack onto the floor. Green apples danced across the floor, rolling all over the room like small, round, shiny bullets.

Everyone picked an apple. Marat bit into one and made a face.

"It's sour! Spit it out!" he told his sisters. "Ganna and I'll go to the river; we'll bring you sweet ones from the garden!"

Ganna obeyed, threw away the apple.

Charlie and Bulkin rushed to the apples. Charlie loaded them under his shirt, Bulkin stuffed his pockets. Freckles ran between them, taking a bite out of every apple, one after another, so that nobody would take them.

"That's my apple," she'd say. "And this one's mine, too. And this one."

Her face was contorted from the sourness, but she kept biting into them; she couldn't stop. After each bite she chanted, while chewing, "Vitamins! Vita-a-amins! That's why it's sour!"

19

Ganna and Marat went down to the Akhtuba River.

"Put it in the water." Marat pointed to the bedsheet. "Let

it soak. We'll weigh it down with a stone. And meanwhile we'll go for a swim. Don't worry—it won't float away."

Marat undressed and stood in his briefs. Ganna took everything off. She stood naked, with a cross on her chest.

"What're you doing? Why take everything off? Put on your underwear, at least," Marat felt awkward for her sake.

Ganna looked at him without grasping what he wanted.

"Okay, let's swim." Marat sighed.

Ganna shook her head: *No.*

"You can't swim?" Marat guessed. "Let me teach you."

Supporting her with one hand, he helped her along the shore. "Move your feet! Move them faster! Splash only in the water, don't splash me. Now try swimming on your back!"

Ganna turned over; Marat was as if blinded: two gentle pink nipples on Ganna's chest, and below her stomach—a golden triangle burning like a red-hot coal. . . .

He couldn't take his eyes off her.

"Dive!" he shouted, but his voice failed him. "Swim underwater!"

Ganna dived with her eyes open. She saw small silver fish swimming beneath and swam after them. They swam in a lively silver shoal and played with her, touching her face with their cool silver faces. She wanted to kiss them, extended her lips. They laughed like silver bells and sped away. Ganna surfaced. There was a ringing in her ears.

"You're a real ace!" Marat shouted. "You swam about twenty meters. I thought you'd drowned! You've got real talent! I'll teach you everything! Do you want me to teach you to read?"

Ganna splashed her arms in the water, drunk with happiness and the splashing, and nodded: *Yes, I do.*

She swam toward him. He swam toward her.

All of a sudden, a snake swam between them, like a flashing string, like lightning. It held its head high above the water, as if stretching out its neck. It gazed menacingly at them.

They froze.

"A snake," Marat exhaled. "It's making for the shore. It doesn't sting in water. . . ."

Ganna stood motionless. She was afraid to stir.

"What's wrong? Let's swim to the other shore," suggested Marat. "There's a mill over there. Maybe we can nab some flour."

They swam side by side. Ganna got frightened and splashed with her arms.

"Don't be scared, I'm here. I'm with you . . . ," Marat said.

20

At the mill, a Red Army soldier was standing with a rifle. Marat and Ganna ran around the corner. Marat bent back a board. "Get in!"

They crawled through the opening and found themselves in what seemed a different world: the noise of machines, white dust. The millstones were working methodically, the water streamed noisily, and the grain came pouring in. The white flour was suspended in the air like white fog.

"Get over here and stay here! Let the flour sift down on you!" Marat whispered in Ganna's ear. He stood, arms spread, demonstrating to Ganna how to do it. Ganna stood next to him and raised her arms.

They stood there, getting covered in flour. The bearded, red-faced miller, drowning in the flour and the sun, saw them. The Red Army soldier approached him. The miller winked at Ganna and led the soldier away.

Marat and Ganna crawled out into the daylight—white, all covered in flour, including even their eyelashes. They walked slowly, their arms spread wide, so that the flour wouldn't fall off.

21

Ganna licked Marat's back. She licked the flour off his back. Marat scrunched up, guffawing. "This is your breakfast. It tickles! Ganna, you're like a cat. Ah, I can't take it anymore! Let me lick you!"

He turned around and began licking the flour off her. Her head thrown back, Ganna laughed: it tickled. Her white eyelashes quivered, and the flour on them scattered.

"Ganna, stop laughing! Stay still! Don't shake, or you'll shake off the flour."

He was licking her back and suddenly licked—a birthmark. Right at the bottom of the neck. He touched the birthmark with his lips. Caressed a curl. Ganna became quiet, stopped laughing. Her back tensed, then straightened.

"Ganna," Marat said in a thick voice. "I love you."

Ganna turned around helplessly. Marat understood.

"You're no fool! You're not! You're beautiful! I'll marry you!"

He kissed her on her white lips. Then hugged her tight. Ganna, her arms resting against his chest, tried to push him away. But he pressed her tighter and tighter to himself, attempting to kiss her.

"Why not? I'll marry you, honest. Don't be scared. . . ."

Ganna kept turning her face away.

Then she turned her head in the direction of the river. The current was carrying off the bedsheet. She mumbled, struggling in Marat's arms.

"What?" He let her go.

She pointed. "*Ga!*"

Marat looked at the river. "So the bedsheet's gone. We'll catch it!" He sighed. "You're really something!"

He set off at a run, following the river. Ganna ran after him.

They raced along the shore. The river widened and turned.

Suddenly they saw a raft on the sand. It was old and cracked. They pushed it into the water and floated off on it.

22

Her dress tucked up, Ganna was rinsing the bedsheet on the shore while Marat hid the raft under an old willow. He covered it up with leaves, branches, and grass.

"It might come in handy."

He approached Ganna. He turned her face toward him.

She was looking at him in a new way: with love, without taking her eyes off him for a second.

"Do you love me, Ganna?"

She closed her eyes: *Yes.*

He removed an eyelash from her cheek.

"Ah, if only we could sail away from here, Ganna!"

They looked at the river. Beyond the river, the sun was setting.

23

In the evening, Kharyta washed the floors and went to pour out the water. She was passing the watchman's hut when all of a sudden the door opened. The watchman was trying to push Traktorina Petrovna out. Traktorina was clutching the doorpost with her powerful hands.

He hit her with a fist right in the soul.

"Get lost! I'm sick of you!" He shut the door.

Traktorina Petrovna rolled head over heels off the porch. She landed on all fours, the dress pulled up on her rear. She crawled into the bushes.

"*O! O! O!*" she howled like a beast.

Kharyta came up to her and called, "Arina!" Kharyta put her hand on Traktorina's shoulder. "Arina, dear!"

Traktorina glanced back at her, her face tearstained. "You talking to me?"

"Is anything wrong?"

"Are you spying on me?" In an instant Traktorina Petrovna's tears dried up.

"I was walking by. I wanted to help you, Arina."

"I'm not Arina!" she yelled. "I'm Traktorina."

"You're a human being," Kharyta said. "Your name should be human, too, the one you were baptized with," Kharyta said.

"Soviet power baptized me," Traktorina Petrovna said proudly as she stood up. "And it gave me the name I have— Traktorina! And I'm not a human being! I'm a Communist! Understood?"

"I understood long ago that you're not humans."

"Get out of my way!" Traktorina Petrovna yelled and walked away, then glanced back. "Your tongue will get you into trouble—and somebody will cut it off. You're not dealing with your own kind, Kharitina Savelyevna, for sure, not your own kind!"

Kharyta emptied the dirty water from the pail. She looked at it for a long time, until the water had soaked into the ground.

24

At night, the whole room could hear the moans. Freckles was crying, holding her stomach.

"Ay, Mama, my stomach hurts something awful!"

"Let us sleep!" Charlie shouted at her. "You're wailing like crazy!"

Freckles ran to the door, body doubled up.

She returned with Kharyta.

"Where does it hurt?" Kharyta asked, feeling Freckles's stomach. "Does it hurt here?"

"Everywhere!" Freckles moaned.

"She's got diarrhea!" Charlie said. "Keeps going all the time. Shitting up a storm!"

"I'll brew some sorrel for you. It'll get better! Hold on a bit," Kharyta said.

"I can't hold on! I can't!" Freckles jumped up and ran to the door.

"Where are you going?"

"Outside, to do it!"

"That runny shit!" Charlie said, snuggling down more comfortably. "She's driven everyone up the wall!"

25

Next morning Ganna was initiated into the Young Pioneers.

The children were lined up in the steppe. Traktorina Petrovna said, "Today we're admitting a new member into our close ranks of the Young Pioneers, our new comrade

Ganna. . . ." Traktorina Petrovna hesitated. "Ganna Doe. Ganna, come to me."

Ganna approached her.

"You know that Ganna's mute. So I'll read the Young Pioneers' oath instead of her. And you, Ganna, listen and repeat in your head. Traktorina Petrovna cleared her throat. "As I enter the ranks of Young Pioneers, in front of my comrades I solemnly swear! To fight for the cause of the Communist Party of Bolsheviks! To ruthlessly exterminate the enemies of Soviet power! To give all my blood, to the last drop, for the workers' and peasants' cause!"

"Let me through!" Charlie whispered to Bulkin. "I've got stomach cramps."

He ran to the bushes. Sat there, just his red tie visible.

And another child ran to the bushes, then a third. . . . By the end of the oath, all the Pioneers were sitting in the bushes, Traktorina Petrovna wanted one of the Pioneers to put the red tie on Ganna and looked around: nobody was there. She put the tie around Ganna's neck herself; while she was struggling with the knot, the wind lifted the tie and carried skyward: it floated in the air, winding like a red snake.

Traktorina Petrovna ran after the tie. She jumped up and fell.

"Traktorina Petrovna!" the three sisters called her. "Come quickly to the children's room. Freckles is lying there. She's not breathing!"

"And she's cold as ice!"

26

Freckles lay dead on the bed.

Traktorina Petrovna touched her forehead. Pulled back her hand and raised her eyes to Kharyta.

"She's dead?"

"Passed away," Kharyta answered tersely.

"From simple diarrhea?"

"Looks like cholera, Petrovna," Kharyta said sternly.

The boys ran into the room.

"Charlie's collapsed in the bushes!"

"Is he dead?"

"No, he's alive. . . . He's talking nonsense, though, seems delirious."

"We've gotta isolate him," Traktorina Petrovna said dismally. "But where can we put him? There's no place. . . . Bring him here, into the room. What are we gonna do, Kharyta? There's no doctors in this village, nothing. . . ."

"Well," Kharyta said. "We'll prepare ourselves to die."

"I have to go." All of a sudden, Traktorina Petrovna seemed in a hurry. "I'll phone into town—Tsarev. You'll call me . . . if you need to."

27

Charlie was dying. Eyes open, he lay on the bed, changed, pale, looking stern.

He was talking quickly. "You run along the left side of the field, and I'll run to the center. . . . You'll lob the ball toward the goal and I'll hit it with my head. . . . Hit it! Go on, hit! Hit!" He almost got up in bed, then sagged and fell back. "Missed . . . I'm thirsty. Water . . ."

Ganna rushed to him with a mug. Kharyta wouldn't let her come near.

"Get away, I'll do it myself. You'll catch it."

Ganna shook her head: *No.* She gave Charlie some water. He closed his eyes, then opened them again, looked lucidly at Kharyta, and asked her, "Am I going to die?"

"God is merciful, perhaps you'll get well," answered Kharyta.

"I know I'll die," Charlie said. "I'm scared. Tell me, Aunt Kharyta, where'll I go after I die? Where does life disappear? And what will I be when I die? Or will I not be? Tell me. . . ."

"Your life's eternal, my dear. Your soul's immortal. And you'll be an angel in heaven," Kharyta said. "You'll be in heaven. Are you baptized?"

"No."

"Good Lord!" Kharyta threw her hands up. "Ganna! Bring a tub. And warm up some water. We're going to baptize Charlie."

28

Ganna poured a bucket of water into the tub. Kharyta chose two children.

"You'll be Charlie's godparents. Stand here."

The three sisters approached Kharyta.

"Don't bother me now, sweeties," Kharyta asked them.

"It this a game, Aunt Kharyta?" Vera asked.

"No, this is for real."

"Then I want to become an angel, too," Vera declared. "Baptize me, too."

"And me. I also want to fly," Nadia said.

"We want to be together when we die—in heaven," Liuba said.

"I want to be an angel, too," said Bulkin.

"Me, too. . . ." Other children came up.

"Ganna! Marat!" called Kharyta. "Stand here. You'll be godparents to everybody. Take them by their hands." And she said loudly, in an unexpectedly low, unfamiliar voice, "Exorcise from him any evil and unclean spirit, hidden and nesting in his heart." She blew on Charlie, whispering, "On his mouth, his forehead, and his chest."

Then she asked Charlie loudly, "Do you renounce Satan, and all his deeds, and all his angels, and all his services, and all his pride?"

"I do," said Charlie.

The children jostled about a little, then chorused, "I do."

"And now turn to the west. Both children and their godparents. Turn here, toward the door. There, in the west, lives the Prince of Darkness, Satan; when I tell you, spit. And blow and spit on him!!!" she shouted.

The children spat. Suddenly the door opened and Traktorina Petrovna came in.

"Oh!" Vera became frightened.

"What's going on here?" Traktorina Petrovna asked.

"Baptism," Kharyta said sternly. "Get out of here, Petrovna."

"Me? Get out?! Stop your religious tricks! This is an outrage. These are Young Pioneers, our Soviet children. . . . Children! Leave the premises. There is no God!"

"Go away, Satan," Kharyta sternly told her. "We gave you everything: our flesh, our possessions, our works, and our thoughts, and we gave you our motherland, Satan. Leave our souls to us. Get thee behind me!" And she pointed authoritatively at the door.

Traktorina Petrovna ran out in a rage.

29

Traktorina Petrovna was calling on the phone.

"Hello, miss, connect me with the local NKVD office."[19]

30

The baptism ceremony was almost over. Charlie lay in a white shirt, with a cross on his chest. Vera, Nadia, and Liuba climbed into the tub. Covering their nostrils and mouth, Kharyta immersed the girls' heads under the water three times.

"God's servant Vera is being baptized. God's servant Nadezhda is being baptized. God's servant Liubov' is being baptized![20] In the name of the Father, amen! In the name of the Son, amen! In the name of the Holy Spirit, amen!"

Many people in military uniforms entered without knocking and surrounded the children and Kharyta.

"The demons have arrived," Kharyta said and smiled. "You're late. They're not yours anymore."

One of the men, with a scar, said, "Citizen Mova? Kharitina Savelyevna? You're under arrest."

"Let me say good-bye," Kharyta said.

"Now I'm not afraid," Charlie said, "to die, Aunt Kharyta."

"Forgive me, dear children." Kharyta bowed to the ground. "Farewell."

Ganna clung to Kharyta, not letting her go.

"We'll see each other again, Ganna. If not on earth, then in heaven. Don't cry! Marat, take care of Ganna. . . ."

In the tub, surrounded by military men, the defenseless naked girls stood like angels: Faith, Hope, and Love.

31

Marat ran through the steppe, holding Ganna by the hand. They were running breathlessly.

"We must avenge this! Exterminate her, you hear me? We'll poison her. Remember? We saw a snake in the river. We'll get poison from it and poison Traktorina!"

Ganna sat on the ground, hanging on to Marat. *No,* she shook her head, *no!*

Marat squatted down.

"Don't you understand? Traktorina Petrovna's a murderess. Aunt Kharyta won't survive in prison. Traktorina's killed her. And what about Freckles? And Charlie? They fed them apples till they died! Vitamins! A death for a death! Let's go!"

Marat was searching for the snake's lair.

"It was crawling here. Then it crawled over there. Here's the hole!" Marat shoved a stick in the hole. "Come out, viper! Come out, you gray beast!"

The snake slowly crawled out of the hole. Marat hit it with the stick. The snake hissed. He hit it again, jumped sideways, and grabbed the snake by the head.

"Ganna, give me the jar! Stick it under the fang!"

Ganna hesitated.

"Hurry up, Ganna! I can't hold it long, it'll bite me!"

Ganna went to him. Marat squeezed the snake's head; the snake opened its jaws. Ganna placed the glass jar under the fang. Yellow rosin-colored liquid slowly flowed down the glass.

"Poison," Marat whispered.

The snake gazed menacingly at Ganna and Marat.

Marat wanted to finish the snake off with the stick. Ganna intercepted the stick and snatched it from Marat.

Like a dirty gray rope, the viper crawled away, raising dust.

"Ganna, we've got to kill it. Snakes bear grudges. Did you see the way it was looking at us? It'll remember and get revenge on us sometime. Like we're doing now with Traktorina Petrovna!"

No! She shook her head.

They lit a campfire. Marat took a rag out of his pocket, unwrapped it.

"Flour," he said.

He kneaded the dough, shaped it into a flat bread, and with his finger made a hole in the bread. They bent over the bread, their faces touching: Marat poured a drop of poison from the jar into the hole. The poison was quickly absorbed. They placed the bread on a tile, placed the tile with the bread in the fire.

They waited till it baked. They were silent.

"Done!" Marat said, removing the cake from the fire. He placed it meticulously on the rag and wrapped it up. "Instant death!"

Ganna looked at him in fear. Reluctantly, she got up and followed him, limping slightly. As she walked she rubbed her leg: it was numb from squatting.

32

While the food was distributed, Marat came up to Bulkin. The latter, wearing a white cap, was carrying millet cereal to the tables. Marat pulled the cap off his head, put it on his own, and snatched the plates from Bulkin's hands.

"I'll be on duty today instead of you," he said.

He set the plates on the tables. Looking around, he unwrapped the rag, took out the flat bread. Put it instead of the regular bread next to the biggest plate.

33

The children were sitting at the table when Traktorina came in. As usual, she recited, as if it were the Lord's Prayer:

"Pioneersbereadytostruggleforthecauseof theCommunistParty-ofBolsheviks!"

"*Ga-ga-gagaga!*" The cafeteria thundered as usual and fell upon the food.

Ganna and Marat waited.

Whereupon Traktorina Petrovna sighed, then tasted the millet with a spoon.

"There's not enough salt in the millet," she said. She took the salt and added some to the cereal. She stirred it for a long time, sitting over it and thinking about something. Engrossed in her thoughts, she took the flat bread, raised it to her mouth.

"*Po! Po! Po!*" Ganna suddenly cried out, jumping to her feet. Marat held her while she struggled to break free.

Traktorina Petrovna looked at her in surprise, biting off the bread.

Ganna broke loose, raced over, snatched the bread from her mouth, and threw it on the floor.

Her face blood red, Traktorina Petrovna bent to pick up the bread.

Ganna pushed her away.

"Po!" she shouted, stamping on the bread with her foot.

"Poison?" Traktorina Petrovna realized. "Who's on duty today?"

Marat was slowly rising to his feet.

34

That night the sounds of whipping and Marat's screams came from the tower window. Ganna stood under an old maple tree. Her whole body shook at each blow. On the ground the watchman's huge shadow raced back and forth. Then all of a sudden everything grew quiet. Ganna spat on her palms and started climbing the tree. Carefully she peeked through the window.

35

The huge back of the watchman was moving in front of the window. One moment it bent down; the next, it straightened up. At each movement of this back, Ganna hid behind a branch. Finally, the back moved aside, then walked away.

Dead Marat, hanged by the watchman, looked right at her.

Marat's face was tearstained.

36

Ganna gave such a scream that the leaves trembled.

The watchman came up to the window, blindly peering into the darkness. Then he ran downstairs, his boots clattering.

"Ganna! Get down!" Ganna heard Traktorina Petrovna's voice. "And don't yell like that. You'll wake up the children. Get down, you hear me?" Ganna clasped to the tree more firmly as she hid. She heard a quiet exchange below.

"Is he dead? Have you checked? Did she see everything? What are we gonna do, Egorych? We have to get rid of her. . . ."

The watchman approached the tree and shook it as hard as he could. The tree swayed as if in a storm. Ganna pressed herself firmly to the trunk. He shook it again, then left.

"Ganna, get down from the tree! You're a good girl. You're a kind, honest girl. You saved my life. I won't hurt you. Why're you scared? Because Marat's dead? It was his own fault. Why did he want to poison me? He hanged himself from fear! From fear of punishment. He hanged himself! Himself! Get down, Ganna. Get down, dear child. . . ."

Ganna climbed still higher.

Suddenly the tree shook from the blow of an ax. Again and again.

The watchman was furiously cutting the tree down.

Ganna looked down in terror. Traktorina Petrovna shouted up to her, "Get down, you scum! I'll strangle you with my own hands! And nobody'll ask any questions! I'll say you died from cholera! They won't dare come near!"

Ganna climbed to the highest branch. Got ready to jump to the tower roof.

"Go ahead, jump, jump! You'll fall and kill yourself! It's at least three meters to the tower!"

Ganna whispered something inaudible and—jumped. The tree immediately collapsed.

It was huge. And it began falling right on Traktorina Petrovna. Traktorina Petrovna ran, screaming, from the falling tree. The tree caught up with her, knocked her down, and crushed her.

37

Ganna got down from the roof, climbed over a fence.

She set off at a run through the village and looked back: nobody was following her. She slowed down to a walk. Out of habit, she made for the marketplace. Next to a wooden store, she lay down in the dust and curled up.

PART TWO

I

In the morning Ganna walked around the market stands. She stood in front of the saleswomen, her eyes begging for alms. The women weren't locals. They didn't know Ganna. One of them, with a big, fat face, was wiping the smoked head of a pig with a rag, tenderly, as if it were a child.

"Go on, girl. We've nothing to eat ourselves. We're swelling from hunger!"

Ganna then sat by the store and started singing:

> "Rain in the street, rain's
> Watering the earth,
> Watering the earth—
> Brother's rocking his sister.
> Brother's rocking his sister—
> Humming a song:
> Ay, sister, dear sister,
> You'll grow up,
> You'll grow up—
> I'll marry you off
> To an alien village.

Men there are mean,
They fight with stakes.
Rain in the street, rain's
Watering the earth . . ."

People walked by, busy with their morning tasks, without paying attention to Ganna.

A young peasant woman stopped and said, biting into a pastry, "What a depressing song you're singing. . . . I wouldn't give anything for such a song."

Another woman was walking with a yoke, carrying pails filled with milk. Without addressing anyone in particular, she said as if into a void, "She's singing about our village. Only we have mean women, not men." She turned to Ganna. "Give me something, dear, to pour milk into. . . ."

Ganna looked around, but there was nothing. She held out her cupped hands. The woman poured milk from the pail into them.

Ganna started drinking. The milk disappeared through her fingers into the dust.

Another beggar crawled up to Ganna and hit her hands. The milk spilled.

"Get lost! This is my spot."

He sat down beside her, started pushing Ganna away. They didn't notice a policeman approaching.

"Stop hurting the girl! Hey! Aren't you the one we're looking for?" He peered at Ganna. "Are you from the orphanage?"

Ganna moved away, nodding: *Yes.* Then shook her head: *No.*

"So, is it yes or no? Say something! Are you dumb? That's right, you are dumb! They said that girl was dumb, too. She poisoned some children and the teacher! They're searching for her all over the district, and she's sitting here, right under our noses. Get up, let's go! There's a warm spot in prison for you!" The policeman painfully grabbed Ganna by the shoulder.

"How can she be dumb? She was just singing!" intervened the woman with pails.

"Singing?" the policeman sounded dubious.

Ganna broke free and set off at a run.

"Grab her!" yelled the man. "It's her, her for sure."

Ganna ran through the market square. The policeman was on the point of catching up with her.

All of a sudden a cart drove out of the gate. Ganna raced after it, jumped on. The peasant driving it glanced back, whipped the horse with all his might.

"Giddap, darling! Giddap! Giddap!"

"Freeze or I'll shoot!" The policeman took the gun out of his holster, shot in the air.

"Don't try to scare us, we've been scared before!" Standing upright, the peasant drove on triumphantly.

2

The horse plodded along the road. The peasant asked, "Were you the one singing at the market?"

Ganna nodded.

"I heard you. . . . You sing well, plaintively. Did he shoot at you for your singing?"

Ganna raised her shoulders, meaning *I don't know.*

"He shot because of the song! I know!" the peasant said confidently. "They've cleaned us out completely, now they're taking away the last thing we've got—song! The Russian people will die out without a song!" The man got excited, then thought a while and said to Ganna, "Don't be scared. I'll hide you. You'll sing in my orchard!"

3

In the orchard the man took the clothes off the scarecrow and handed them to Ganna.

"Dress up. You'll sing your songs in the orchard and scare away the birds. They've taken to pecking at my cherries. Walk around, play the tambourine, sing songs. Sing revolutionary songs, the birds are afraid of their songs. They're birds—but they can sense it. Only don't fall asleep. We've got these birds. During the famine our birds got used to eating human meat. They'll peck you to death!"

4

Ganna walked around the orchard, amid the cherry trees. She banged at the tambourine and sang vehemently:

> "We'll go bravely into battle
> For Soviet power
> And we'll die as one
> In this struggle!"

The birds sat on a big poplar tree, listening.

Ganna grew exhausted. She sat down to rest and fell asleep.

She woke up at somebody's touch. Opened her eyes— there were birds walking on the ground, hundreds of them.

"*Ga! Ga! Ga!*" Ganna shouted at the birds. The entire black cloud of birds flitted up, above Ganna. Drunk on cherries, with red beaks.

"*Ga! Ga! Ga!*" they shouted over Ganna's head.

Ganna looked at her feet: her bare feet were red up to the ankles—from the squashed cherries. She was running on the earth—bloody from cherries.

"*A-a-a!*" she rushed at the birds with a stick. The birds were young crows. But now the old black crows took off from the poplar tree, circling very low over Ganna's head. Ganna got scared, started running away from them.

Like a black flock, they flew after her, cawing maliciously. They chased her for a long time, until she reached a house.

5

She ran into the unfamiliar house without knocking. She entered the first room—nobody there. Entered the second— nobody there. She saw bowls on the table, with hot cabbage soup in the bowls. The bread was sliced. She stretched out her hand toward the bread. Pulled it back. Her mouth was watering.

Somebody coughed from under the floor. Ganna looked: a cellar. She pulled on the cellar door.

Three men with guns and three women with children stared at her in fear.

"Save us, people, save us!" one of the women suddenly screamed.[21] "Burglars!" And she swung her ax at Ganna.

Terrified, Ganna slammed the cellar door shut, ran out of the house. As she ran through the vegetable gardens, she heard behind her, "Save us, people, save us!" The woman was standing on the straw roof, waving her colorful scarf.

And someone was beating on a rail, as during a fire.

6

She was making her way through a field when all of a sudden she saw a boy and a girl plowing. The boy had harnessed himself instead of a horse to the plow. The girl was walking behind the plow—a tiny girl, collapsing from exhaustion.

"I'm tired, Brother dear, I'm thirsty," the little girl complained.

"One more round, Masha, then you can drink as much as you want."

"I can't, Vania. I've no strength left. . . ."

Ganna went to the little girl, took the plow handles in her stead. She followed the boy with sweeping strides. The boy glanced back and gave a smile.

"Neigh! Neigh!" He kicked up his heels like a horse and quickened his pace.

Ganna laughed.

7

In the evening, they sat around a campfire. The boy was baking potatoes, using a twig to check whether they were done and rolling them back into the fire.

"They arrested our mom and dad a week ago. And our older brother, too. Masha and I are the only ones left. They said they'd take us somewhere, too. They said they'd drive us in a car, a real one. But for some reason they're not coming.

Maybe they'll forget about us. Who'll give us food in the winter? That's why we plow. . . . Mashka, don't fall sleep!"

8

Masha fell asleep in Ganna's arms. Ganna bundled her up in her shawl. Pressed the girl against her own body.

Suddenly headlights blinded them. The children leaped up. A car drew up.

The driver came out of the car.

"The Beklemishev family?"

"That's us," the boy said.

"Let's go."

"The potatoes haven't baked yet. Wait," the boy said.

"There's no time. They'll give you food there."

Ganna stood holding Masha in her arms. The boy said, "Come with us. You'll have a nice drive."

They got in the car and drove off. They looked at the road.

"Great, isn't it?" The boy glanced back at Ganna.

She nodded happily.

"A hare! A hare!" the boy shouted. "We're driving fast."

"We'll be there in an hour," the driver answered.

"And where are you taking us?"

"You mean you don't know? To the orphanage. To the neighboring village, where the deaf-and-dumb people are."

Ganna started knocking on the window with her fist.

"What's up?" the driver asked. "You wanna pee?"

They stopped. Ganna ran to a small woods. The driver and the boy produced their own gurgling stream by the car as they talked.

"Is it good there, at the orphanage?" asked the boy.

"They feed the kids well."

"That's the main thing," the boy said in an adult manner.

Ganna was running across the field. She was running away.

"Hey, girl! Come back! Come back! Let's go!" they shouted.

They flashed the headlights. Ganna's huge shadow was running ahead of her.

They left.

9

She came to a house. Sat down on the porch. She didn't dare knock. She sat for a long time. A housewife came out to pour the slops. Saw Ganna.

"Oh, you scared me! Why are you sitting out here so late, girl? You can't sit over here."

Ganna got up but didn't leave.

"You don't have anywhere to spend the night?" the woman surmised. "All right, you can sleep in the cowshed."

She heard a male voice and responded, "Coming!"

She took Ganna to the shed. Poured slops for the pig.

In the dark Ganna moved in the direction of the squelching sound. The pig, chomping noisily, was eating slops from a tub. Ganna sat down beside it. She took a bread crust from the tub and started chewing. Then fished out a potato. Ate it.

10

In the morning Ganna helped her hosts. She carried wheat sheaves in the field.

The wife was standing on a haystack; with a smile, she said to her husband, "She's a good girl. Let's keep her!"

The husband maintained a gloomy silence. Then he said, "Let's go dig potatoes instead of prattling. . . . I've got to go work at night."

"At night?" the woman started.

"A gang of kulaks has appeared in our area. Lyoshka Orliak's their leader."

"Lyoshka? But he used to be such a quiet man. . . ."

"He's not loud now, either. He kills quietly!"

Ganna collected potatoes in the bucket. The master dug them out. He was constantly looking down at Ganna with a gloomy expression. Ganna raised her head: she saw a scar on his face and lowered her eyes in fear.

In the evening they had dinner. They poured milk for

Ganna and gave her bread. As Ganna ate tiredly, the man went behind a screen.

He came out wearing an NKVD uniform. Ganna recognized him then: he'd arrested Kharyta.

"Well, I'm going."

"God help you." His wife made the sign of the cross over him. "And the girl and I'll be going to bed."

"Lock the girl in the cowshed," the man said sternly. "No call to spoil her."

11

At night, as Ganna slept, the door suddenly opened. Ganna woke up. Quietly, stealthily, the husband came into the shed. He groped his way through the darkness. Ganna raised herself and crawled away. The man turned around, moved in the direction of the rustling. Ganna got up, took a few steps back, and hid in the corner. There was nowhere else to hide. The man approached her.

"Here's where you are, Ganna," he whispered.

Ganna shuddered to hear her name.

"I recognized you at once. You're from the orphanage. I checked it out today. Fine mess you left there."

Ganna shuddered at his words as if they were blows.

"I should turn you in."

Ganna covered her face with her hands in terror.

"But I won't."

Ganna looked at him in surprise.

"I'm not a beast!" he shouted. "I'm not a beast! I don't want to be a beast! You all think we're beasts! But we're human beings, just like you! We're human beings! Human beings!" He suddenly burst into tears. "We're the same human beings as you!"

He was crying. Ganna stroked him, trying to calm him down.

Then she walked lightly to the door. Opened it. Stood at the threshold. He raised his eyes.

"Where are you going? You'll live with us. Not in the cow-shed. In the house. We don't have children. You'll be our daughter. My wife'll be your mother. I'll be your father."

Ganna shook her head: *No.*

"Not good enough for you? Even you're squeamish. . . ." He hung his head.

Ganna stepped outside and set off along the deserted road.

"Stop!" the host shouted. "Come back!"

She broke into a run.

12

In the morning Ganna lay down by the road, in the warm dust, and fell asleep. A camel was walking down the road, walking as if it were floating, and pulling a wagon. In the driver's seat was the Canary family—husband and wife—their hair yellow, faces pockmarked, already tipsy, though it wasn't yet sunrise. They sat with their arms around each other, singing songs.

The woman saw Ganna, shouted to the camel, "Whoa! Stop, Suleimen!!!"

The camel wouldn't stop: it didn't understand Russian.

"Whoa! What did I tell you? You're a real piece of work! Heathen!" She pulled on the reins as hard as she could. "Stop! You devil!" The camel glanced at her with his velvet heathen eyes and stopped.

They came level with Ganna. Ganna was sound asleep. They shook her. Ganna didn't wake up.

"She dead?" Canary-wife asked her husband.

". . . e-ad. . . ." He was roaring drunk.

"Hold her by the feet, I'll hold her arms. Throw her in the wagon!"

They threw the sleeping Ganna in the wagon. Then continued on their way.

13

Ganna kept sleeping and wouldn't wake up. She dreamed that she was lying on something soft. Driving somewhere. It was nice. Only some sweet smell was choking her, rising to her throat.

She woke up, turned her head: a dead man was sitting and staring at her without winking.

She turned her head the other way: a peasant woman with a blue face, wearing a kerchief, was lying there; the kerchief was clean, white.

A green fly was gleefully sitting on her white kerchief.

Ganna looked around: she herself was lying on corpses—men, women, children, were all lying in a haphazard pile. There was a sweet, nauseating smell.

Big flies were wildly flying in zigzags, buzzing; they'd settle on the corpses, restlessly and quickly crawl all over them, then suddenly take off, bursting with a buzzing sound—*z-z-z*—as if sawing through her soul.

"Whoa! You damned creature!" Ganna heard.

The wagon stopped at the cemetery, beside a large pit.

The Canaries jumped off the driver's seat, walked over to the corpses, and pulled out the dead man by his feet.

With several wide swings, they threw him into the pit.

They got hold of the woman and, with a swing, threw her in.

Ganna lay in the wagon, petrified. They grabbed Ganna by her hands and feet and started swinging her over the pit.

"And-a one!" Canary-wife counted. "And-a two! . . ."

Ganna now started struggling to break free. They threw her to the ground in fear.

"Looky here! She's alive!" Both bent over Ganna. "Are you hurt?"

Ganna gazed up at them in silence.

"Hey! I know you," Canary-wife said. "You're the dumb one, from the orphanage. They're looking for you. The police are looking."

Ganna looked back in silence.

They moved away from her.

They threw the corpses into the pit quickly, silently. Poured brown earth over them.

They climbed back onto the driver's seat.

The wife turned to Ganna. "Sit yourself here, girl, come along with us! We'll hide you so well, the devil himself won't find out where you are! We'll hide you at the watermelon patch, on the other side of the Akhtuba!"

14

They drove along. The wife took out a bottle of homemade vodka from under the seat. Poured a full glass for her husband—he drank it—then a full one for herself, too, and drank it; then poured one for Ganna.

"Here, take it." She held out the glass.

Ganna shook her head: *No.*

"Drink it! So that the infection won't stick to you!"

Ganna took a gulp, choking.

The wife laughed, finished off Ganna's glass, and grew drunk and talkative. "Not a single bit of infection gets us! Year before last we were hauling dead bodies—there was typhus—but we didn't get it. Last year people were dying from hunger—we carted them off, too. This year we're driving all over Tsarev *uezd*. . . ."

"Region," the Canary-husband corrected.[22]

"That's what it's called now," the wife agreed. "We drive from Tsarev to Lake Baskunchak, collecting the dead. All around—from Tsaritsyn to Astrakhan—the cholera's raging! Let it croak! But we don't catch it! That's 'cause we've got a remedy for all diseases."[23]

She took out the bottle of home brew and shook it. "This is it, the remedy!"

She poured some for her husband. "Drink!"

She poured some for herself and said, "We live like birds! By spirit alone! That's why the disease won't stick to us!"

They drank and started singing like birds, whistling and warbling—like two birds—two tiny ones, sitting on the seat, driving the camel. Ganna burst out laughing.

At the outskirts of the village, there were men with home-made guns, looming there like a dark woods.

"Stop!" They released a shot. "Stop, you unclean spirits!"

The men surrounded them.

"Don't bring the dead to our village, you Canaries!" They shouted. "Don't drag your disease in here!"

"That's not for you to decide!" Canary-wife shouted at them. "That's the authorities' decision! The order was to pile them up in one pit! It's an epidemic! You should understand that!"

"The authorities ordered one thing, but we're ordering something else. You bring any in tomorrow, and we'll kill you! We'll break your neck like a canary's!" they roared with laughter.

"But where can I take them? The dead bodies?" the woman asked them. "Where?"

They whipped the camel. The wagon sped off.

All the way the woman sat worrying, "Where?"

15

They arrived at the watermelon patch.

There were watermelons everywhere, lying left and right, watermelons enormous as pigs. Ganna stumbled across one as she walked: it cracked and split in half. Ganna plunged her teeth into the sugary, scarlet flesh; her whole face disappeared in the scarlet, sweet pulp.

"Leave it! It's overripe!" The Canary-woman grabbed her by the hand, dragging her farther. "We'll cut another watermelon for you! This one! Look at it: terrific looking, isn't it! And this melon! Just look at it, what a beauty! It's a lady, not a melon!"

She ordered her husband, "Cut this watermelon and this melon for us!"

The husband plunged a crooked knife into a watermelon, drew a circle, as if cutting someone's throat: it turned crimson under the knife and started dripping. Then he ripped open the melon and gutted it. He cut it into slices.

The Canary-wife followed her husband's movements.

"You'd make a hell of a bandit!" she praised him. She asked Ganna, "Do you want some Astrakhan-style *tyurya?*" She mixed some bread with watermelon in a bowl. "Here!" she said. "Eat!"

She filled the glasses.

"Let's have a drink, old man!" she said to her husband. "Look what a daughter we got for ourselves!" She hugged Ganna. "And you, dearie, do you like it with us?"

Ganna nodded.

"Really? This is our home!" the woman traced a circle with her hand up to the horizon. Pointed at the sky with her finger. "And that's our roof." She laughed. "When it breaks, the rain pours down. We didn't always live like this." She glanced back at the field and whispered, "We used to have a real home, a household, and kids—five of them."

"You'd better keep quiet, woman!" her husband said.

"She's dumb," the wife dismissed him with a wave of her hand. "Whatever you tell her won't go any farther. . . . So they started herding us into the collective farm and expropriated those who were well off. . . .[24] We see they're getting around to our house. We got ready in one night, threw what we had in the wagon, put the children on top of the bundles, took the horse by the bridle, set the house on fire—and off we went in search of happiness. Looking for freedom where there are no collective farms. We're from around Voronezh; we're not afraid of trouble. We went as far as Tashkent. People said there were no collective farms there. We walked through desert sands. We sold our horse, sold all our goods—bought Suleimen, the camel, to trek through the desert. The wagon couldn't get through, got bogged down in the sand like it was snow. . . . So we walked, and walked, walked for a long time, got to Tashkent, but they had a collective farm there! We started back. On the way we lost our kids—they burned up with typhus—all five of 'em!" She burst into tears. "One after another, they burned down like candles. Pour me some!" she suddenly yelled in a horrible voice, got up, swayed, overturned the bottle, and rushed to pick it up. She poured some vodka, offered it to her husband. "Drink!"

"I don't want to."

"Drink!"

"I won't!"

"Drink!" she hugged him around the neck, wanted to kiss him. The camel came up, stuck his shaggy head between them. He tried to push the Canary-woman away from her husband.

"L-o-o-ky here!" She laughed! "He's jealous! He's jealous of all men!" the woman told Ganna with joy, then turned to her husband and said, "If you hurt me—I'll leave you for the camel. Will you marry me, Suleimen? Do you love me, Suleimen?" She hugged the camel. "Come here, I'll kiss you!" She was laughing as she kissed the camel's hairy muzzle.

The husband spat and walked away.

"Where are you going?" she called him.

"I don't feel so good," he said and went to the hut to get some sleep.

Ganna and the woman made a campfire. The woman laid Ganna's head on her lap, running her fingers through her hair, searching for lice, and said, "You'll live with us, sweetie. We stay here in summer, but in winter we'll go to the Caspian Sea, where it's warm. We're like birds of passage. Russian birds . . ."

Ganna gazed at the sky. The stars were shining.

A big yellow moon lay in the starry sky as if in a melon patch—it smelled like melons.

16

In the morning, the Canary-woman tried to wake her husband.

"Get up! It's already past sunrise!"

There was no response. She crawled into the hut herself.

He lay there dead, motionless. She gave a wail.

She dressed him in a white shirt.

Put him on the green grass.

He lay on the grass as if sleeping.

"Vania!" she called. "Wake up!"

She picked a blue wildflower and put it in his hands—instead of a candle.

She woke up Ganna.

"Our old man's died. Let's go and bury him!"

Together with Ganna she loaded him on the wagon and drove off.

"I kept telling him yesterday: 'Drink, Vania! Drink, so that the infection won't get you'!" the Canary-woman said. "He didn't listen to me." She started crying.

At the outskirts of the village, there was a cordon of men with guns waiting on a hill.

From far away they shouted, "Hey, Canaries! Turn back! Or we'll shoot! We told you yesterday: 'Don't bring your plague to the village'!"

"This isn't the plague, it's my husband!" the woman said.

"What's with him?"

"He died."

"But he was alive yesterday." They couldn't believe it. "What did he die of? Cholera?"

"I don't know," she said, slowly driving uphill. "Maybe of cholera."

"Stop! Where are you going? Don't let her in, guys!" yelled a peasant with a black beard. "She's bringing death to all of us! Get her outta here, the mother cholera fucker!"

He fired. The bullet hit the woman in the shoulder.

"Ay, you murderer!" she cried, releasing the reins.

The bearded man on horseback fell upon her. Both he and his horse had eyes bloodshot with rage.

"Turn back!" he barked.

Ganna grabbed the reins, turned the wagon around.

The man whipped the camel.

"Go! Go, you devil!"

They took off at full speed.

The men on horseback followed them. They chased them all the way to the bridge.

Ganna crossed the bridge.

The peasants stopped at the bridge. On the shore they found a barrel with tar, broke it on the bridge, and set the bridge on fire.

They watched as the fire flamed high.

"You won't come back now, you Canary!" they shouted across the river. "This is the end of you, cholera!"

17

Her dress was soaked in blood.

Ganna took the kerchief off her head, bandaged her wound. Dragged the Canary-woman into the hut.

The Canary-woman lay silent, her face deathly pale. Then she opened her eyes, saw Ganna, and whispered with bloodless lips, "Looks like he's hit my lifeline. I'm dying. Forgive us, daughter dear. We invited you to live with us, but have abandoned you. . . ."

The kerchief was soaked with blood.

Ganna started rebandaging her, hands shaking.

The Canary-woman raised herself up a bit. "Beyond that cliff there's a ford. When I die, go away from here. They saw you. Take Suleimen with you. He's yours now. . . ." She leaned back, said plaintively, "I wanted to give Vania a nice burial. . . ."

Ganna took a spade.

The woman looked Ganna in the eyes.

"Dig the grave wide enough for two," she said. "We'll go searching for freedom in the other world. . . ."

18

The camel was sitting at the grave, uncomprehending.

It was already night. Ganna pulled him by the reins: *Let's go.* He turned his head away from her. Didn't get up.

She tossed aside the reins. Set off for the ford on foot.

She glanced back.

Suleimen was sitting motionless, his swan's neck stretched out.

Ganna undressed, lifted her clothes above the head, and entered the water.

19

The Akhtuba, as if waiting for her, embraced her with its strong arms, pulled her along. Ganna bent like a willow twig, and broke free.

Then the Akhtuba started carrying away the sand from under Ganna's feet. Ganna swayed, grabbed at a snag, and managed to stay on her feet.

Slowly, she made her way along.

The Akhtuba grew calm, too, splashed against her side as against a boat, gently murmuring something.

Stars were reflected in the dark water.

Slowly, as if through the starry sky, Ganna walked through the river, separating the stars in front of her with her hands: she moved them away so not to hurt them.

She reached the middle of the river and—as if the Akhtuba had lured her into a trap—fell into a hole, and the water closed over her head. Ganna threw away her clothes, started flapping her arms as she swam out of the hole. The Akhtuba wouldn't let her swim, twisting her like a beast, swirling her into a crater.

Ganna surfaced, wanted to grab a tree that had been torn out with its roots and was rapidly floating right at her, but wasn't quick enough: the tree hit her, knocked her over, deafened her.

The last thing Ganna heard was the ringing of bells. As if the stars in the sky were ringing like bells. Ganna glanced at the sky and sank to the bottom.

Someone grabbed her feet, pulling her down there—with strong, passionate hands.

20

On the bank, fishermen were sleeping by the extinguished campfire.

Suddenly they heard ringing on the river and jumped to their feet.

It was the bells on their fish traps striking. They rang, pealing out in unison—then fell silent.

"What was that?" a young fellow with a forelock asked.

"A sturgeon swam by, snagged them with its tail," answered Pyotr Rybakov, a sinewy little man in a tattered jersey. He turned around, shouted to the others. "Ivan and Iakov! Come on, get in the boats! Let's check the nets! A sturgeon just headed right into them!"

They pulled the nets out.

"Heavy!" said Pyotr in the darkness. "Must be man sized!"

They pulled it out onto the shore, untangled it next to the fire.

In the nets, all covered with silver scales, like a big fish, lay Ganna, looking at the fishermen.

"A mermaid!" Forelock exclaimed. "Guys, we caught a mermaid!"

21

They approached cautiously, started examining Ganna.

"Is she breathing? Maybe she's drowned."

Ganna moved away from them, covering herself with her arms.

"Lo-o-o-ky! A mermaid, but she's embarrassed! Covering herself!"

"She's nothing to hide. She's still a little girl. . . ."

"Pretty, though! She'll be a beauty when she grows up!"

Forelock approached.

"Get out of the way," he said, covered Ganna with his fisherman's jacket, took her in his arms. "Are you cold?" he asked.

Ganna made no response, just snuggled closer to him.

"Watch out, Andrei, she'll tickle you to death," Pyotr told Forelock.[25] "You'll fall asleep and she'll drag you to her place under the snag, to the mermaid's house. . . ."

Forelock settled Ganna by the fire. She sat and stretched her legs.

"A mermaid without a tail," a pockmarked man glanced at her. "She's no mermaid!"

"Not drowned and not a mermaid . . . who is she, then?" Forelock asked.

"I don't know," the pockmarked man answered. "We've gotta question her. What's your name, girl?" Ganna looked at the pockmarked man in silence.

Pyotr was busy with a teapot near the fire. He turned and quickly said, "Seems she doesn't understand our language." He hit himself on the forehead. "This is Tuba! Why didn't I guess from the start!"

"Who's this Tuba?" Forelock asked.

"The khan's daughter! The daughter of Khan Mamai—Tuba. Haven't you heard about her?" Pyotr was excited.

"No, I haven't."

"How come? Khan Mamai had a daughter. A beauty and really clever. Her name was Tuba. That was when Old Russia was under the Tartars. Russian princes used to come, cap in hand, to the Tartars, here, to our land, to the Astrakhan region. People say it used to be a kingdom, the Golden Horde.[26] Where the town Tsarev is now—that used to be their capital, it was called Sarai. So princes would come to this Sarai, pay their tributes, and beg for new principalities for themselves.[27] You could say Russia's capital was here; everything was decided here, in our part of the country. Once a Russian, Prince Dmitry, came to Mamai to ask him for a land to rule over. He saw Tuba and fell madly in love with her. And Tuba fell in love with him. She was about thirteen at the time. Now we'd consider her a child, but they used to get married at that age. So he asked her father for her hand: 'Marry off your daughter to me, Khan Mamai!' Mamai was enraged. 'What? A Russian bondsman proposing to the tsar's daughter! Get out,' he said, 'off with you! I'll give no land to a bondsman, nor power, nor my daughter.' Dmitry got angry. 'All right,' he said, 'if you won't give her to me in peace, I'll take her in war.' And he rode back to Russia to gather an army, to go fight Mamai. And he told Tuba to wait for him. 'Wait for me,' he said. Rumors started that he was gathering an army. Khan Mamai got scared, decided to get Tuba out of harm's way—to marry her off to a Crimean khan. She'd been promised to him while still in her mother's womb. That was their Tartar custom. The khan of the Crimea arrived with the money to buy his bride. Was he old and mangy! 'Here's your bridegroom,' Mamai told Tuba. 'The wedding's in three days.' Tuba looked at him, didn't say anything to her father, and left. In her room she started crying. She wrote a note to Dmitry—*Come fast*—and sent the note to Russia with a faithful courier. She acted merry and tender with the groom, smiling, not showing any sign. Meanwhile, she was waiting for Dmitry. She waited one day, then another. The third day came—the day of the wedding. In the morning, they brought a herd of sheep to the house, started slaughtering them; cauldrons were boiling, they were cooking *beshbarmak* for the wedding.[28] They decked Tuba out in her wedding dress, led her to the altar. But she was waiting for Dmitry, waiting until the last minute. So the Tartar priest places the bride and groom behind a curtain—that's their custom—and asks the groom through the curtain: 'Have you, khan of the Crimea, married Tuba?' 'Yes, I have!' he answers. So the priest asks Tuba, 'Have you, Tuba, married the khan of the Crimea?' And she has to say that yes, she has. As soon as she says this, the business is done; the wedding's arranged; you can't go back. That's how the Tartars did it. But Tuba says nothing. The priest asks her again: 'Have you got married, Tuba?' Tuba says nothing. And as soon as he started asking her the third time, she rushed from behind the curtain, ran out of the house and into the steppe, raced to the river, and from this very bridge—the one nearby that leads to the watermelon patch—jumped off and drowned! Mamai came running to the bridge, started crying and screaming. 'Ah, Tuba!' he screamed. 'Ah, Tuba!' From that time the river has been called Akhtuba."

"But what about Dmitry?" Forelock interrupted. "Didn't he come?"

"Of course he came. He did. . . . Only he came a bit too late. He didn't come alone, but with an army. That's why he was late! Mamai learned that Dmitry was approaching with the army and sent a dark host—that's what they called the Tartar army—to meet him.[29] The light and the dark—Dmitry and Mamai—clashed on Kulikovo Field.[30] Damask swords shine, golden helmets roll under brave horses' hooves. Many a knight's head fell from the brave horses onto the damp earth. They fought for three days and three nights. Russian blood mixed with Tartar blood, flowed like a river through ravines as if through riverbeds. Blood kept streaming into the Volga; the Volga was all red. We, the Russians, won. The Tartar yoke ended for Russia. After the battle, Prince Dmitry came to Kulikovo Field, stood at one end. After the battle Khan Mamai came to Kulikovo Field, stood at the other end. They stood at Kulikovo Field, looking: the field's covered with dead bodies, both Christian and Tartar. The Christians are flickering like candles, and Tartars are lying like black tar. And they see the Virgin Mary herself walking around the field, God's apostles are following her, and archangels—holy angels with bright candles, reading services for the Orthodox dead. The holy Virgin Mary herself is burning incense over their bodies, and crowns come down from heaven onto their heads. Mamai was terrified: 'Great is the God of the Russian land!' he said and rushed off to the Golden Horde. He arrived there and told the Tartar women, 'All your men have been killed by the Russians, now they're coming here for you. They'll be here soon. Save yourselves while you can!' He said this and fled; together with the Crimean khan he made off to the Crimea. And the women? They had nowhere to go. They sat down in the steppe, the whole horde of them, and started crying, crying over their slain Tartar men. They cried for nine days and nine nights. They cried two lakes of tears—Baskunchak and El'ton—to this day they extract salt there. Then the Russians

came, snatched up the Tartar women, and took them home—
to Russia."

"And Dmitry? What about him?" Forelock interrupted again.

"Dmitry arrived in Sarai ahead of his army. He arrived, galloped up to the khan's palace, got off his horse, entered the
palace, but there was nobody there. He found only one servant.
'Where's Tuba?' he asks the servant. 'Tuba's not here,' the servant
says. 'And where's Khan Mamai?' he asks. 'He ran away with his
son-in-law,' the servant answers. 'What son-in-law?' 'The
Crimean khan, Tuba's bridegroom.' Dmitry trembled; her
bridegroom? 'So my beloved Tuba didn't wait for me?' he asks.
The servant's silent, afraid to tell the truth. Dmitry stood there
for a while, turned, and went away. He left the palace and went
to the river. He fell facedown on the shore, in the deep grass, and
started crying. 'Ah, Tuba,' he cried. 'Ah, you unfaithful one!'

"Suddenly he feels somebody's little hand stroking his curls
as lightly as the wind. He raised his head: Tuba! She stands in
front of him, wearing a crown of white lilies, like a bride.

'I'm not unfaithful,' she says. 'I ran away from my bridegroom, the Crimean khan. And I waited and waited for you,
my fate, for three days and three nights, and then for nine days
and nine nights, and again for three days and three nights. And
now you're here.' Dmitry embraced her, kissed her, couldn't get
enough of her. 'We'll have the wedding today,' he says. 'But do
you love me, Dmitry?' Tuba asks. 'I love you,' Dmitry answers.
'Do you truly love me?' Tuba questions him. 'Truly,' he
answers. 'And will you go with me?' 'With you I'll go to the
ends of the earth!' 'Let's go, then. . . .' She took him by the
hand and led him into the river.

"Dmitry follows her as if in a dream: farther and farther.
It became really deep! And in front of him—just a step
away—a pit: black water is boiling over it like fish soup in a
pot, tumbling, swirling splinters and sticks into the crater.
Tuba pulls Dmitry into the pit. He follows her. The only
thing he asks is 'Where are we going?' 'To my new house,'
Tuba answers. 'Everything's ready for the wedding. . . .'

"Whereupon she pushed Dmitry into the pit! And she jumped in after him. And the black pit spun them around, whirled them, and sucked them in."

22

"Dmitry recovered and looked around. He sees himself, the bridegroom at his own wedding. He's sitting at an oak table on a golden chair, in a crystal palace. Beside him is his bride, Tuba. Servants with red sashes are rushing about, placing dishes on tables. Around him, young fellows and girls wearing wreaths are singing and dancing, singing in praise of the newlyweds.

His soul's desire had come true.

"Only Dmitry has a bad feeling, as if a heavy stone lay on his heart; it oppressed him, didn't let him breathe. An old man—his gray mustache reaching his shoulders—raised his goblet: 'To the young couple's health,' he said. 'To Tsar Dmitry and Tsarina Tuba.' Dmitry was surprised: What kind of tsar was he? And the old man took a sip of wine and shouted, 'It's bitter! Make it sweeter!'[31]

"Everybody shouted, 'It's bitter!' Dmitry got up. Tuba got up, too. Dmitry gazed at his beloved and forgot his sorrows and woes: Tuba was looking at him, her eyes like clear stars, offering her scarlet lips for his kiss. Dmitry suddenly felt merry, felt good!

"And he held Tuba tighter, embraced her, drawing her to him for a kiss. Only all of a sudden he feels something slippery beneath his hands, as if he's embracing not Tuba but a slippery burbot, as if it's fish slime beneath his hands and he can't grab it! He glanced down—and instead of a dress Tuba has a fish tail! Dmitry guessed where he'd ended up. He took a better look around: that wasn't an old man with a mustache reaching his shoulders, shouting 'It's bitter'— it was a mustached sheatfish blowing bubbles. Those weren't servants with red sashes—they were crawfish with claws, placing dishes with dead meat on the tables. Those weren't young fellows and girls singing and dancing, but victims of drowning.

"Dmitry pushed Tuba away from him. He yelled at the top of his voice. He picked up the oak table and hit the crystal walls of the palace with it. The walls shattered. Dmitry grabbed an oak board, pushed himself off the river bottom, and shot up to the surface.

"He surfaced and made it ashore but couldn't tell whether he was dead or alive. Then he sees—he is alive. He called his dun horse. He was getting ready to return to Russia. But in a flash the mermaid was there. She splashed in the river beside the shore, begging Dmitry in a plaintive voice: 'Don't leave me, Dmitry. Don't go!' 'You deceived me, Tuba,' Dmitry said. 'You didn't tell me you'd turned into a mermaid.' 'I gave my life for you! I became the river tsarina! Come back and you'll become the river tsar! There are countless treasures in our river kingdom. . . .' 'No,' Dmitry answered. 'It's better to be a prince in holy Russia than the tsar in the river kingdom.' He mounted his horse. He set out across the ford. Tuba seized hold of the reins, started crying. 'I won't let you go,' she said. 'I can't live without you. I love you more than life.'

"Dmitry, too, started crying. 'I love you too,' he answered. 'Only we're not fated, it seems, to be together in this world. Maybe in the next God will take pity on us. . . .' He kissed her. 'Forgive me and farewell!' he said. Tuba released the reins."

23

"So he just left?" Forelock asked.

"Yeah. Found someone he married in Russia, people say her name was Evdokiia. They had a lot of children."

"And what about Tuba?"

"Tuba became the river tsarina. She still lives in the Akhtuba. In the daylight, she splashes around, swims with people. But if someone is not careful—she catches him, grabs him by the feet and drags him to the bottom where she lives. She especially likes drowning little kids and young girls. You can understand that: it's boring at the bottom of the river; she wants to play with them; she's still a child herself. . . . But when night falls, Tuba calls her golden horse and gallops on this golden horse under the steppe. . . ."

"Under the steppe? On a golden horse?" Forelock raised his head.

"Yeah. People say that when Khan Mamai was fleeing, he melted all his gold and cast a golden horse—and to size! He buried the horse in the steppe."

"And where'd he bury it?" The pockmarked man licked his dry lips.

"Nobody knows that. People have been looking for that horse for hundreds of years but can't find it. At night, the story goes, the golden horse and Tuba gallop under the steppe, its golden hooves thumping under the ground. And during the day, it returns to where Mamai buried it: it sleeps all day long," Pyotr said. "There's just one night a year Tuba won't call the golden horse, won't summon it. Once a year, on Midsummer's Night—that's Ivan Kupalo—Tuba comes ashore, sits on a willow tree, and calls Dmitry, saying: 'Where are you, my bright sun, my red sun, Prince Dmitry! Come to me, to the beautiful maiden! And shine all day, all day long. Shine over me. . . .' And all night long she cries for Dmitry. And she cries so plaintively, in such a thin voice. . . ."

Suddenly somebody cried in the night—plaintively, in a thin voice—and stopped.

"Sh-h!" Pyotr half rose. "You hear that? That's her crying!"

And again somebody cried plaintively, like a child—then stopped again.

The fishermen jumped to their feet, peering into the pitch-dark steppe.

And someone cried a third time, bitterly, uncontrollably.

They looked around.

The crying came from nearby, by the campfire.

They approached—Ganna was sitting by the cracked boat, muffled in the fisherman's jacket, and crying.

They uncovered her face: tears were streaming down it like rain. Her shoulders were shaking with sobs.

"Then it's true, it's her! Tuba! The khan's daughter!" Forelock said, astounded. "Just look: she heard us talking about her Dmitry and started crying."

"The khan's daughter?" the pockmarked man asked him. "Then we've got to turn her over to the authorities!"

"What for?" Forelock was surprised.

"'Khan' means 'tsar' in Russian," the pockmarked man said. "Right?"

"Well, yeah," Forelock agreed.

"If that's so, then she's the tsar's daughter. Right?"

"Well, yeah," Forelock agreed again.

"So it follows," the pockmarked man said in a solemn voice, "that we're harboring the tsar's daughter!"

Everybody fell silent. They looked wordlessly at the pockmarked man.

Pyotr, in his tattered jersey, sidled up very close to him, and glanced in his face.

"Wow!" he uttered in incomprehensible delight.

And suddenly he slammed his fist into the pockmarked man's forehead!

The man fell, and Pyotr bent over him, removed a mosquito from his forehead.

"Here," he showed the mosquito to the others. "I killed a mosquito! Blood-sucking scum. . . ."

He laughed. "Stepan Razin did well in not conjuring the mosquito.[32] Our fishermen from Astrakhan kept bugging him: 'Conjure up the mosquito. We're sick and tired of mosquitoes!' But Stepan answered, 'I won't conjure it, or you won't be able to get any fish!' And he didn't conjure it."

Pyotr moved away from the pockmarked man, sat down beside the campfire, and threw in some logs.

Grunting, the pockmarked man got up, wiped off some blood, and stared at Ganna with his coal-like eyes.

"Still, we've gotta interrogate her!" he repeated threateningly.

"Are you at it again?" Pyotr turned to him.

"Let her tell us where the treasures are!" the pockmarked man shouted. "Where her father Mamai buried the golden horse. And if she won't tell, let's hand her over to the authorities! Let them interrogate her. They'll make anyone talk!"

Ganna looked at the pockmarked man in fear. Then ran and hid behind Pyotr's back.

Pyotr rose.

"Listen, you. . . . Leave the girl alone!" he told the pockmarked man. And added sternly, "Don't take sin upon your soul! Remember! We're fishermen, Christ's people: we don't turn in anybody. We don't betray anybody! When Christ comes down from heaven to earth again, he'll come to us first, he'll ask us first: How did you live here, without me? What are we gonna answer him?"

He bundled Ganna up warmly.

"Sleep," he said. "And we'll catch some fish for you, we'll make fish soup in the morning. . . ."

Pyotr turned to the others and shouted, "Hey! Fishermen! Get up! Andrew! John! Jacob the Older and Jacob the Younger! Simon! Thaddeus! Philip! Matthew! Bartholomew! Thomas! Let's go to the boats! We'll put up the nets: the fish will come soon. . . ."

The boats splashed in the river.

The fishermen threw their nets in.

It grew quiet.

Pyotr could be heard praying by the river.

"Our honorable angels-archangels! Keep and protect our fishing: every hour, every day, and every night. Jesus Christ, crucified on a tree-cross, protect us, fishermen, with the power of the Lord's honorable and life-giving cross! . . ."

Ganna closed her eyes. Lay down on the ground. Put her ear to the ground. She heard the golden horse galloping under the earth, its golden hooves thumping.

She fell into a deep sleep.

. . .

24

At dawn Ganna felt somebody carefully stepping over her.

She opened her eyes. Saw somebody's back, moved.

The man glanced back at her—it was the pockmarked man. He leaned down.

"Sleep—sleep—sleep," he whispered in frightened tones.

And, looking around, he set off for the road.

Ganna turned over and fell asleep.

25

In a minute she woke again. Jumped up, as if stung.

She ran to the road. The pockmarked man was quickly walking to the village.

Ganna was scared. She ran to tell the fishermen.

The fishermen were lying by the extinguished campfire, like slaughtered *bogatyrs*, fast asleep.

Ganna rushed to and fro. She didn't know where to hide.

Then she ran to the river, to the ford.

She made her way down to the water and saw Suleimen, the camel, swimming in the river like a ship.

She walked toward him. Suleimen swam to her. She put her arms around his neck, climbed onto his back, and settled there.

26

The sun was rising.

The camel, with Ganna on his back, was coming out of the water.

Forelock woke up and saw them.

"Ah," he exclaimed, "Tuba! The khan's daughter!"

Ganna spurred the camel with her bare heels.

The camel ran into the steppe.

27

Ganna rode along the steppe on the camel. She was hungry. She saw some wild blackthorn growing on the slopes of a gully. She slid off the camel, climbed down the slope.

Blackthorns were hanging on prickly bushes like ink drops.

She stretched her hand toward the thorn—the thorn scratched her hand.

She licked the blood off, stretched out her hand again: now she pricked her finger.

Ganna got angry at the blackthorn, marched determinedly at it: the bush bristled its thorns, wouldn't let Ganna approach.

She sat on the ground. The pricked finger hurt. She raised it to her lips, blew on it.

Suddenly a dragonfly came from nowhere, as if descending from the sky. Rustling its mica wings, it landed on her finger.

Seeing Ganna, it froze. It fixed its gaze on her, staring in surprise.

Ganna froze, too. She examined the dragonfly, afraid of exhaling.

The dragonfly had a light, almost weightless, dry body, as if it were superfluous. The dragonfly had light wings, as transparent as air. Its round head had two huge eyes. Those eyes took up, and replaced, the whole head. It was as if it thought with its eyes. Like a light and weightless soul, the dragonfly had been lowered from heaven to earth—to look.

When it had finished looking, it would fly back to heaven.

With its bulging, hard, watchful gaze, as if trying to retain Ganna in its memory, the dragonfly raptly looked at Ganna.

So they looked into each other's eyes.

"Seeing as the camel's here, she must be here, too." Ganna suddenly heard a familiar voice. "They couldn't have gotten far. I bet she's hiding in the gully!"

At the slope of the gully, next to the camel, stood the Director of the collective farm. He was looking right at Ganna but couldn't see her: the sun was blinding him.

He was thinking out loud. "We'll catch the girl and take the camel to the collective farm. A camel can go two hundred days without food. It works without food. A profitable animal for the farm."

The pockmarked man came up to him: he, too, looked blindly at Ganna without seeing her.

Ganna backed up. A twig crunched under her feet, gave her away.

"There she is!" turning his head, the Director yelled and pointed at Ganna.

The pockmarked man rushed down the slope, ran toward Ganna.

Ganna quickly lay down on her stomach, crawled under the thornbush like a grass snake. The bush hid its thorns, let Ganna in.

It bristled in front of the pockmarked man, not letting him through.

The pockmarked man started breaking the bush. His hands stained with blood, he pulled the bush out. Ganna hid behind another bush. He pulled that out, too.

Ganna set off running through the prickly thicket. The man plowed straight through after her. Ganna glanced back: the pockmarked man was catching up with her. She hid behind a stunted bush. Sat behind the bush, breathless.

"There she is!" the Director said from above, pointing at Ganna.

The pockmarked man turned and headed straight for Ganna. He burned Ganna with his coal eyes. He grabbed at the bush, started breaking it. The branches cracked like bones. He bent down, intending to grab Ganna—and the thorns thrust into his eyes like knives. The coals grew dim. The man snarled like a wounded beast. He swirled in place, his bloody eyes looking blindly at Ganna, his bloody hands trying to catch her.

Ganna evaded him and ran through the thicket, making her way through the blackthorn. She made it up the opposite side of the gully. Ran into the steppe.

"Stop! We'll catch you anyway!" the Director shouted

from the other side of the gully. "Come back! You'll croak in the steppe from the heat, you fool!"

28

Ganna moved farther and farther into the steppe.

The sun already stood high in the white, burnt-out sky. The steppe, steely in color from the wormwood, was gradually heating up like a skillet. It was getting hotter.

Ganna's hands and body were scratched bloody by the thorns, and the wounds burned.

She was thirsty.

Ganna turned back, and there, far below, she could see the river that she was leaving farther and farther behind. The river shone in the sun and grew smaller and smaller, as if it were drying up while Ganna watched: you already could fit the whole river into a mug.

Ganna felt like drinking up the river.

She licked her parched lips.

Drops of sweat surfaced on her face and dried up, leaving traces of salt—and new drops would appear. Her hair grew wet, dark—and the sun's rays fell on Ganna's dark head like arrows on a target. Covering her poor head with her arms, Ganna started running.

She had nowhere to run. The steppe was all around her. It emanated heat like an oven. Exhausted, Ganna sat down. She wanted to drink, drink, drink. . . .

She saw green blades of grass under her and picked one. Stuffed it in her mouth, started chewing. She picked up another one: milk streamed from the stem in white drops. Ganna rejoiced, put the stem in her mouth: her lips and tongue grew bitter—it was wormwood. She spat it out, burst into tears. Her tears fell onto her hands, and Ganna started licking them off. But they were as bitter as wormwood. As the tears on her face dried, the skin under her eyes tightened, itching from the salt.

She turned to look at the distant river with the cool water. Shining and winding, the river suddenly smiled maliciously at Ganna, a shiny snakelike smile as it slyly slipped away and disappeared.

And Ganna suddenly understood that she wouldn't make it. She looked with reproach at the sun as at a murderer. And in the white sky, burnt-out like the steppe, she saw a little wrinkled sun, as lonely as Ganna, walking, suffering from the heat that emanated from God knows where. But the sun stubbornly walked on through the sky.

She also had to walk.

Ganna got up and set off, swaying.

She walked for a long time. Her head was swimming. The wounds on her body were bleeding. Sweat poured down her face, but she kept on walking, looking at the ground under her feet, feeling pain in her heels from the dry stony ground and thorns, sharp as needles.

But when she suddenly raised her head, she stopped, astounded, unable to believe her eyes.

In front of her there was an immense blue lake that filled her range of vision.

Ganna raced happily toward the lake. Running, she jumped into the water.

Salty water suddenly burned her body. The salt ate away at her wounds.

As if her soul was burned through.

Ganna screamed with pain, "*GA-GA-GA!!!*"

Her scream reached the sky.

"*GA-GA-GA!!!*"

It was Baskunchak Lake, created from the Tartar women's tears.

PART THREE

I

Ganna was going around the backyards, begging for food. Winter had come.

Muffled in rags, she stood at the door of a house.

She knocked. They opened.

"We don't have anything. Go away, girl, go on." The woman slammed the door.

2

Ganna went into another yard. Approached the house. Knocked. Nobody answered.

Suddenly, a huge shaggy dog quietly attacked her unexpectedly from behind, toppling her over. The dog pulled Ganna about like a doll. Ganna silently tried to fight it off. Growling, the dog rolled Ganna up to the gate. Ganna leaped outside the gate.

The owner came out on the porch.

"Good dog, Buran," he praised the dog.

He threw a piece of meat to the dog. The dog caught and swallowed it without chewing.

3

Ganna dragged herself along. It started snowing. The snow fell slowly, in flakes.

Ganna whirled, catching the flakes with her mouth. Whenever she caught one, she'd laugh happily. Boys attacked her like malicious puppies.

"Little fool! Little fool!"

Ganna sat down by the wall of the empty church, bristling. The boys left her alone. She sat there, shaking from cold. The snow kept falling, covering the earth.

Suddenly there was a clang above Ganna's head.

"*Boom!*"

The earth shook.

And again.

"*Boom!*"

The sky shook.

She raised her head: Father Vasily stood in the belfry, ringing the bell.

"*Boom! Boom! Boom!*" The ringing flowed out of the bell slowly, in a thick flow, like honey flowing out of a pitcher, flooding the world.

People came running out of their houses. Lifted their faces.

"Look-y! The clapperless bell's started talking!"

"Father Vasily cast a golden clapper for it!"

"Where'd he get all that gold?"

"He found a treasure. People say Stepan Razin's treasure was revealed to him."

People—old and young—were hurrying to the church.

"Today's a holiday, Orthodox folks! Epiphany!"

4

After the service they went to the Podstyopka River.

Father Vasily, carrying the golden cross, led the procession, all the people following him.

Ganna brought up the rear.

5

In the middle of the river stood a cross, carved from ice, light blue.

It shone fiercely in the sun.

The local men cut an ice hole beside the cross.

Father Vasily blessed the water.

"In the name of the Father, and the Son, and the Holy Ghost. Amen."

He turned to the people.

"Today's Epiphany, you of Orthodox faith!" he said. "Happy holiday!"

The daring men and young fellows in the congregation threw off their clothes and jumped into the ice hole in their birthday suits.

They splashed the women with the ice-cold water from the hole.

The women shrieked, then burst out laughing. They bombarded the naked men in the ice hole with snowballs.

"Just like in the old days!" the old women whispered. "Everything's like it used to be!"

A thin woman came driving a sled to the ice hole. There

was a sick man in the sled, swaddled like a baby, who gazed at the heavens.

She drove him up to the ice hole and unwrapped the swaddling clothes.

"Take my husband, Christians. He's not been able to get up for a year. Just lies there. Maybe the holy water will help him?"

The men accepted the pale body, emaciated like a relic. Passing it from hand to hand, they plunged it in the water.

They placed him in the swaddling clothes like a newborn, wrapped him up.

For a while the man lay there, swaddled, then all of a sudden yelled at his wife at the top of his voice, "My damn cock's frozen because of you!!! How am I going to use it on you?"

People roared with laughter. "Look! He's cured! Seems the holy water helped! The holy water!"

Others picked up on the notion and yelled, "Holy water! Holy! Holy!"

All the other men, young fellows, and boys started undressing. Laughing and shouting, they threw off their hats, dragged the felt boots off their feet, pulled off their sheepskin coats, pants, and shirts—and leaped into the icy water: it took your breath away!

Ganna came up to the ice hole, scooped the holy water into the palm of her hand, and drank it down—one icy gulp after another.

All of a sudden there came the sound of whistling and whooping in the distance.

Ganna looked into the distance. A dark crowd was running across the ice—the ice trembled as it approached.

"Hey, fellas! Get outta the water!" shouted a young fellow next to Ganna. "The Komsomol's coming!"[33]

They leaped out of the water, pulled on their pants, and formed a solid wall of bodies.

. . .

6

The Komsomol members ran up and formed their own dark solid wall of bodies opposite them. Like fledgling crows, they opened their mouths wide.

"There is no God!!!" they shouted. "There is no God!!!"

The men stood in silence, like a solid wall.

Hat cocked on his curly head, hands on his hips, a well-built Komsomol member—the secretary—stepped forward. He cast a penetrating glance at the men.

"Take away the cross!" he shouted.

The men stood like a solid wall, silent.

Behind them the icy cross shone in the sun. It blinded the secretary.

"Cut the cross down!" the secretary yelled, shielding himself from the light.

Without any words, silently, the men joined hands to form a chain.

Father Vasily stood next to the cross, shielding it with his body.

"Cut it down!!!" the secretary yelled, mad with fury and foaming at the mouth. "There is no God! None! . . . Your God has kicked the bucket!"

"You're lying!!!" someone suddenly cried behind the crowd.

The crowd parted in two.

A small man—hardly reaching the well-built secretary's waist—emerged and moved toward him. His whole body was covered in scars from bullets and saber cuts. He faced the secretary, threw his hat to the ground.

"You're lying, you dog! God is alive! God's alive!"

"Dad?" the secretary was surprised.

"Yes, son," the other answered.

"Go away, Father," the son ordered.

He moved determinedly toward his father.

"But, Father, you were in the Red Army, you spilled your blood for Soviet power!"

"I never fought against God!" his father answered.

He stood determinedly in his son's way.

The secretary's eyes grew bloodshot.

"Get out of my way!" he yelled insanely. "Get away!"

He pushed his father as hard as he could. His father fell, hit his head on the ice. Blood flowed from his mouth.

People gasped.

But the father got up, swaying, spat out blood, and went up to his son.

"Devil's seed!" he said, swung his arm, and hit him in the teeth.

White teeth poured out of the son's mouth like a necklace, rolled on the ice like pearls.

"A-a-a!!!" the son yelled terribly with his bloody mouth. "I'll kill you!!!" and he moved for the attack.

As if embracing, father and son came to deadly grips with each other.

"They're beating our men!!!" both sides shouted.

And the fun began.

A fistfight started.

7

Everything got into a confused tangle: men naked down to the waist, Komsomol members wearing devilish-black leather jackets, women in colorful shawls, little boys scurrying here and there. . . .

All around were the sounds of whistling, yelling.

Then came moaning and wailing.

They beat one another with all their strength, without pity, as if they were cutting oaks—strong, damp oaks—with damask axes.

"Aa-akh!!! Aa-akh!!! Aaa-akh!!!"

A man hit a Komsomol member in the nose with his fist.

The Komsomol member wiped off the blood with mucus, hit the man with a sneaky blow—below the belt.

The man doubled up, eyes bulging, gasping for air. He drew a few breaths, then swung his arm—and shifted the

Komsomol member's cheekbone from the right side to the left. Then he spat on his fist and smashed it into the other fellow's ear.

The young man's head rang. He got mad. He picked up an icicle from the ice, swung back his arms, and hit the man with his whole might—right in the temple. The man collapsed on the ice like a felled tree.

. . . The red-faced miller stood like a windmill in the middle of the crowd.

"Come here, Komsomol!!!" he roared. "I'll grind your bones!"

He kept grabbing Komsomol members by the collar like flour sacks, banging one forehead into another. Heads cracked like nuts. Bodies drooped like empty sacks—then he'd cast them aside. Empty bodies flew through the air, to fall on the ice with a thud.

. . . Anna Pshenichnaia—her fists like pumpkins—rushed into the fray. She grabbed one of the Komsomol members by his carroty forelock. She silently pulled him back and forth, back and forth, by the forelock, repeating, "Act like a human being, act like a human being. . . ."

The Komsomol member couldn't take it any longer, begged her, "Hey, Mom! That hurts! Let go my forelock, Mom!" His freckled face contorted in a wail.

She took pity on her son, released his forelock.

"Act like a human being, Nikola!"

He ran some distance away from his mother.

"There is no God!" he shouted to her from afar.

Anna Pshenichnaia chased her son again.

She slipped, fell, hurt herself, and burst into bitter tears.

Cries and moans accompanied the melee; blood was flowing all around, while bones cracked.

Friend was beating up friend, brother was beating brother, son hitting father, father hitting son.

The combatants fell on the ice like chips flying from a damp oak.

"Brothers! Come to your senses! Remember God! Brothers!"

Father Vasily walked among the fighters and appealed to them. "Deliver us, Lord, from hatred and evil, conflict and lovelessness . . . ," he appealed to heaven. He kept coming between the antagonists. "Brothers. . . ."

They blindly beat him from both sides: from left and from right.

8

Ganna was sitting, hiding behind the crowd, shaking.

Suddenly she heard a heavy clatter, like the pounding of a stone heart.

The clatter drew closer. Ganna looked up from behind the cross.

Horsemen in military caps were galloping at top speed on the ice.

They raced up.

"Disperse!" they yelled.

They whipped both parties.

They whacked a Komsomol member: the scar on his face swelled up.

"NKVD," he said gloomily, his eyes following them as he wiped off the blood.

Their horses trampled those lying on the ice.

One horseman was making straight for Anna Pshenichnaia.

Father Vasily rushed to the horse from one side, carrot-haired Nikola from the other side; they grabbed the horse by the reins.

The horse reared.

The rider rolled headfirst off the horse.

Other riders immediately swooped down on Father Vasily and Nikola, seized them under their arms, dragged them to the ice hole, hit them full force on the head with whip handles, and pushed both into the black water.

The crowd gasped.

The people came to their senses and ran to the ice hole.

. . .

9

The black water was motionless in the ice hole, freezing.

"Father! Father Vasily!" Maria Bokaneva, Father Vasily's goddaughter, was crying over the ice hole.

Anna Pshenichnaia was crawling to the hole over the ice.

She crawled to it, looked down into the abyss.

"Nikola! Son!" she called.

She called for him to come out of the ice hole as if calling him home for dinner, away from his buddies in the street.

"Where are you, Nikola? Nikola!!!" she yelled.

And, as if hearing his mother, somebody sighed down there at the bottom. Bubbles rose to the surface.

Nikola's carroty head floated up to the surface. Anna grabbed him by his carroty forelock, and, straining every muscle, pulled her son out. Nikola lay motionless for a while, then opened his freckled eyes.

"Mama," he said. "It hurts!"

And closed his eyes.

His mother started wailing.

10

"Disperse! Disperse!" the NKVD men shouted.

With whips they herded the people to the shore.

Anna Pshenichnaia walked in front, carrying her son in her arms.

He lay there as if asleep.

Maria Bokaneva remained at the ice hole. She sat by it as if it were Father Vasily's grave. On the grave stood the icy cross, shining in the sun.

"Get going! Get going!" The men on horses returned for Maria.

"I won't!" she cried.

They seized Maria, threw her over a horse's back, and rode off.

"Monsters! Monsters!" she yelled.

Ganna ran with everybody else.

One of the riders caught up with her, hit her with a whip. She glanced back: the rider had a scar—it was the man from the cowshed. He saw her.

"Ganna?" He recognized her.

Ganna set off for the other shore at a run. He turned his horse, galloped after her.

"Ganna, wait!"

There were wooden logs lying on the shore—the horse couldn't get through—she jumped on them and ran.

He stopped the horse at the logs. Got down, followed her along the logs.

Ganna emerged into an open field. Ran over a layer of frozen snow.

He raced after her, floundering in the snow up to his waist.

"It's not my fault!" he cried to Ganna. "They sent us here!"

He couldn't keep up.

11

Ganna ran for a long time.

She came to an unfamiliar village.

She sat in the snow by the fence, in front of a tearoom.

It started snowing.

She sat there, shaking.

A girl with slanting blue eyes, who seemed drunk with joy, came out on the porch. She looked at the snow.

> "Winter! . . . The peasant, feeling festive,
> Breaks a new trail with sledge and horse . . . ,"

she recited.[34]

She saw Ganna. "Come here, girl, I'll give you some *shchi*."[35]

12

"Eat, my darling, eat, my treasure." The slant-eyed girl poured *shchi* for Ganna, then sat down opposite her and watched her. Ganna moved the spoon around in the soup for a while, then dropped it.

"You don't like it?" The girl gave a start. "Oh, you're burning up, darling. Go lie down, I'll make up a bed for you right here. Let me tuck in the blanket around you. That's it."

She gave Ganna an herbal concoction and settled her on a bench in the corner, covered her with a patchwork quilt.

13

Ganna tossed and turned. Through the fever and haze she saw sweaty men walking around the tearoom, drinking vodka, drunkenly hugging and kissing one another. The girl with slanting eyes brought food to the tables, collected dirty dishes, and responded to the calls.

"Hey, Katerina! Give us another!"

She walked like a queen.

Whenever there was no work, she'd sit beside a fellow with a forelock, telling him something, laughing sonorously, tenderly. She would come to Ganna, put her cool hand on Ganna's burning forehead, and ask, "You feel better? Right?"

They'd call her, and she'd leave.

Two men were sitting at the table next to Ganna: one was stocky, with a black beard—the blacksmith Danila—the other one was young, his dark blond hair lying on his head in a stack like rye, the groom Yeryoma Popov. Their heads bent close together; they were talking quietly.

Through the fever and delirium Ganna heard:

"Did you hear? Today in Kapustin Iar, they drowned Father Vasily in an ice hole," the black-bearded blacksmith said.

"You don't say!" the fair-haired fellow exclaimed, and, covering his mouth with his hand, asked, "Who drowned him? Those guys?"

"Yeah. . . ."

"What for?"

"He was ringing the bells. Today's Epiphany. He put up

an ice cross on the Podstyopka, baptized people in an ice hole. Like in the past."

"And he wasn't afraid?" The blond was amazed.

"No . . . people say"—the black-bearded blacksmith looked around, leaned closer to the blond, and whispered—"the Virgin Mary herself ordered him to ring the bells. 'Go ring the bells!' she said."

"Did he see her in a dream? Or did he have a vision?"

"Neither. She came to him in person."

"In person?" the blond asked in amazement.

Eyes closed, the black-bearded man nodded and said, "In person! She came from the heavenly hold. An old woman on a small horse. People say she rode all over Russia on that horse. She'd see a beggar and give him bread. She'd console widows. Bandage the wounds of the sick. Wipe the tears of kids in orphanages. Now, they say, she's going to the prisons, to help the innocent. She'll collect all of Russia's woe, show it to her Son in heaven: 'Lord,' she'll say. 'Help the Russians! They've suffered plenty. They've had enough!'"

For a while they were silent.

The blacksmith continued, "She confided in Father Vasily alone. Maria Bokaneva also saw her. . . ." The black-bearded man grew thoughtful. Moved closer to the blond and whispered, "Father Vasily came to my smithy half a year ago, asked, 'Danila, can you make a clapper for our bell?'"

"What did you say?"

"I said I could. If there was something to make it from. For the bell, I told Father Vasily, you need a lot of silver and copper and plenty of gold—the bell's huge. In olden times they brought it to us by ship on the Volga! It weighs five hundred fifty poods! Its clapper must be real heavy!"

"What did he say?"

"'We've got the material,' he said. 'Get a cart,' he said, 'and let's go!'

"No sooner said than done. I harnessed a horse. 'Where,' I asked, 'should I drive?' 'Drive to Tsaritsyn, and there I'll show you,' Father Vasily said. We drove the entire day. It was already night when we approached a village. 'What's this village called?' I asked. 'Peskovotovka,' Father Vasily answered. 'Turn in the direction of the Volga,' he said. 'See that burial mound?' My heart leaped! For I knew that Stepan Razin's treasure was buried in that spot. The whole ship was buried, full of gold and silver. Stepan brought it there in high water, and when the water got low, he built a mound over the ship, and he stuck an apple branch in the ground on top. The branch grew into an apple tree; only its apples, they say, are seedless.

"We drove up to the mound. And what people said was true! Apples shone in the darkness.

"'Do you recognize it?' asked Father Vasily.

"'Yes, I do!' I said. 'Stepan Razin's treasure is buried here.'

"'Get a shovel,' he said. 'Let's go and unearth the treasure.'

"I got scared.

"'No,' I said. 'I won't go. Everyone knows that the treasure's under the mound, but it's scary to dig: this isn't an ordinary treasure but enchanted, cursed for many generations. A lot of people perished on account of it, but Stepan Razin's treasure wouldn't reveal itself to anyone!'

"'But it'll show itself to us!' Father Vasily said. 'The Virgin Mary herself ordered Stepan to reveal the treasure to us. Don't be afraid, Danila! Let's go!'

"And we went to the mound. As we passed the apple tree, I picked an apple and ate it: it really was seedless, that was no lie!

"We climbed to the very top. We dug down: once, twice. We see something like a pit, but more like some kind of cellar, with a door. The door's bolted, locked. We just touched the door, and the bolts fell off, the door opened. We went in. There was an incredible number of different things! Barrels of silver, barrels of gold! Gems of all sorts, tons of silverware! And everything glittered like gold.

"Father Vasily and I started rolling out the barrels of gold and loading them onto the cart. We loaded all the gold, then went for the silver. We get to the door—but the door's already closed, the pit's covered with clay! The treasure had closed itself off under the ground.

"And we went home.

"I melted the gold in my smithy, cast a clapper for the bell, forged it.

"A golden clapper—from pure gold!"

The blacksmith stopped and closed his eyes, deeply affected.

The blond said with regret, "The Komsomol folks will tear the bell's clapper out when they find out it's gold."

"Let them try!" The blacksmith laughed, opening his eyes. "As soon as they take it down, the gold will turn into bits of pottery in their hands."

"How do you know?" the blond asked.

"I know. I took a gold coin for myself, put it in my pocket." The blacksmith lowered his eyes in shame. "Just as a souvenir."

"So?"

"Later I was looking for something in my pocket. . . . And there, in my pocket, instead of the gold coin there lay . . . what do you think?" the blacksmith asked the blond and shouted, "Fresh cow dung!" and he roared with happy laughter, opening his mouth like a scorching red furnace. "Stepan Razin played a joke on me!!!"

A young fellow with red cheeks, as if painted with rouge, ran past them with beer mugs. He stopped.

"Sten'ka? Razin?" His eyes lit up. "Did he used to come here?"

"What, were you born yesterday, lad?" asked the blacksmith, surprised. "Where do you hail from?"

"From Tula," the red-cheeked fellow answered.

"Comes from Tula and eats bullets. Tula folks put a flea on a chain," the blacksmith teased him.[36] "You're not a local, that's clear right off. Anybody born by the Volga learns about Sten'ka before he learns about his own dad. Mothers rock babies in the cradle and instead of a lullaby sing a song about Stepan Razin. Stepan Timofeyevich left a memory behind him, that he did! The Volga remembers him: Tsaritsyn, Saratov, Samara! . . . Astrakhan remembers!"

The blacksmith raised his voice, so that entire tearoom would hear. From all the corners of the room the men thronged to him.

Katerina, too, sat down to listen. Sat down beside Forelock. He put an arm around her shoulders.

The blond threw more logs on the fire. It blazed up.

Ganna was also all ablaze. She listened.

"Under Stepan Razin there was a free kingdom here," the blacksmith started his story. "Astrakhan freemen, haven't you heard of them? Those looking for truth and those looking for freedom and those poor and those crippled and those who were kind at heart and brave of soul—everyone would come here from all over Russia—to the free land of Astrakhan.

"Astrakhan accepted everybody, fed everybody. Such a rich land! Sturgeons swimming in the rivers, grapes ripening in the orchards, watermelons and melons lying in the watermelon patch, pumpkins the size of your head in the gardens. . . . The sun's hot, the sky's blue. . . . A land of paradise!

"So Stepan Razin gathered downtrodden folks from all over the Russian land and made a decision: here, in Astrakhan, there'd be a kingdom, not of falsehood, but of truth. To the enslaved he gave freedom, to the poor he distributed the goods he'd amassed, he set free those who'd been unjustly imprisoned, and he bowed to the homes of the Mother of God—the churches.

"The people of Astrakhan wrote a letter: 'Let us live here, in Astrakhan, in love and peace, and hurt nobody in Astrakhan, and stand up for each other like one man. . . .'

"They had driven out all the rulers. Now, they said, all our affairs will be decided by the circle. They would gather in a circle—old and young, Cossacks, townspeople, Kalmucks, and good Christians—and decide what to do and how to live. Everybody would say what he thought; everybody's word would be of value.

"Stepan would stand in the middle of the circle, taking council with everybody. If the people liked his word, they'd yell: 'Your word is to our taste, boss!' If they didn't like it, they'd make a commotion: 'Not to our taste! Do it like this,' they'd say. . . . Stepan would stand beneath the Cossack banner and listen.

"But he was also strict with everybody. There was order. If anyone stole something from someone, even a needle—they'd tie a shirt over his head, put sand in his shirt, and toss him into the water. . . . He was strict, was Stepan Timofeyevich, real strict!

"But his heart was kind. . . . A guy fell in love with a girl. . . . But the parents wouldn't agree to their marriage. The couple came to Razin: 'What should we do, Stepan Timofeyevich? We can't live without each other.' Stepan took them by the hand, led them around a birch tree: 'Here, you're husband and wife now,' he says. 'Love is more important than anything.'

"People lived well under Stepan! But not for long.

"Stepan's soul felt profound pain for all Russian people. He decided to march on Moscow with an army, to expunge falsehood and treason from the Kremlin.

"He fought and fought against falsehood, but it conquered him, that falsehood, twisted him around its finger, the crooked thing.[37] It deceived him!

"And they captured the brave fellow! They tied his white hands, brought him to Moscow with its stone walls.[38] And on glorious Red Square, they cut off his reckless head!"

Forelock gasped, rocking as if in pain. "Why, why did he go fight Moscow!" he regretted. "He should've stayed here to rule. There would've been two Russias: one Russia here—the free one—the other Russia there, the unfree one. . . ."

"Russia is one," the blacksmith said sternly. "Dividing Russia is like cutting a man into pieces: he'd be dead. And how can you live without Moscow? Moscow is the head. How can a man live without a head? No, he decided everything right, Razin did; only he himself perished. . . . There had never been a man like Sten'ka in Russia, and there won't be ever again. He was one of a kind!"

"They say he was friends with the devil himself," the blond said, stirring the coal in the stove.

"They ain't saying the truth! He was of Orthodox faith! It's just that he was an extraordinary person!" the blacksmith said. "Bullets didn't touch him; cannonballs would miss him. He'd sit down on his bedding of sheep's wool—and be off to the Don River. Next time he'd sit on it—and sail up the Volga. They'd put him in prison, he'd take a piece of coal, draw a boat on the wall, ask for a drink of water, splash it—and it would turn into a river. He'd get in the boat, summon his comrades—and the next thing you know, he's sailing! That's the kind of man he was! He led a charmed life. There was no way to kill him. . . . And people say he didn't die. He'll be back. Just wait. He'll come again, they say, from the Don. He'll drive falsehood from the Kremlin and put truth on the throne. He'll give freedom to all Russia. He'll dig up his treasures, give them away to the poor. . . . Sten'ka Razin's treasures won't give themselves up to just anybody." The blacksmith laughed. "I myself saw how they disappear underground. They're waiting for their master, that's why. . . ."

"That I don't believe! These are miracles! It's not true! I don't believe it!" the red-cheeked young fellow said.

"Ha, you Tula gingerbread!" The blacksmith was indignant. "He doesn't believe! There are a lot of miracles in this world," he said. "Like people say a camel is spreading cholera throughout Astrakhan, trumpeting, heralding the end of the world."

"I don't believe it! These are all old wives' tales!" the red-cheeked young fellow shouted in response.

"Miracles!" blond-haired Yeryoma was talking to himself as he sat by the stove, thinking deeply about something.

"And yet others say Khan Mamai's daughter gallops at night through the steppe on a golden horse, looking for her fiancé. Whomever she meets she drags right away to her place underground," the blacksmith said.

"Well, I don't believe it! As God's my witness, I don't believe that!" the red-cheeked fellow shouted.

"Miracle!" the blond said pensively.

"And yet others say this summer some fishermen in the Akhtuba caught a mermaid in their nets!"

"I don't believe any of this!" the red-cheeked fellow was practically crying, as if being tortured.

"Andrei!" the blacksmith invited Forelock. "Tell us, is it true or not?"

"True," Forelock said, staring at Katerina.

Katerina got up, went to Ganna, fixed her blanket, tucked it in. Then moved over to the window, anxiously listening to the men.

"They say the mermaid tickled you?" the blacksmith interrogated Forelock.

"What?" Forelock said absentmindedly, looking, spellbound, at Katia.

"It's another girl who's tickled him!" Everyone laughed.

Katerina came up, embraced Forelock, and confirmed, "I won't give him up to anybody! Yesterday, when we saw each other—we realized that it's forever!"

"That I believe!" Suddenly the red-cheeked fellow burst out laughing. "Now I do believe."

Katerina laughed happily.

Forelock continued looking at her as if enchanted.

14

Through her fever and haze Ganna saw a peasant run into the room and shout, "Lyoshka Orliak's gang is in the village! They're coming here."

The men jumped up, rushed to the door.

The door opened with a bang: an ataman stood on the threshold.[39] Katerina paled. Armed men entered the room.

"Alyosha?" Katerina asked the ataman, shielding Forelock with her body. "Why have you come? I asked you not to come here. . . ."

"I came for you. Get ready. The cops are at our heels. We're leaving, going beyond the Caspian Sea."

"No," Katerina said quietly. "I won't go."

"Why not?"

"I love someone else, my dear."

"Well. . . ." The ataman hadn't expected that. "Another time—another love? Only yesterday you were in love with me. . . ."

"Time's not to blame—it's the heart."

The ataman pushed Katerina away. Saw Forelock: "You fell in love with a barefoot ragamuffin?"

"Barefoot or not, I don't care. He's dear to my heart."

The ataman pulled out a sawed-off rifle. "I'm asking you peaceably: Let's go! You know you're the only one dear to me."

"No, my dear." She shook her head.

"No?"

Before she had time to answer, the ataman shot her in the heart. He glanced at Forelock. Forelock stood there, pale, without stirring.

The ataman cried "We're leaving!" and went out.

15

The armed men started running around the tearoom.

"Get some vodka!" one yelled to another. "Semyon!"

"Grab the girl, Stepan!"

Ganna's hair straggled all over the pillow; one couldn't see her face. They seized Ganna together with the blanket and dragged her off.

"Set it all on fire—our farewell!"

The village was burning. Horses were galloping at full speed. Ganna lay in the blanket in the cart. She lay there and watched as if the fire were already raging inside her; house beams were crashing; people were burning.

"All you care about is drinking vodka, Stepan."

"And all you care about is making it with girls, Semyon."

"Vodka and girls—there's nothing sweeter in the world."

"Oh, come on. . . ."

"Well, what, then? That's my point. . . ."

The bandits were partying in the woods. They sat around the campfire, drinking, examining what they'd managed to steal. Stepan was trying on rings.

"Hey, this is the last time we'll be celebrating on home ground, guys!"

In the woods, the ataman was sitting alone at a tree stump. He was drinking vodka from a tin mug without eating anything. He was thinking about something.

Semyon came up to him. "Ataman! The guys have brought us a trophy, they're calling for you."

"What kind of trophy?"

"Female kind. A girl, in short. The guys are restless. Go, take a sample, then we'll follow you through the plowed soil."

"Leave me out of this," snapped the ataman.

16

"Bring her here, Stepan," Semyon ordered.

Stepan brought the blanket with Ganna. Put it on the snow. They unwrapped it. Ganna gazed in fear from the patchwork cover.

"Pah, she's so small!"

"Small or not, as long as she has *it* . . . ," Semyon said.

"She's a village idiot, a fool. She's a cripple." The same fellow sounded doubtful. "It's a sin."

"We'll burn in hell anyway," Semyon answered. "As for being a cripple . . . it's these very cripples that've taken our whole life away from us. . . . Goddamn them! Hold her, guys! I'll be her first!"

They fell on Ganna from all sides. Ganna twisted her body, hit Semyon in the face, bit them. The fellows held her arms and legs. She lay on the snow as if crucified.

"C'mon, Semyon, go for it. . . ."

Suddenly they heard a gunshot.

A man came running.

"The ataman's shot himself!"

. . .

17

The ataman sat, his face buried in the stump.

"All because of Kat'ka." Semyon spat. "He's traded us for a broad!"[40]

A sentinel ran by. "Watch out! The cops are coming!"

"On your horses!" Semyon ordered.

18

Horses galloped over Ganna. Then came other horses, with people in military coats; they briefly poked about the campfire, then rushed where they could hear shooting.

They didn't notice Ganna.

19

Ganna got up, dragged herself along to the woods, following the people. She made her way in a torn white shirt, falling through snowdrifts and walking on again.

She emerged in a clearing. The moon lit up the clearing. Suddenly she saw Stepan's severed hand, covered in rings. A bit farther she saw Semyon, dead. Next to him lay Stepan, embracing a man in a military coat. Dead bodies lay here and there. She saw the scarred face of the NKVD man. The snow around him was black from blood.

Howling with fear and terror, Ganna walked through the clearing.

Getting stuck in the snow, she walked from tree to tree. She sat down to rest beside a thick fir tree. She sat there, trembling. Closed her eyes. She didn't notice when she fell asleep.

20

Was this Ganna's dream or a vision?

Ganna saw a shining cloud floating over the earth. And on that cloud or snowdrift there stood a woman with an unusually beautiful face. It was a face familiar to Ganna, a dear face. She'd seen that face on Kharyta's icon.

"The Virgin Mary," Ganna whispered.

The Virgin Mary gave an imperceptible nod, smiled. "You are the Lord's beloved daughter," she told Ganna.

"Me?" Ganna asked, surprised. "But why me?"

"You have suffered," the Virgin Mary said lightly.

Her voice was like Kharyta's.

"What do I have to do?" Ganna grew agitated.

"Go and heal people. When the ice on the river moves— sail to other people."

"Should I heal them, too?"

"You'll find out there."

"But maybe I've died?"

"You won't die. Go." And the Virgin Mary melted away. Only the cloud was left, burning like silver.

21

Ganna opened her eyes and squinted: her eyes were blinded by the snow shining in the sun.

It was daylight. The snow around Ganna had melted. Ganna got up, stepping with her bare feet. Something sizzled under her feet. Ganna looked down: snow was melting around her foot with a sizzling sound. She took another step: the snow under her foot melted.

22

In a torn white shirt, barefoot, bareheaded, she entered the village.

"Ganna's a little fool! A fool!" some boys shouted as usual.

Light was radiating from Ganna. The boys fell silent and made way for her.

Ganna entered an empty church: all the candles lit up by themselves.

"Ganna's a saint! A saint!" people around started whispering.

They led a beggar to her. He was blind, covered with scabs.

"Where's the saint? Let me touch her . . . ," he asked.

Ganna touched him: the scabs fell off, his unseeing orbs turned into blue eyes.

"I can see! I can see!" the beggar cried.

"It's a miracle! A miracle!" Everybody fell to their knees.

23

Spring came. Ganna was sitting by a mighty tree.

A line stretched all the way to the tree, the whole road was flooded with people and carts.

People from all over the world came to Ganna to get healed.

"From all over the world people come to her," they were saying in the line.

"She's one of a kind in the world, there isn't anyone else like her!"

They stood, waiting their turn: blind and deaf, lame and leprous.

24

A lame man on crutches stood in front of Ganna.

"Daughter, save me. I'm all alone now, my wife died. How will I live without my wife and without my legs? Tell me?"

Ganna rubbed ointment on his leg, whispered something, tapped it with her palm.

She took the crutches away from him, moved away. The old man stood there for a while and then walked like a one-year-old: a step, another step, then another one. . . .

"Am I really walking?"

"Try to dance," someone from the crowd suggested.

He started dancing, squatting. People clapped their hands.

"You can still find yourself a young wife!" They laughed.

25

They brought in a woman. She was writhing, foam coming out of her mouth. She didn't want to come, kept resisting.

"Demons have made their nest inside of her," her mother explained. "At night they cry in different voices. Help her!"

Ganna approached the woman. The possessed woman began shrieking in different voices. She howled like a wolf and barked like a dog. Ganna stood in front of her. She started repeating all the movements of the possessed. The possessed would raise her hands, and Ganna would raise hers. The woman would swirl, and Ganna started swirling. The possessed swirled faster and faster. Then all of a sudden she collapsed as if knocked off her feet. Her body twitched and shook. Ganna stood over the body. It looked as if she were pulling something out of it, a string or a root. She pulled it out, sat down, exhausted, wiped her moist forehead, and smiled.

The woman got up, came up to her mother, and said to her as if nothing had happened, "Mama, what are we doing here? Let's go home."

26

A father came.

"My daughter's dying! She's all feverish, burning out like a candle!"

Ganna ran with the girl's father to his place.

The girl lay at home, delirious. "Give me the scarlet flower, Dada! Please, give it to me! Give it, I'm begging you, give it, Daddy, do!"

Ganna gave her a drink from the bottle she had brought with her. She sat by her side for a while, eyes closed. The girl regained consciousness.

"Daddy, I just had a dream about you. . . ."

27

Ganna was walking back. Some people were carrying a coffin with a little boy in it. They stopped near Ganna.

The mother threw herself at Ganna's feet.

"Bring him back to life!" Her eyes were full of entreaty and faith. "Bring him back!"

Ganna shook her head: *No!*

"You can do anything! Bring me back my son!"

No, Ganna shook her head. She went away and started crying.

She made her way through the crowd of diseased, sobbing.

28

A blind man who had just regained his sight asked Ganna, "Is that the sky?"

Ganna nodded, smiling.

"Is that a tree?"

Ganna nodded.

"Is that the sun?"

Ganna didn't have time to answer. They were already carrying someone on a stretcher to the tree in the yard.

"Let me through! Let me get to her immediately!" could be heard from the stretcher.

Ganna shriveled in fear. Traktorina Petrovna lay on the stretcher, looking at Ganna.

"Ganna? I can't believe my eyes. You! Heal me. . . . You made me a cripple, you heal me!" she ordered.

Ganna backed away, turned around, and ran behind the tree. She stood there, drew in an agitated breath. She kept breathing and breathing but couldn't calm down.

The man who'd regained his sight came up to Ganna, asked, "You don't want to heal her?"

No, Ganna shook her head.

"Do you want me to drive her away? Let me do that!"

No, Ganna shook her head. Stood there for a while. Then made up her mind. Came out.

She went up to Traktorina Petrovna, turned her around, started massaging her vertebrae.

"It hurts!" Traktorina Petrovna cried. "It hurts! I can't take anymore! Ganna!"

Ganna stepped back, her gaze commanding Traktorina Petrovna: *Rise!*

As if spellbound, Traktorina Petrovna rose and walked toward Ganna.

They stood there, looking at each other.

"So you're the saint?" said Traktorina Petrovna. "I always knew you'd come to a bad end."

29

At dawn, crashing sounds came from the river. The ice had begun to move.

Ganna woke up, listened. She grabbed her shawl, ran out.

"Where's she running off to?" a sick man asked.

"She's sensed something," an old woman answered.

Ganna ran along the shore. She was running to where Marat once had hidden the raft.

She removed the leaves and stones. Got all muddy. Pulled out the raft.

She looked at the river: huge ice floes were crowding, jostling one another.

30

On a bright sunny day, the village gathered to see Ganna off.

Men carried the raft to the water. Put Ganna on the raft. Pushed the raft off.

The people stood on a high bank, watching.

"Why's she leaving us?" a young fellow asked an old woman.

"The Lord gave her an order," the woman answered.

"And what did he say?"

"He told her: '*Sail!*'"

The raft was already in the middle of the river. Ganna bowed from the waist to everyone.

Everyone on the shore bowed to her, too. Women, men, children.

"Sail," repeated the young fellow.

. . .

PART FOUR

I

Creak.
Creak.
Creaky-creak. . . .
Creak.
Creak.
Creaky-creak.

The swing's creaking, flying higher and higher.

I'm lying on the roof and watching Nad'ka.

I look right into her pupils.

"Nad'ka! Where did you come from?" I ask her. "Where did you set out from, Nad'ka? What did you come for? After all, we used to live without you. Where did you come from, Nad'ka?"

For a second, her confused face is suspended next to mine. She's silent.

For a year and a half now, I've been the brother of a mad girl who had sailed in on a raft.

That spring there was a big flood. At the time, I was sitting by the Akhtuba, fishing, and I saw a raft sailing on the river, and on the raft there was a really pretty girl; I waved to her, she sailed over to me, came ashore, and started watching me fish. What's your name? She didn't answer. I collected my fishing rods and set off; she followed me. My mother and father were in the garden, planting carrots. Here, I told them, some girl sailed over here on a raft, she's following my every move. My mother slowly sank to her knees, right on the carrot bed. "Nadia!" she said. "Oh, Lord," my father said. "Oh, Lord!"

It was their sin that had come floating back: Long ago, thirteen years ago, their daughter was born, my sister Nad'ka, a retarded girl, a little fool; they were ashamed—before the military town, before the officers and their wives—my father had reenlisted in military service. My mother and father put the girl in a crib—Mom cried when she told the story—on a crimson pillow, put the crib on a raft, and sent it down the Akhtuba, out of sight. Nad'ka grew up somewhere and came back. That's how I got a sister I hadn't had before.

Everyone laughed at her, but I loved her more than life; she was better than all of them, even though she was crazy. She's better than all of you, I kept saying—better!

"Nad'ka!" I say to her and make a face.

"Marat!" my father shouts, raising his head from the car. "Stop teasing Nadia! She'll fall!"

"Marat! Stop the swing!" my mother shouts. "She shouldn't go so high. . . ."

I come down from the roof, stop the swing.

Nad'ka slowly gets up. She walks, swaying, her hands holding her big round belly.

Mama looks intently at Nad'ka, turns away, covers her face with her sleeve, and cries.

Our Nad'ka is pregnant.

2

My sister Nad'ka conceived by a poplar seed.

Poplar down was flying then like snow, a hot wind blew from the south, there was heat and a white blizzard; the down would stick to sweat-dampened skin, everything itched, and that southern wind inflated her. The wind inflated Nad'ka, they said, and in the fall her stomach began swelling like a balloon when it's inflated with a bicycle pump. And I decided to have a look.

"Nad'ka, take off your clothes!" I shouted when we were home alone. I shouted right in her face, even though she was deaf, totally deaf, didn't hear a thing. "Hey, deaf post! Take your clothes off! You fool!" I yelled, while she kept smiling that foolish smile of hers, which made me want to bury my head in shit and howl. I pushed her roughly, I kept pushing her toward the door, then dragged her by the hand down the wet autumn garden paths, shoved her into the wooden

LITTLE FOOL

227
▾

summer shower, and locked the door with a rusty hook. Inside, it smelled of bast. Nad'ka remembered that people showered here in the summer and that she had to undress and slowly began taking off her clothes, hanging on a nail her green woolen cardigan, maroon flannel housecoat, dark blue man's knit undershirt, and, as I watched, her pink flannel drawers; the drawers—large, pink, as if alive—slipped off the nail and fell into the dirt. Bending down, she picked them up, feeling sorry for them, shook them out, and smoothed them, and I watched as she hung up the black sateen men's boxers that she'd inherited from me (I was still attached to them), and it was strange, as if a part of me looked black, crucified on that soft, pink flannel. . . .

She stood, huddled up, looking at the gray square of sky from which the rain was falling, an interminable, fine, cold autumnal rain; behind the gray clouds—with the *craah-craah* of crane calls—invisible birds were flying off, while I kept looking at the huge, round, suntanned, leather balloon of Nad'ka's belly, with the patterned imprint from the elastic; that balloon grew bigger and bigger with each day, and I was afraid, really afraid, that the taut skin wouldn't hold out and would burst, but it kept growing, this balloon, I secretly started expecting that one day this balloon of hers would lift my sister Nad'ka up there, from where the rain was falling, from where there came the *craah-craah* of cranes, and she would hover above our sad, gray military town and float in the sky like a blimp or like the sun and, from there, from the sky, would smile her foolish, senseless smile, which made me want to howl. And perhaps then compassion and happiness would begin on earth.

There was golden hair under her round belly.

"Get dressed!" I said.

She kept looking up at the rain and didn't hear either me or the birds.

"Get dressed!" I yelled. I patted her on the back, her shoulder blades protruded from her back like sharp wings, and her skin was covered in goosebumps.

She turns around, and I hold out her black sateen boxers, stretching the elastic. She understands and steps into them.

"Good girl," I told her as if she could hear me. I always expected something from her. Every day I expect her to suddenly hear me or start speaking or stop being a little fool. I always think that any moment now . . . or tomorrow. . . . It's because I strongly sense Nad'ka's kind, beautiful soul, encased, for some reason, in a stupid, deaf-and-dumb body, as if confined in a prison utterly devoid of sound.

And I also expect Nad'ka to give birth to that beautiful soul of hers—and that soul will be strong, smoothbore, rustling, green, growing up to the very sky, like the poplar from whose seed she conceived.

3

"Let's go to the dugout," I tell Nad'ka when we come out of the shower room.

We go into the depths of the orchard. We dug a shelter there against the atomic bomb. Dad and I dug it half a month ago. Dad used a big spade and gave me his military shovel. We did the digging on Sunday. In every orchard, people were digging. Everybody was expecting a nuclear war. We'd exchange remarks with our neighbors over the fence. We talked about Cuba, about missiles in Cuba, about Kennedy, about Khrushchev, about America, about the nuclear attack, about who'd attack first: them or us. We lived in the missile town of Kapustin Iar, and everyone expected the American missiles to hit our military town first.

"Oh, Khrushch will get it for his games! America will hit us hard, you bet it will!" Uncle Boria Sinitsyn, our neighbor to the left, was saying.[41]

"They'll be afraid," Dad said. "Because we'll hit them, too, then!"

"It's the end of the world!" Aunt Masha, our neighbor to the right, said with quiet conviction. She had no husband living with her and was digging the shelter with her six-year-old daughter. "It's written in the books of old. Nobody will be saved."

"Why are you digging, then?" Uncle Boria asked.

"For my daughter," Aunt Masha replied and added, with hope, "What if she's able to save herself?"

We dug a pit, covered it with twigs. Threw some earth over the twigs.

"If they strike, nothing will help," my father said.

We built an excellent shelter.

Me and the other boys would hide in it, playing war. Dad said they used to live in dugouts like that during the war.

Nad'ka and I crawled into the shelter, sat on the bench. It was dark but not overly so. Some earth fell off the roof, and through the twigs we could see the sky. Rain leaked into the dugout.

"This is a civil-defense shelter," I told Nad'ka in an important tone. "The nuclear war will soon begin."

Nad'ka seemed to be listening to me.

"We'll hide here when the atomic bomb falls on us."

Nad'ka was listening.

"An atomic bomb explodes noiselessly." I started retelling her what I'd heard at school in civil-defense class. "A dazzling flash is what tells you the explosion's happened. You shouldn't look at the burning ball, or you'll go blind. You've got to turn your back to the burning ball and lie facedown on the ground. The next thing you feel are the effects of the thermal radiation, then you experience the shock wave and finally hear the sound of the explosion, which resembles a peal of thunder."

Nad'ka shrank. I got scared, too.

"Don't be scared," I said. "We won't see it. We'll be sitting in the shelter."

The rain intensified, and the cold drops fell on our heads.

"We should stay here at least a minute, so not to be subjected to the gamma radiation."

I stopped talking and started counting a minute.

Nad'ka sat and trembled.

The water dripped down.

All of a sudden it seemed to me that there actually was a war and that we were sitting in the shelter for real, hiding from a bomb.

"Let's go," I said and got up. "Now we might be subjected to radiation. We might not even notice it. The main symptom of having received a dose is vomiting."

I took Nad'ka by the hand.

"If a person vomits for an hour after the explosion, it's a bad sign. It means he's got a fatal dose of radiation. If vomiting appears several hours later—"

I hadn't finished when Nad'ka suddenly bent down, covered her mouth with her hand, and began vomiting. Then again and again.

"What's wrong, Nad'ka? What's with you?"

I dragged her home, dragging her through the autumnal paths of the orchard, but she kept stopping, bending over, and vomiting.

We ran into the house.

"Mama! Mama!" I shouted.

Mama ran out of the kitchen.

"What's happened?"

"Nad'ka's sick," I said. "She's vomiting!"

Nad'ka stood in front of our mother, her face greenish pale and exhausted, then bent down and threw up again.

"Food poisoning," Mom said.

And she led Ganna to her room.

4

"Looks like it'll start soon," Father told Mom a week later.

He stood in the doorway in his military coat, getting ready to leave for the site—he worked there in the missile silo—unsmiling, stern, looking at us as if he were saying good-bye.

Mama went up to him, ran her hand over his face, and suddenly threw herself onto his chest, crying. He hugged her tightly, tenderly, then took her by the waist and put her aside like a liqueur glass and admired her for a while. Turned to us. Nad'ka and I got up from the table and approached. He hugged and kissed us.

"Take care of your mother and sister!" he told me.

Nad'ka suddenly wailed like a siren, in a low-low voice: "*Oo-oo-oo!!!*"

Father turned and left.

We went outside and stood for a long time in the road, watching him go. As if we were seeing him off not to work but to war. Not for a day but forever.

5

Father didn't come home from work anymore.

A week later he phoned Mother at the computer center and said only one word: "Tonight."

6

On the evening of 28 October 1962, a siren wailed throughout the town. It used to wail before, at night, during tests.

But today it wailed for real, as if it were alive, as if a huge man—as tall as the sky—were wailing with misery all over town.

It wailed in a low, heartrending voice—Nad'ka's voice.

"*Oo-oo-oo!!! Oo-oo-oo!!!*" without stopping.

The nuclear war had started.

Mama, Nad'ka, and I ran out of the house, and, just as we used to during tests, we ran to my school, number 232.

All the streetlights were out.

People were running toward us: soldiers with rolled-up blankets on their shoulders were running in formation and getting into a truck; officers holding their caps were running to the checkpoint to board a troop carrier.

Parents were running with children, men, women, and old folks. Each of them was supposed to know where to run: it had been rehearsed during test alarms. But many of them were confused and, upon reaching the site, stopped: though it was dark, there were crowds there, and so it wasn't as frightening. A man with a loudspeaker was trying to persuade people to go to their workplaces.

Nobody would leave.

We got through the crowd and ran on.

They didn't allow parents inside the school: parents were supposed to go to their place of work and wait for further instructions.

At the school doors, everybody was crying. Parents were saying good-bye to their children.

We began saying good-bye, too. Mama didn't cry. She was as if in a fever. She looked at Nad'ka as if from a distance, with stern, dry eyes, peering not at us but inside us, into our souls. She hugged and kissed Nad'ka, then me. She kissed me on the cheek, and her lips were so dry and hot, it felt as if she'd burned me.

"Mama!" I said.

And the crowd pulled Nad'ka and me inside.

7

In the gym, they lined up our whole division according to our unit in the Young Pioneers organization. Our leader, Trakto-rina Petrovna—a gray-haired old woman in a red tie—came out to the middle of the hall and said, "We'll be going to the steppe now, farther from the town. Tonight, the ultimatum expires, and it'll be zero hour. First, those who have remained in town will die with the first missile drop. We'll perish with the second strike, but we'll be the only victims on our side. Then our missiles will strike and will exterminate America in a few minutes. You, children, will become heroes just like Pavlik Morozov and Volodia Dubinin.[42] The whole country will learn our names. They'll make us into legends and sing songs about us. Young Pioneers! Be ready to fight for the cause of the Communist Party!"

"Always ready!" we shouted.

They distributed dry rations: plastic bags with Ritsa Lake

chocolate candy, wafers, cookies, and tangerines—just like in New Year's gift baskets. Either because they'd already been prepared for New Year's or because all this was for the last time.

8

Holding hands, we ran in pairs along the dark streets to the buses. First, we ran along Victory Street, where our school was located. Past the Officers' Club, where our whole family used to attend movies and concerts. Then along Soviet Army Street, past our house: number 8. Along Aviation Street, past the store that stayed open after-hours, where we used to buy bread—black bread at fourteen kopeks a kilo and white bread at twenty kopeks a kilo—they used to add a piece to the loaf of white bread: a crust, which Nad'ka and I used to finish off even before reaching our house. Past Lenin Street, along which we used to go to parades every year. Past the Avenue of the Ninth of May, where the bathhouse was located: my dad used to scrub me there with a branch of wormwood—birches didn't grow around there.[43] Past Soldiers' Park, where we used to ride on the merry-go-round: two airplanes would rush around in circles, with Ganna and me at the controls. As I ran I said my farewells to the town. It had been my whole life.

9

Buses stood at the checkpoint. I ran faster, to get in first. Nad'ka withdrew her hand from mine and stopped. I looked back. She was standing in the headlights' golden light and, breathing heavily, was holding her belly. It looked as if she were holding a golden balloon, pressing it to herself, so that it wouldn't fly away.

"Here! Here!" shouted Traktorina Petrovna, waving her red tie at us from the bus.

Nad'ka and I approached the bus. Traktorina Petrovna was letting the children onto the bus, checking them against a list. When it was our turn, I said, "Marat Sidorov. Nadezhda Sidorova."

She checked me off, but couldn't find Nad'ka on the list.

"She's not on the list," she said. "What grade is she in?"

"She doesn't go to school," I said.

Traktorina Petrovna looked at Ganna in surprise.

"Oh, yes," she said hastily. "They told me. Sidorova—she's the retarded one, right?"

You're retarded yourself! Fool! Idiot! I wanted to tell her but said nothing.

"She's the one who was raped by soldiers?" she inquired.

The color rushed to my face.

"No," I said.

"How's that? Our school got a letter from the Department of Education. In winter, in Soldiers' Park, three soldiers took Nadia Sidorova, a feebleminded girl, into the water tower and raped her. . . ."

"Nobody raped her!" I yelled.

"Oh, yes, of course." She smiled slyly, looking expressively at Nad'ka's belly. "Right, it was the wind blew it in. . . ."

"Let us in!" I said.

Traktorina Petrovna shielded the bus door with her body.

"No. She won't be going! She's not on the list!" she said spitefully.

"What do you mean 'won't be going'?" I couldn't believe it. "She'll die here alone!"

"Creatures like her," Traktorina Petrovna said with hatred, "should be exterminated right in the hospital. She's not a human being! Let her stay. . . ."

My brain stopped working. I saw darkness. I didn't understand anything anymore. Suddenly, to my own surprise, I bent down, picked up a stone from the ground, and brandished it at Traktorina Petrovna.

But somebody from behind grabbed my hand.

"Don't, sonny." I heard the voice of Granny Manya, a cleaning woman at our school. "Don't take the sin upon your soul!"

"Bandit! Bandit!" Traktorina Petrovna shouted. "You'll not be going anywhere!"

"Move aside, Traktorina," Granny Manya said. "Let the boy in the bus! And her, too—a living soul. This isn't the orphanage! And times have changed!"

And Granny Manya advanced upon Traktorina.

Unwillingly, Traktorina Petrovna moved aside and, writing something down on her sheet of paper, let Nad'ka and me into the bus.

"You, Maria Bokaneva, have stayed the same kulaks' accomplice as you used to be!" she told Granny Manya in a fit. "Even prison hasn't straightened you out!"

"But the grave will straighten us all out! Including you!" Granny Manya said lightly, getting on the bus after us.

10

Nad'ka sat next to Granny Manya. I sat in the front, right by the driver's seat, so not to see anybody. My face was burning with hot blood. My temples were pounding.

"Traktorina's a fool! A fool! Fool!"

But by and by I calmed down. I looked out the window. We were driving through the endless steppe. The moon was shining. It silvered the wormwood. The bus seemed to be rolling through an enormous silver dish.

Is it really possible that we'll be killed tonight? I thought.

It turned out I'd spoken out loud.

"It's awful." Manya sighed. "They dug their heels in on this. Both our leaders and theirs. And children suffer. . . . Better not think about it. God is merciful, we might survive. . . ."

But the horrible thought of death had nested in me and wouldn't give me any peace. I turned to Granny Manya.

"Granny Manya, tell me, where will I go when I die?"

Before Granny Manya could answer me, Traktorina Petrovna said, as if taking revenge on me, "Nowhere! You'll turn into molecules!"

I looked ahead at the dead steppe, as if flooded with mercury, and swallowed my tears.

Somebody came over to me from behind and caressed the short hair on the back of my head with her hand.

I turned around—Nad'ka stood there, looking into the silver distance at the steppe.

II

The bus stopped in the middle of the steppe. It unloaded us and went back to pick up another grade.

We got out. Children were scattered all over the steppe: they'd been brought there from schools and kindergartens. Here and there in the dark you could hear laughter, shouts, and conversation. We weren't supposed to light a campfire, so not to make an easy target for the enemy, who was watching us from a satellite. But our Traktorina Petrovna ordered us to gather some dry steppe grass.

She built a campfire in the night.

"Let America see us, let it aim better at us," Traktorina Petrovna said to the black sky—right into the starry eyes of America, which was aiming at us.

Everyone sat around the fire and started singing passionate songs from the 1920s—Traktorina Petrovna had taught us to sing these songs from her youth. At first, it was all like a camping trip, with singing by the Pioneer campfire.

I sat next to Nad'ka without singing. I was thinking: What if the Americans strike right now? It was alarming.

Then everybody started eating their dry rations, rustling the plastic bags and candy foil, crunching wafers and cookies. It started to smell of tangerines. And suddenly everyone recalled New Year's Eve, everyone at once began laughing and talking. A kindergarten girl started singing in a thin voice:

> "A little fir tree was born in the woods,
> It grew up in the woods. . . .
> In winter and in summer it was
> Shapely and green."

Everyone joined in.

I also sang that silly song and looked, with hope, at the sky.

It suddenly seemed to me that over there in America they'd see us, and our campfire, and how we're sitting beside the fire singing; they'd hear our songs—and would understand that there was no need to attack us. They wouldn't be able to strike a blow at us, singing children, they wouldn't dare. . . .

My fear disappeared.

The starry sky was so full of round bright stars, it was hard to believe that death could come from it.

There will be no war, I thought.

Granny Manya started telling a fairy tale to some little kids, and the tale ended well and happily, and I—overwhelmed by that happy ending as I gazed at the clear bright stars hanging like festive garlands on a huge New Year's tree from a fairy tale—I was overcome by sweet sleep.

I awoke as if someone had nudged me, in complete darkness, awoke from the clear and horrible thought that pierced me: It was all over.

I was completely alone. There was no one next to me. Darkness as dense as a blanket surrounded me from all the sides. There was no sky or stars. There was no steppe. Only darkness above and below me.

And I realized that the end of the world had come.

I realized that I'd slept through the explosion, that everybody had been killed, and I was the only one left.

I felt my face, arms, and legs—they were intact. I couldn't tell whether my eyes were blind or not—I couldn't see anything. For some reason, I was unable to shout—my throat was pulled tight, as if by a rope, I could hardly breathe. My heart, by contrast, had grown huge—it was pounding in my ears. It was pounding so loudly that I got scared they'd hear it and aim at it from the satellite, and I set off at a run, so that they'd miss; and suddenly something started running after me, lumbering forward like a beast, some horrible monster, banging and rustling with a crunching and breaking sound, right at my heels—IT was running very close. I ran faster, but, as if in a game, IT ran faster, too, banging, clanging, and squealing louder and louder, with increasing glee.

It was as if death itself were chasing me in the pitch-black darkness, and, feeling my hair stand on end in terror, I lost my head and yelled, and, yelling, I fled from it, panting breathlessly, as fast as I could; but it followed close behind, breathing hoarsely right near me and suddenly called me by my name in a loud, inhuman voice, grabbed me, and pushed me to the ground. . . .

For a long time I rolled in the steppe in a hysterical fit, while Traktorina Petrovna stood over me.

"What were you scared of? Me? I heard someone rushing about in the steppe like an elk at night, so I ran after it."

She was speaking, but I couldn't see her face. It was as if darkness were talking to me!

I got scared, my lips trembled, and I crawled away from Traktorina into the night, thick as evaporated milk.

I crawled through the steppe.

Here and there in the steppe lay piles of sleeping children, looking like they'd been killed. I looked for Nad'ka among them.

She was nowhere to be found.

I crawled and crawled. I was afraid to get up. I crawled just like my dad had, at the front, under fire.

At dawn, I met a Kazakh shepherd with a flock of sheep. He didn't know anything. I told him the whole story.

"What will be will be." He made a dismissive gesture and, looking at the field scattered with sleeping children, said, "They're lying like lambs."

12

I found her far from the campfire. Nad'ka was sitting with Granny Manya and Svetka—the six-year-old daughter of our neighbor Masha. The three of them were sitting by a gopher hole. Svetka took out a Ritsa Lake chocolate candy from the plastic bag and put it next to the hole.

Then she took out the cookies and tangerines and put them next to the hole, too.

"Why?" I asked.

"The gophers—they'll be the only ones left after the nuclear war," Svetka explained to me. "They'll survive in their hole, like in shelters. After the war they'll come out, and there'll be the candy. . . . They're about to strike," she said like an adult. "At four o'clock sharp."

Hearing our conversation, the children started gathering around us. Even Traktorina Petrovna came up, wrapping an old shawl around herself. It had gotten really cold. I was shaking like crazy, I was so terribly cold.

We waited for the end.

I imagined Mama and said my farewells to her. Dad was down below, beneath the steppe—in the missile silo. I said farewell to him, pressing my cheek to the earth, saying into the earth: *Farewell, Father.* I scratched my cheek against the prickly steppe, as if it were Dad's stubble.

Then I sat down to wait. This was the most terrible thing—to wait. It was impossible—to wait. All of us were shaking by now.

"I'm scared. I don't want to die," a girl said. "I don't want, I don't, I don't! . . ."

And all the little kids immediately burst out crying. They cried right into the sky, with heart-wrenching howls.

And that's when I said to Nad'ka, "Nad'ka! Do something!"

I don't know why I said it; I just did. I was shaking, and I said, "Nad'ka! Do something!" I said.

Nad'ka looked at me. She looked at me intelligently, clearly, as if she'd heard me.

Then she got up. She stood, shaking, just like that time in the shower, raising her face to the cold, gray sky. She stood, awkward in her green wool cardigan and maroon dress, with her enormous belly, as round as a ball.

She stood for a while, then put her arms around her belly as if around a balloon—and all of a sudden floated above the ground.

Slowly, she rose higher and higher, as if screwing herself into the sky. Above me, I saw her heels, dirty and cracked, she always walked barefoot. . . .

"Sidorova! Where are you going?" Traktorina Petrovna suddenly shrieked and actually leaped up and rushed after her but fell to the ground. "Sidorova, come back!"

Staring at Nad'ka, Granny Manya fell on her knees.

"A miracle!" she said, lifting her arms. "Oh, Lord! A miracle!"

And Nad'ka looked down at us from above. The way she looked at us!

And everything seemed to stop. The children stood motionless, tipping back their heads. Granny Manya kneeled motionless in the middle of the steppe. Without stirring, looking at Nad'ka with horror, Traktorina Petrovna lay on the ground. The shepherd stood, leaning on his staff and looking upward. The sheep stood, raising their meek faces to the sky. And birds froze in their flight. The air, too, did not stir: not a wind, not a breath. Everything stopped at that moment.

Only Nad'ka was flying up, higher and higher. We couldn't see her anymore.

And in a few minutes, a sun appeared. It was born right before our eyes, where the earth and the sky met, a huge red sun, all sullied by Nad'ka's blood.

Nad'ka was giving birth to the sun.

It rose higher and higher, and suddenly, beaming, it fully revealed itself.

The sun was totally different than before.

It was a new sun.

The sun lay in the sky like a newborn baby in swaddling clothes and gazed at the new world spread before it.

And suddenly I realized that there would be no war, that today Nad'ka had saved us, that there would be no nuclear strike, no missiles. . . . There would be no death! . . .

I fell on the ground, facedown on the steppe, and sobbed uncontrollably, feeling no shame. Something rustled next to my face. I raised my head and saw a gopher with its agile little paw pull a Ritsa Lake chocolate candy down its burrow.

Kasputin Yar—Moscow
1993–98

. . .

Translator's Notes

1. A *gazik,* or GAZ, is a jeep introduced during World War II and subsequently manufactured by the Gorky Motor Works, of which GAZ is an acronym.

2. The name "Kharyta," the shortened form of "Kharitina," phonetically evokes the Christian virtue of *caritas* and in Christianized Greek means "grace" or "benefaction." (Thank you, Mark Possanza.)

3. Kulaks were rich or prosperous peasants who, after the Bolshevik Revolution of 1917, were either killed or exiled to remote areas of the country, their property nationalized by the state.

4. Kharyta is quoting Saint Ephraim of Syria (circa 306–377) from Saint Paul's Epistle to the Corinthians 1:27.

5. Traditionally, the beautiful (red) corner is the place in Russian peasant domiciles reserved for icons. During the Soviet era, red banners and portraits of Communist leaders occupied the "red" corners in public places.

6. Young Pioneers comprised a Soviet youth organization in which membership was obligatory for children nine to fourteen years of age. The Soviet regime viewed Young Pioneers as junior "builders of communism," with their own regalia and solemn oath.

7. Ganna's rendition substitutes the words "human being" for "pioneer," which appears in the official Young Pioneers' "hymn."

8. Kalmucks are an Asiatic ethnic group in the lower Volga region.

9. Five hundred and fifty poods equal approximately nineteen thousand eight hundred pounds.

10. Traditionally, the Volga River is the symbol of the Russian nation's spiritual and material strength and the subject of countless folk songs and legends.

11. The tsar bell is a church bell reputed to be the largest in the world, cast in the 1730s for the Belfry of Ivan the Terrible in the

Kremlin. The bell proved too heavy (exceeding two hundred tons) and, since, has been displayed at the foot of the Belfry.

12.   Since the Russian words for "tongue" and for "clapper" are the same, Vasilenko here refers simultaneously to the Soviet destruction of everything religious and the brutal suppression of anyone who speaks out against the new order (as the following lines make clear).

13.   The majority of names here derive from various grains, animals, or birds: "Pshenichnaia" from "wheat," "Lastovkin" from "swallow," and so forth.

14.   The observation evokes Friedrich Engels's famous dictum "Religion is the opium of the people."

15.   A *paskha* is a pyramid-shaped cake made either of cottage or cream cheese and eggs, traditionally served at Orthodox Russian Easter.

16.   Henbane is a plant that produces dizziness and delirium.

17.   Borscht is a Ukrainian soup consisting primarily of beets, meat, and potatoes.

18.   "Black Maria" is a slang name for the vehicle used by the Soviet secret police when making arrests under Stalin, especially during the purges of the 1930s.

19.   "NKVD" was the abbreviation for the Soviet secret police under Stalin.

20.   In their full form, these Russian names mean "faith," "hope," and "love."

21.   In the original, this statement is in Polish.

22.   *Uezd* is an old Russian term for "region," replaced after the 1917 Revolution as part of the country's modernization.

23.   Tsaritsyn is a town whose name means, literally, "Queen's residence." Vasilenko's characters use this name, although by the 1930s, when the events of the novel take place, the name had been changed to "Stalingrad."

24.   The Russian neologism here is *raskurochivat'*, one of the novel's many instances of word play pretending to educated speech. The word blends the Communist Party term for "expropriation of peasants" with the word for "brutal handling."

25.   According to folk belief, mermaids tickle men, especially those they love, to death.

26. The Golden Horde was the name of the Tartar state, which dominated Russia for more than two centuries (1240–1480).

27.   This is a pun, for in contemporary Russian *sarai* means "barn."

28.   *Besh-barmak* is a traditional dish of meat and rice.

29.   The Russian word *t'ma* literally means "darkness" and designated a unit of ten thousand in the Tartar army.

30.   The reference is to the historical battle between the Tartar khan Mamai and the Russian prince Dmitry. The battle marked the beginning of Russia's liberation from the Tartar yoke. The novel blends historical facts with folk legends and beliefs.

31.   The old man is referring to the standard toast at Russian wedding celebrations, whereby guests exhort the young couple to transform bitterness into sweetness through their kisses.

32.   Stepan Razin was the leader of the massive seventeenth-century Cossack and peasant revolt in Russia, which started on the Don River. Razin is also referred to by his more common name, "Sten'ka," in the novel.

33.   The Komsomol was the Communist Youth League, a Soviet youth organization, the "younger brother" and helper of the Communist Party.

34.   The passage is from the fifth chapter of A. Pushkin's novel in verse, *Eugene Onegin.*

35.   *Shchi* is a traditional Russian soup, with cabbage, meat, and potatoes.

36.   Tula is an old Russian town famous for its forges and metalwork. The phrase here refers to the nineteenth-century novella by Nikolai Leskov, *Lefty,* about a Tula blacksmith who forged a flea in natural size.

37.   In Russian folklore, falsehood is often portrayed as an ugly, one-eyed, old woman.

38.   "White hands" is a folkloric formula, as are "beauteous maiden," "open field," "bright falcon," "brave horse," and so on.

39.   An ataman was a Cossack chieftain, but more broadly the word also referred to gang leaders.

40.   The reference is to a famous folk song about Stepan Razin, who supposedly fell in love with a Persian princess and focused on her until his men accused him of treason, whereupon he threw her in the Volga River.

41.   Nikita Khrushchev was the Soviet premier who assumed power after Stalin's death in 1953. This part of the novel deals with the Cuban Missile Crisis: Khrushchev's deployment of nuclear mis-

siles in Cuba during October 1962 and the subsequent confrontation between the Soviet Union and the United States.

42. Both Pavlik Morozov and Volodia Dubinin are iconic heroes of Soviet history. Morozov was a boy who denounced his kulak father to the Soviet authorities for concealing grain and was murdered by his father and older brothers. Dubinin was a Young Pioneer killed by the Nazis during World War II for helping the Soviet army. Both became behavioral models for Soviet children.

43. May 9 is Soviet Victory Day, for on that day in 1945 Nazi troops surrendered to the Soviet army in Berlin.

■ □ ■ □ ■

WRITINGS FROM AN UNBOUND EUROPE